ONE HELLUVA NIGHT

Other books by Stephanie Sparks:

Scream, Queen

Kill the Babysitter

The Stepchildren

Mandy

ONE HELLUVA NIGHT

Written & Published by

Stephanie Sparks

CONTENT WARNING

One Helluva Night contains subject matter and themes related to violence, death, and murder (of both animals and humans); domestic violence; sex and sexuality; profanity and vulgar language; police brutality and injustice; automobile accidents; and body horror.

Reader discretion is advised.

This one's for all you lovers out there...

ONE HELLUVA NIGHT

PLEASE NOTE

The document you are reading is a record of the last twelve hours of T#00526829 (aka ███████, aka "Paradise," ████.).

Names, locations, and other details that may incriminate notable high-ranking government officials and their respective agencies and departments have been redacted.

As this document contains the true accounts of what happened the night of ████████ ██, 20██, it has in no way been tampered with by anyone associated with any government body.

Totally, for real.

THE MORNING AFTER

DEAN DILTON'S COLD, bloody hands are cuffed to the steel table. The only person he can bitch about it to, for the moment, is his weary reflection in the mirror. He's being watched, he can feel it. The mirrored glass reminds him of a bad cop, a not-so-friendly one—one of the reasons he's in this icy interrogation room now. He shifts uncomfortably, knowing he had better get his story straight, and quick.

But what even is his story?

Well, there's the judge... No, wait—the arrest came first... But actually, it was her. *She's the whole reason I'm in this mess.*

In the chaos of everything that came after, he lost her. Then someone shoved a bag over his head (and not for the first time that night), cuffed him (also not for the first time), and threw him into an unmarked van.

No one knows what happened to her—or at least they're not saying—and he's left to worry and wonder.

He looks up as the door to the interrogation room opens. Dean's direct report from the agency walks in. Director ████████. *[Names have been redacted to protect the identities of government officials.]*

He shakes his head. "For god's sake, Agent Dilton, you look like shit."

Dean stares down at his cuffs. Blood stains his torn and dirty sleeves. Not all of it is his.

Director ████████ takes a seat across from his disgraced agent. He drops a thick file folder on the table. Dean can't reach it and the director doesn't push it any closer. His steely blue eyes study his young agent for a few beats. His mouth is a hard line; he doesn't speak.

The interrogation tactic works its magic. Dean feels himself cracking. He swallows, almost choking on the lump thickening in his throat. His molars grind together. His shaking hands grip each other. He wants to vomit words all over, explain everything—well, as much as he can. But he holds his breath and waits.

The seconds tick by on the big, round clock over the door. Settling back in his chair, the director strokes his chin. Dean feels a tickle there himself. His skin prickles and itches all over.

Is this part of the interrogation?

Dean rubs at the spot to make it go away. His chin is stubbly and most of his exposed skin is sticky with dried blood. His neck is still raw from the noose that strangled him nearly to death.

How did last night get so fucked up? he wonders.

Finally, the director speaks. "Never thought I'd see one of my men parked across from me in this context. I'm terribly disappointed."

"Sorry, sir," Dean says.

"The assignment was simple. I thought a bright, young man like yourself could handle it. What happened out there, Agent?"

"It's a long story, sir."

The director crosses his arms, rumpling his tie. He glances at his watch, compelling Dean to check the clock on the wall. "I got time."

"You're not going to like it."

"I suppose it's about the girl then. The one you keep asking about."

"Well..."

"I gave you this assignment because all you had to do was keep your nose clean and your pecker in your pants."

"I tried, sir. I really did."

"Not hard enough. My expectations were so low and you still managed to disappoint me." He looks into the mirror and as if talking to his reflection, orders someone on the other side to "get in here."

A deputy pokes his head in. He's thankfully not wearing a leather uniform—just a regular one, bland and tan. Dean doesn't know how far away he'll need to be from that awful town before things start to feel normal again. Maybe never.

"What did you need, sir?" the deputy asks.

Director ▮▮▮▮▮▮▮ snaps his fingers. "Pen."

The deputy fumbles with his pocket protector until he plucks out a chewed-up Bic. He offers it to the director, who grimaces in disgust but takes it. Then the director dismisses him.

Discarding the pen's mangled cap, the director exhales and opens the file folder to a blank page. "Alright. Let's get started."

"What about Marlow?" Dean asks. "Does anyone know what happened to her? Did she get away?"

"She's not important."

"Well, actually... She's a big part of this too."

"Don't worry about her. Right now it's imperative that you tell me exactly what happened in T#00526829."

"Sorry, sir?" The jumble of numbers meant nothing to Dean.

"*Paradise*, Agent Dilton. The town you were not authorized to enter."

"Oh, right... Everything?"

"Yes, Agent," he hisses. The ballpoint of the pen bends under pressure. "I want every last goddamned detail of how the hell you managed to wipe an entire town off the map in a single night."

1.

THE TROUBLEMAKER

(Side A)

THE TOWN WASN'T exactly on the map to begin with, but first off, Dean wants it on the record that he's not a bad guy. He worked really hard to be a good, law-abiding person. Bad stuff just sort of happened. Every opportunity he struck out on or royally botched started with the best of intentions.

Like when his mother signed him up for Boy Scouts so he could try something new and develop leadership skills from positive role models (and also presumably to learn how to play nice with others). Instead, he led a mutiny against the scout leader and kept a rogue troop of boys alive for six days in the wilderness before being rescued. (Records of the event used the term "forcible extraction" and described an *Apocalypse Now* situation.)

Or like when Dean continued his troublemaking ways in high school, and his father and the school principal arranged for him to go on a police ride-along. *That'll scare the boy straight*, they figured, figuring wrong.

Dean "borrowed" the squad car and went for a joyride with the principal's daughter.

When the police officers finally caught up to Dean, they tried scaring him by yelling and throwing him to the ground, but Dean was riding high on adrenaline.

It wasn't until they brought him home to his weary and worried mother and father, standing on the doorstep that he began to understand what a little shit he'd been. His mother wrung her hands until her knuckles turned red, but neither parent made a scene.

Instead, they hugged him and sent him off to bed. They promised to talk about it in the morning, and they did, and while Dean didn't remember the exact words of their lecture, the key takeaway was that they weren't mad, just severely disappointed. While that sentiment let him off the hook, it was way worse than if they had threatened to ship him off to military school.

He promised to do better. Much better. He couldn't shake the image of his teary-eyed mother from his memory, but he could try to replace it with one of pride.

After ekeing his way to graduation and narrowly avoiding juvenile detention, Dean enlisted in the military. His parents thought he had finally decided to turn his life around, to straighten up and fly right for once, but shortly after he started basic training, there was an incident.

For reasons of national security, the investigation records were sealed and Dean was discharged. His commanding officer threatened him to never speak of it again.

So Dean went to college to pursue a degree. To get in the good graces of the hardest-grading professor on campus, he volunteered to become the man's teaching assistant. But Dean could only grade so many boring, repetitive essays before he found himself in bed with the prof's much-younger wife. Despite having to dodge accusations from the professor until graduation, Dean managed to finish a degree in criminology on time.

He then applied for positions with the CIA, the FBI, the DEA. No one wanted him, not with the black marks on his records. Only one agency dared to recruit him, and it was because either its background check process wasn't stellar or no one in charge cared about his record of "mild anarchy," as one therapist put it. (Another cited his "lack of impulse control.") And to his parents' surprise, Dean made it through the training academy without a single mark against him.

Buckling down, he stayed focused and worked his ass off. He took on all the grunt assignments without pitching a fit or screwing around. His parents thought he had finally turned his life around.

And then one morning, Director ███████ summoned Dean to his office. Dean had made a good impression on his superiors, and they wanted to give him an opportunity to prove himself worthy of a promotion, or at least a better location detail than Milwaukee.

The news couldn't have come at a better time. In the weeks prior, Dean had been stuck in the archives filing paperwork. He was slowly going mad from the tedious assignment. Boredom was the trigger for his troublemaking ways. Working for the agency, he had been able to keep himself in check by snapping a rubber band against his wrist, but his skin was irritated and red on both arms now, and if he didn't get a better assignment soon, he didn't know what kind of mess he would get himself into. For one thing, the redheaded archivist leading the project wore black, velvet heels, and all Dean could think about was what those would feel like with her legs wrapped around him.

[DIRECTOR ██████████: *Why are you telling me information I already know?*]

[AGENT DILTON: *You knew about the archivist? Sorry, sir. I just— Wait, how do you know her? She's not related to you, is she?*]

[DIRECTOR ██████████: *No, you fool. Not the red-head. I mean, why are you telling me about the mission I assigned you to? I already know all about it. Just cut to the chase.*]

[AGENT DILTON: *Sorry, sir. I'll get there. But this is all important background info, I swear.*]

Director ██████████ gave Dean his first mission. "It's very simple—you're on security detail for a couple of white coats."

Dean leaned in, fingers laced across his black tie and unbuttoned suit jacket. "Can you tell me more, sir?"

"Of course," said the director.

```
Attention: Agent Dean Dilton — you will
be stationed at T#00526829, also known as
██████████,    also    known    as    "PARADISE,"
██████.)  ████████████████████████████████
████████████████████████████████████. Your
assignment  is  ████████████████████████████
████████████████████████████████████████████
████████████████████████████████████████████
████████████████████████████████████████████
████████████████████████████████████████████
████████████████████████████████████████████.
```

strictly prohibited.

soil

dirt .
You are responsible for

Information will be provided to you
on an as-needed basis.

"I see," said Dean.

Despite assurances that the mission was of the utmost importance, the experience was boring as fuck.

For one month, Dean was stationed at undisclosed coordinates in the middle of the desert, outside a dumpy roadside town that he was prohibited from visiting, so that a couple of soil scientists could collect and analyze dirt samples from one of two trailers. Dean lived (i.e., ate, slept, and shit) in the second trailer.

He tried making conversation with the two egg-heads, but they told him nothing. When he asked questions about their work or research backgrounds, they snickered and insinuated that he was too stupid to understand.

But at least he was far enough away from the redheaded archivist who continued to haunt his daydreams.

For weeks, Dean woke up at the ass crack of dawn, shaved, put on his suit, and went outside to see what Dr. Burke and Dr. Gelman were doing—either collecting dirt or studying dirt or talking about dirt. Then a fax might come in on one of the machines in their trailers (yes, a fax—in this day and age), and Dean would ask them questions that came in on the printout. Proving their assumptions about his intellect correct, Dean didn't understand a lick of what they responded with; he simply scribbled some notes down to fax back to head office. Then he fussed over the instant coffee machine that shat out swampy diarrhea-like liquid before planting himself in a lawn chair to supervise the scientists.

Occasionally, a follow-up fax would come in for Dr. Burke who would read it before taking it to Dr. Gelman who would scan it quickly before crumpling it up and chucking it into the surrounding desert.

Sometimes a police car from the town would cruise by on the highway. The officer never pulled in to say hi or ask what they were up to. Never even stopped. Dean figured it had something to do with his agency's presence. His director likely told the local law enforcement to stay the fuck away, albeit in more polite terms.

And just as the officer didn't step foot anywhere

near the trailer, nor did Dean venture into the town of Paradise—though it wasn't much of a town. All he could see from the highway that circumvented the need to go anywhere near the place was Paradise's roadside attraction (a giant cupid statue) that had fallen into disrepair. It was hard to miss the enormous, winged man-baby in a diaper, aiming its bow and arrow squarely into the center of town.

Dean ate his breakfast, lunch, and dinner out of a frozen food tray or scrounged up something from the supplies cooler in the back of their shared station wagon. The scientists' mini fridge (filled with cups of dirt) was off limits.

Unable to go into town, Dean had no one to talk to other than Burke and Gelman, and he wasn't even allowed to talk to them about anything other than their security detail.

By day six, he would have smothered them both for a fresh coffee.

But he had to be a good boy for his folks, a good agent for his agency, and a good security guard for the scientists, so he tried not to dwell on his downward spiral. For twelve hours each day for four long weeks, Dean wandered around the perimeter that the scientists had roped off, keeping an eye out for trouble (there was none, not even a rattlesnake to contend with), or he would doze off under the trailer's awning in a lawn chair (which gave him a crick in the neck), listening to Burke and Gelman bicker about dirt.

He was so utterly bored by the second week that he started to play finger fillet with a plastic knife. The blade snapped off after ten minutes.

By the fourth week, he imagined hanging himself in

the tiny trailer bathroom. Not to kill himself—rather, he was toying with the idea of autoerotic asphyxiation.

One night he scribbled *I'M SO FUCKING BORED* on the wall by his mattress. *KILL ME NOW.*

Before he could lose his mind, the month-long assignment came to an end. As the scientists packed up their dirt and grumbled about not having more time to do their research, Dean was shaking with excitement to go home. He dreamed about sleeping in his own bed. He dreamed about a fresh cup of coffee. And he dreamed about the redheaded archivist. His palms were sweaty just thinking about all the filthy things he would let that woman do to him when he got back.

He just had one more night on the outskirts of Paradise before he could begin the long drive back to the nearest airport and back to civilization.

So he had twelve hours to kill.

A smart man would have retired early, like Burke and Gelman, and though Dean was fairly smart, he had been prone to making impulsive decisions in his younger years, pushing boundaries, and bending rules for the sake of his own amusement. Also, he was painfully horny.

One of his director's rules had been to refrain from browsing the internet. Director ████████ must have known how dull the mission would be and therefore didn't want the young agent to spend all his time scrolling social media—or other, more unsavory sites. Dean's task was to babysit the scientists. But now that the scientists were almost out of the picture and the security detail was coming to a close, Dean didn't see how browsing could get him into any trouble.

So he took a deep breath and checked his email.

Spam, spam, spam—his inbox was a Monty Python musical. His own mother hadn't bothered to send him a check-in email, one of her warning missives about the dangers of modern dating ("They lie about themselves, Deanie! It's called catfishing!"), or even one of those hokey chain letters—*forward this email to ten people or you'll be cursed!*

No, his dear old mom spent most of her days on Facebook, trading gardening tips with Aunt Shaye or arguing about the damn liberals with Aunt Linda, and god knew he wasn't about to waste his time opening that awful app.

He tried Twitter, but what a pile of flaming garbage that was. Even his shit-spewing commander in chief couldn't help being a raging asshole there.

Sitting on the corner of his mattress, he kicked off his shoes and tugged on his tie until it loosened. His free hand scrolled and tapped through various apps, looking for something to pique his interest.

He didn't have to search long to find trouble. Trouble found him in the form of a clickbait article extolling the virtues of online dating and hook-up culture.

The writer—a "certified sex columnist," whatever the hell that meant—had reviewed the latest dating apps and applauded them for allowing hook-ups of the twenty-first century to be "no fuss, no muss."

Dean rubbed his chin. Right on time, his five o'clock shadow was starting to sprout. Instead of thinking that he had better make time to shave in the morning, he decided to poke around in one of those dating apps.

Naughty or Nice's logo was a pin-up devil woman

promising its users a "sinfully sweet time."

Dean swallowed, his thumb hesitating over the sign-up button. There was no way in hell he was going to match with anyone. Not out in the middle of nowhere. No way, no how. The town's population had to be fewer than ten people. It wasn't even a town by that standard. It was a *ghost* town. And even if by some random chance he matched with someone, he'd be spammed with junk emails from this company for the rest of his life.

So then, what do I have to lose?

He tapped the sign-up button and filled in all the boxes. Name, email, password, re-enter password. Verify login information. Log in with credentials.

WELCOME TO NAUGHTY OR NICE! CREATE PROFILE. TELL US ABOUT YOUR SEXY SELF (25-word limit).

Dean groaned. What could anyone really share about themselves in twenty-five words? He figured it didn't matter. The app was for hooking up, not for finding a life partner. So he wrote, *Tall, dark, and handsome. The end.* Short and sweet.

ADD PHOTO.

Dean groaned again. He hated having his picture taken. Though he was tall and had dark hair, like his bio noted, he didn't like looking at himself for too long. That was what vain assholes did. His mother always said he was a good-looking boy, but his eyes were like mud and his Adam's apple stuck out on his scrawny neck like a snake trying to choke down a mouse. In other words, he had a few eccentric features on a good bone structure.

But if he was going to go fishing, he needed something for his lure. So he sucked up his feelings about selfie culture, propped himself up by the window where the setting sun cast a soft, orange glow, and snapped a picture of himself. Then he fiddled with his phone's auto-edit function to touch himself up before posting it to his profile.

Dean, 33

Tall, dark, and handsome. The end.

Stupid, but whatever.

And doubt swept in.

His phone signal was weak and the internet connection was poor, and certainly there were no attractive women for miles. This wasn't going to work. It was a waste of time. All this trouble for a one-night stand.

He tapped FIND ME A MATCH!

NAUGHTY or NICE?

His brow furrowed. *What's this? I get to choose?* "Hmm..."

On the left side, a sweet-faced angel chick in a halo and mini-skirt sucked on the tip of her finger. On the right, a leering devil woman reminded him of the redhead back home.

His thumb barely touched the NAUGHTY button before a big, red heart with devil horns filled his screen. *Loading... Loading... Loading...*

Dean stood up and tossed the phone on the mattress. He wasn't going to think about it. He was going to take a cold shower and go to bed early, and tomorrow while he waited for his flight, he would delete his profile, delete the app. He would return to Milwaukee, back to his original assignment in the archives, where he would politely ask out the smoking hot redhead. And if she said no or maybe some other time, then she wasn't interested and he would back off like a gentleman.

YOU HAVE A MATCH!

"Huh?"

He knelt down next to the bed and scooped up his phone. He didn't want to appear too eager, but he was very curious about the kind of small-town troll woman who browsed his profile and deemed him worthy.

He flipped to his match's profile.

Marlow, 29

A good man is hard to find. A hard man is good to find ;)

"Fuck me," he breathed.

His match was a smoking hot redhead with pouty lips and overly nerdy librarian glasses perched on her nose. Her face and duck lips filled most of the photo, but her breasts managed to squeeze in at the edge of the frame.

He tugged on his snug collar and swallowed. The app was almost too easy.

He checked the location results for this unicorn of a match. Miraculously, she was in town—that was about as much detail as the app would share with him, and that was close enough for Dean.

Rubbing his fingertips together, he had to come up with some clever way of messaging her. He thought about it for five straight minutes, just staring at the screen. And then he came up with the perfect ice-breaker. It was going to make him sound so cool.

Hunched over the phone, he typed out his message and hit send.

Hey.

He grinned, nodding at the clever coolness he was obviously conveying.

Now he could sit back and wait.

2.

THE TROUBLEMAKER

(Side B)

WHAT THE HELL? was tattooed in cursive around Marlow's wrist. Her ex, Tony, had warned her about getting tattoos.

"No identifying marks. It's harder for them to make you if you get caught."

Make you. Tony liked to sound like he was an Italian mobster by way of Portland. He was also a major hypocrite because he dressed loud and proud like he was the second coming of his rock hero, Jerry Lee Lewis.

It rubbed Marlow the wrong way when people told her what to do, even if what they told her made perfect sense or was the right thing to do. So the day after Tony told her no tattoos, Marlow took her cut from their latest job and got *What the hell?* inked onto her skin—because what the hell? *You only live twice.*

Except for Marlow. She had more lives than a street cat. In her last "life," she was a redhead with big, dorky glasses she found in a Value Village. The lenses gave her a headache, but she popped them out and wore them without. She was surprised how many men she could attract with that look, but not surprised when the scummy bastards asked if her carpets matched her drapes, wink-wink, nudge-nudge. Like her life was a Monty Python sketch.

Men were sleazy, but they did have their uses. Like Tony. He taught her how to make fast cash, how to drive like a bat out of hell, and how to never get caught. And he "donated" his 1971 Dodge Demon 340 to Marlow when she needed to disappear from his life.

Sorry, Tony.

By the time Marlow settled into her no-tell motel room at the Shady Palms Motel in the middle of the desert, a four-eyed redhead in New Mexico was wanted for questioning. Luckily, Marlow had long since ditched the copper wig in a gas station bathroom and tossed the glasses out the window on the highway.

Gotta keep moving—she was thinking that would eventually be the tattoo on her right wrist.

Paradise seemed harmless enough. It didn't appear on her GPS or any of the roadmaps in Tony's car.

The town was flatter than her chest in junior high and looked like a bunch of random buildings had dropped down from the sky to land wherever: a bank, a second-hand store, a police station/courthouse with excessively tall columns, an all-night diner, and the motel with a sleepy-eyed clerk behind the desk. But on the edge of town, the earth broke upward, a rocky bump in the middle of a chaotically hilly graveyard, on top of which sat a dilapidated antebellum-style mansion.

It was a weird sight. The architectural style of the house didn't match the 1950s-style diner, which didn't mesh with the 1920s art deco bank, which didn't jive with the early '70s chic of the motel, which didn't gel with the Wild West facades of the rest of the scattered buildings.

And at the center of town, a giant cupid statue aimed an arrow into the ground.

On top of that, the air smelled stuffy, like the people of Paradise were ants trapped under a dome intended to slowly suffocate them.

Marlow didn't pay any of it much mind. She had bigger things to consider, like where to go next. She wasn't planning to stay in this place any longer than one night, and unless she forced herself to go to bed early, it promised to be one long, lonely, boring night.

When she checked in—as "Dixie Normous," to which the clerk (whose name tag said "Billy") either ignored or just didn't care—she asked if there was anything fun to do around town.

The gangly, greasy-haired Billy scratched the crust out of the corner of his one milky eye and said, "TV, I guess."

"Okay."

"But cable's out."

"What about a liquor store?" she asked, pressing her breasts against the counter and giving him her sweetest smile.

"Nuh-uh," he grunted, selecting a key from a wall of other room keys. The folks of Paradise were still living pretty analog lives. "It's a dry country."

"Boo," she pouted, wondering if he must have meant dry *county*.

"You need something else?" Billy asked, sliding the key across the counter. One of his fingernails was black and just about to fall off. "Somethin' I can give ya a hand with?"

She studied his knobby fingers, his skinny wrist, and patchy forearm, all the way up his arm to where it disappeared under a baggy bowling shirt. His shoulders were narrow and his chest concave, and even if she were desperate, she wouldn't dry hump the brim of his trucker hat.

"No," she said, squeezing her thighs together. "Nothing I can't take care of myself."

The room was a dump, but at least it was far enough away from greasy Billy. She lifted the ugly paintings off the wall to check for peep holes, cameras, or any other creepiness she had found at seedier motels. The place was clean and clear.

On the nightstand was a yellowed brochure for the town. *Whatever your heart's desire... Find it in Paradise! Voted Best Roadside Destination for Honeymooners 1960!*

"Gross," she muttered. *Who would want to honeymoon in this dump?* She bent the brochure in half and used it as a fan. She tried to turn on the A/C, but it was too hot to think, let alone figure out air conditioning mechanics, so she gave up.

Outside, the sun was setting, bleeding red across the horizon. Darkness wasn't going to take the sting out of the dry, relentless heat. She tugged on her bra where sweat collected under the band. Though she wanted to take it off, first she needed to retrieve her bags from the car. A small overnight case with a change of clothes, her makeup, and toiletries, and a black duffle bag with a sports team logo emblazoned on one side. She didn't know or care who the team was or what sport they played; it was just a bag.

Just a bag she unzipped once the motel door was locked and chained behind her. It was just a bag that she lifted upside down over the bedspread and shook the contents out. Cash in small denominations—fives, tens, twenties—fluttered out and covered the bed. Then she tossed the bag aside.

She took her time and laid out each bill until the cash was perfectly spaced together like a money-patterned coverlet. Other than applying her cat's-eye eyeliner, the money ritual was the only thing she was meticulous about. It had to be perfect.

How else would she manifest more cash from the universe?

She kicked off her boots and jeans. She peeled off her t-shirt and unclasped her bra. She threw everything into a corner and faced the bed. Then she tucked her thumbs into the waistband of her undershorts and stripped them off, letting them collect around one ankle before flicking them aside.

Taking a deep breath, she dove head first onto the bed. Bills flew everywhere. She rolled around and stretched out, grabbing fistfuls of dirty cash and rubbing it all over her body. Between her legs and under her sweaty breasts. She traced it up her chest, shoulders, and neck, moaning at how wrong—and yet so right—it felt.

"I love money and money loves me," she gushed.

Marlow didn't believe in gods or religion—though she dabbled in astrology and appreciated the art of tarot card readings. She worshipped at the altar of only two things: money and sex. And though she loved rolling around in big piles of dollar bills, it wasn't enough to get her off, and eventually she had to seek out a helping hand. And if Billy was any indication, she wasn't going to find it in town.

Regardless, she opened her Naughty or Nice app and hit FIND ME A MATCH! As she watched the throbbing heart search the internet for her next piece of meat, she peeled a bill off her skin and began to build a pile. The only thing sadder than not getting to spend her hard-earned dollars was having to put the money away after playing in it.

She was about to give up on the stupid dating app when it chimed at her. YOU HAVE A MATCH!

"Huh," she said, and tapped to see.

Dean, 33

Tall, dark, and handsome. The end.

He didn't look too bad. A little dorky, but she had slept with worse. She tapped to confirm it was a match. *Ball's in your court, dude.* Then she left her phone on the bed while she had a shower.

The water was too cold and the towels were too small, but she managed to clean up nicely. She primped her hair and painted her lips bright red. She checked her phone before getting dressed.

Hey.

"That's it? Fuck me." She rolled her eyes, typing her response.

Hey to you. Can't believe there's someone else alive in this place. You hungry?

She waited for his response.

Haha. I'm alive, aren't I?

She shook her head. It might be worse than she expected—he thought he was funny. *Meet me at that weird diner at seven. Flo's or Jo's or Moe's, or something like that.*

It's a date, he replied. *See you then.*

Neither of them could have anticipated that they were about to go on the date from hell.

And then their evening would get much, much worse.

3.

THE DINER

THE DINER'S ACTUAL name was Happy's. Marlow was way off with the name, and it made Dean wonder if he was even in the right place. Or if he should even be in the town at all.

Most definitely not. He had "borrowed" the car he shared with Burke and Gelman, so he hoped neither one of them noticed and decided to report it stolen. Or report *him*. Burke might be cool, but Gelman would squeal.

The roads in town were crumbling, threatening to warp and sink under the weight of the car. Foul steam erupted from jagged cracks in the pavement. *Is this why the town is off limits? Well, supposed to be off limits. Is this why Burke and Gelman were collecting soil?*

Because there wasn't another diner that fit Marlow's poor description, Dean took his chances on Happy's, a throwback joint with Formica tables and chairs, red vinyl booths, and tabletop jukeboxes. He wandered in and took a seat in the corner booth with a wide view of the parking lot. While he waited for his date, he tried to pull up the location information about Marlow on the app. Maybe she wasn't actually in town...

His thumb clumsily tapped an ad for longer-lasting erection medication and his dickbag of a phone blasted out the very loud first seconds of a fast-talking voiceover asking, *"Does YOUR PENIS have you feeling DOWN?"*—followed by a sad slide whistle.

He fumbled around, dropping the phone under the table.

"Not able to SATISFY the ladies?"

"Fuck." He scrambled as the waitress shuffled over. Halfway under the table, he grazed the screen.

"Ever wish your ERECTION could last up to eight minutes LONGER?"

"Fuck, fuck, fuck."

He grabbed the phone as the waitress, Delores, hovered nearby. Face burning, he settled back in his seat. He turned off his phone and stuffed it in his jacket pocket, alongside his wallet. He was dressed in his usual black suit and tie, so he didn't *look* like an erection-obsessed creep, but when he offered Delores a befuddled smile, her blank expression gave him no hints as to what she thought of him.

"Coffee?" she grunted, barely lifting one of her two decanters.

"Uh, yeah. Please." He flipped over one of the white mugs already on the table. "Fill 'er up," he added with a nervous chuckle.

She filled his mug and shuffled away. "Be back to take your order."

Dean tapped his fingers on the table, waiting for his

coffee to cool or for his date to arrive, whichever came first. He was about to check his phone, but the erection commercial was still too fresh in his memory.

The clock on the wall claimed it was after eleven. Broken. The second hand was caught, ticking between the same two seconds.

He tapped his foot.

The only others around were Delores, a line cook, and a trucker sitting at the counter. He sported a red MAGA hat and was hunched over a yellowed newspaper. Harsh lines etched his grim face. As if aware he was being stared at, the trucker turned. When their eyes met, the trucker frowned.

Dean looked down at the table. He fiddled with the mug's handle.

This is stupid. What am I doing? Hoping to get laid by a stranger in some dumpy town? This is a mistake. I'm not supposed to be here. Not for any reason. I'm leaving tomorrow. All I have to do is keep my nose clean. I don't need the trouble. I need to go.

He reached for his wallet, glancing out the window. Outside, a woman marched toward the diner. She was swinging a purse at her side.

Oh, fuck me, he thought, forgetting about his wallet.

She wasn't a big-breasted redhead with nerdy glasses. She was perky with curly blonde hair and perfect vision. Maybe contact lenses. And she was kind of short—maybe five-foot-two. Not as long and lean as the archivist back home. This woman was compact and curvy.

She chewed bubble gum like it was cud and had a sassy bounce in her step. She was hot in her own way, but she wasn't the woman he was expecting. Although, he didn't mind the sight of her fishnet stockings under a pair of jean shorts and the ripped, white t-shirt that showed off her midriff.

No, he told himself. *I need to leave.*

Before he could act, before his brain could tell the rest of his body that this was a big mistake, a bad idea, and to *move already,* the bell over the door chimed. The woman paused in the doorway, looking around.

Oh, no.

She pulled a phone from her purse and turned on the screen. She held the screen closer to her face, comparing the photo to the only two men in the diner. She looked really hard at the MAGA hat guy before her eyes settled on Dean. Maybe she needed those glasses after all.

Dean sank down in the booth.

Oh, hell no. That can't be her. That's not *her.*

Lowering the phone, she raised an eyebrow. "Dean?" she called from across the diner.

He glanced at the trucker, who watched them both from under his heavy-lidded eyes, still frowning. Dean felt trapped under a spotlight. There was no backing out now. Marlow sashayed toward him, pointing. She showed him her screen as she slid into the seat across from him.

"Looks just like you," she said. "Fresh?"

"What?"

She tapped a fingernail on the screen. "Did you just take it?"

"Uh, yeah."

This is a bad idea. Terrible. If I get caught, it won't even be worth it. What was I thinking? She's not even the hot redhead. I've been catfished! My mother was right.

"Cool."

He took a sip of the coffee. Still too hot, it scorched his lips. He puckered them and shakily set the mug down.

"Too hot for ya?" she asked.

No shit, Sherlock. He cleared his throat. "Marlow, right?"

"Mm-hm." She plucked the gum from her mouth and stuck it under the table.

The waitress came by and offered her coffee or decaf. Marlow turned her down, asking for a chocolate milkshake with whipped cream and a cherry on top. Delores sighed. Clearly the last thing the tired old woman wanted to do was whip up a milkshake, but Marlow was undeterred. She beamed at the waitress until she went away with the order.

"I don't drink coffee," she explained to Dean when they were alone again. "I prefer to run on my body's natural energy."

"What if you get tired?"

"I take a nap."

"But what if you can't take a nap?"

"Why wouldn't I be able to take a nap? It's a free country."

"Suppose you're at work."

She tipped over the jelly packet caddy and began to stack the packets. Marmalade, strawberry, grape, peanut butter. "You know, in Japan, they like, *reward* you for napping? It shows you're a hard worker. We should do that here."

Dean could just imagine how well that would go over at the agency. Federal agents taking a siesta on stakeouts or resting their eyes during a debrief meeting.

What a brilliant fucking idea.

"So what's your full name?" he asked.

"Why?" She smirked. "You gonna Google me?"

"I just wanna know who I'm talking to."

"Isn't my profile enough for you ... Mr. *Tall, Dark, and Handsome?*"

A good man is hard to find and a hard man is good to find. What that bio said about Marlow, Dean wasn't sure. "I guess," he said, struggling to mask his disappointment.

Marlow rose up, sticking a leg under her butt so she could sit higher in the booth. She looked around. "Where's that chick with my milkshake?"

Dean pressed ahead. "So, uh, what do you do for a living?"

"What do I *do?*" She raised her dark brows as if his question came out of left field. "I just live. I don't have to *do* anything."

"You're joking, right? I meant like a job—what do you do for work?"

"I get by," she said, shrugging. "What about you? What do you 'do'?" She used finger quotations, and as annoying as that was to Dean, he couldn't take his eyes off her pouty lips when they curved around the word do, like she was blowing him a kiss.

He adjusted his tie. "That's classified."

She laughed. It was light and joyful with a bit of a rasp. "Same then," she replied with a wink. "Classified."

They sat in silence after that. Dean buried his nose in the menu, wondering how long he could pretend he wanted to be there. Delores returned to take their orders. Dean ordered a club sandwich, and when the waitress asked Marlow what she was having, Marlow clicked her nails on the tabletop and replied, "A milkshake, hopefully."

Delores made a gravelly *hmmm* sound and wandered back to the kitchen.

Marlow turned back to Dean. "What're you, my mother?"

"Excuse me?"

She cocked her head. "Because you seem really disappointed in me."

"I'm not..." But he was, and the longer he talked to Marlow, the harder it was to like her. She just wasn't his type, though she did have some nice features.

"I guess I'm a little surprised," he admitted. He reached into his jacket for his phone. Turned it on. The app was still open, but thankfully the ad had gone away. He pulled up her profile and showed it to her. "You don't look too much like your photo."

She wrinkled her nose. "That was my last look." She scrunched up her blonde curls and grinned. "I'm trying a new one right now. Blondes have more fun, right?"

"I guess..."

"Let *me* guess," she said, leaning in. "You're into redheads."

"Well..."

Her eyes crinkled as she focused on him. "Is it a fetish?"

"No!" he denied a bit too forcefully.

"No judgment here." She poked his screen with her fingernail. "That was a wig, dude. Besides, a person's hair color doesn't reveal anything about the *person*. It's just a color. You should be looking at what's on the inside. That's what counts. Now, where's my stupid milkshake?"

Dean felt like he should feel bad, but he didn't need a guilt trip from a stranger. "Look, I like what I like—what's wrong with that?" She blinked a few times, as if surprised he would talk back. "The app's called Naughty or Nice—I doubt ninety-nine percent of the people that use it are actually looking for their future spouse."

"Maybe I am," she replied, a glint in her eyes.

Dean gave her a hard look. "No, you're not. Otherwise, you would've selected 'nice.' So either you chose naughty by accident or you're playing devil's advocate because you like to rile people up. That's *your* fetish."

She raised her eyebrows. The corner of her mouth perked up. "Dude…"

"That's why you couldn't just order a damn coffee," he continued, on a roll now. "You had to mess with that poor waitress—"

"She's not—"

"*And* it's also why you're telling me you're the one percent of people using a hook-up app to make a love connection. Yeah, okay, sure."

Her jaw dropped. "I'm not the one percent. *You're* the one percent, Mr. Suit and Tie."

Smirking, Dean leaned back and brought the mug to his lips, smug in the knowledge that he had gotten under her skin. "Face it, toots. You're the one percent."

"*Toots?*" She scoffed, fumbling for a retort. "Well, *you're* an asshole." She grabbed her purse.

As much as he loved making her squirm (almost as much as she enjoyed doing the same to him), their date was circling the drain. He stood up and reached for his wallet. "Well, it's been a slice." *A slice of shit pie*, he thought.

Marlow dragged herself out of the booth. In her ridiculous red cowgirl boots, she lost her footing and stumbled against him. He caught her by the elbows and she planted her hands on his chest. They were caught in a delicate balancing act. Her big, green eyes gazed up at him, before trailing down. His suit jacket gaped open, giving her a peek at his service pistol.

Her breath hitched. "Geez, dude—just a head rush," she said. "Hands off."

"Hey, *you* fell onto *me*." He put his hands up, making it clear that he hadn't tried to cop a feel.

She shook her head, storming off. She had one hell of a sexy walk, and if she had not been so repugnant, he might have followed her back to whatever hellhole she spawned from. But the night (and their match) was a lost cause.

He sighed, picking up his coffee to finish it off just as Delores returned with his sandwich—and the stupid milkshake. A perfect red cherry glistened on top of a pile of rich cream.

The little woman was going to be pissed off to see Dean sucking back her milkshake as he cruised past her on his way out of town.

"Any chance I can get that to go?" he said, reaching for his wallet.

Releasing a throaty grumble, Delores looked less than impressed.

Dean grimaced—his wallet was not in his breast pocket. "Excuse me. I seem to have misplaced my wallet."

Delores dropped the food on the table with a loud clatter, drawing the attention of the line cook and the trucker. "You can't pay?"

"No, no, I can pay. I just need to find my—"

He stared into the void Marlow left behind, and a realization hit him like a semi-truck. *Marlow.* She wasn't wobbling from standing up too quickly. *She's a pick-pocket.*

"Fuck," he groaned, smacking his head.

Delores cleared her throat.

Dean held up a finger. "I'll be right back."

"You're not leaving here without paying!"

The scrawny line cook poked his head out from the kitchen. The MAGA hat guy spun around in his seat.

Dean pointed after Marlow, who had disappeared across the dark parking lot. "That woman— She stole my wallet. I just gotta—" He burst out the door, bell ringing, and ran after the blonde thief.

Delores stomped into the kitchen. The line cook and trucker stayed out of her way, but watched as her crepey hand picked up the phone and dialed the number for a man Paradise residents knew all too well.

"Police," grunted the man's voice.

"I got a couple of troublemakers for ya," she said.

4.

THE DASH

TOTTERING ACROSS THE uneven blacktop in her cherry red boots and dodging the sweltering steam spraying up through the cracks, Marlow tucked the wallet into her shirt. All the while, she laughed her ass off, even though there was a fifty/fifty chance Dean would follow her.

Men didn't like being bested by a woman, and they absolutely hated when a woman took all their money and gave them the slip. Sometimes they were too embarrassed to confront her. Those men were her favorite type. But other times, they wanted to make her pay. Sometimes they meant to punch her in the face.

Dean seemed harmless enough, even with the gun in his jacket. Plenty of her exes had carried concealed weapons for one reason or another, but they were all dangerous men who were not to be fucked with.

Dean wasn't like them, and she was a good judge of character. And she only took his wallet because he was such a stuck-up bore and a complete waste of her time.

Oh, well, she thought as she cut through the diner's parking lot.

The only other car was a station wagon.

Ew, she thought. *Is that how he got here? What a drag.*

If what he did for a living was "classified," wouldn't that make him a secret agent? He definitely looked like a fed—boring and beige, which would explain the car.

When she checked over her shoulder, Dean had exited the diner and was waving at her. "Hey!"

Oh, great. She picked up the pace. *Now he's going to accuse me of stealing his wallet.*

She took one more step and before her sole touched the pavement, the ground began to shake. The asphalt shifted, throwing her off balance. She was pinwheeling to stay upright when the ground broke apart in front of her. Hot steam shot out, about to hit her in the face when she was dragged to safety.

"I got you," Dean said, his hand around her wrist.

"I don't need any help," she replied, shaking him off.

"Sure," he said. "Hey, I was calling you."

"Oh, yeah?" She was already walking away, heading back to the motel.

"Yeah. I'm missing my wallet and—"

The earth groaned, a smaller rumble shook under their feet. Marlow froze, reaching out for Dean—just in case.

"What *is* that?" she wondered.

"An aftershock maybe," he said.

"But earthquakes? Here in the desert?"

"Doesn't matter," said Dean. "I don't care. I just need to get my wallet back. Now have you seen it?"

Marlow wasn't about to cop to anything. She had acquired that wallet fair and square.

But the item in question was the least important thing on her mind when a deafening crack rippled through the parking lot, breaking apart right under the station wagon.

"Oh, no..." Dean stepped toward it, but it was too late to do anything but watch.

The crack expanded into a sinkhole, swallowing the sad car. The driver's side leaned into the hole with a scraping crunch sound. The other two tires lifted up toward the sky.

"Oh, fuck..."

"Holy shit," Marlow whispered.

No car, no wallet, no nice meal at a restaurant—Marlow felt bad. She reached into her shirt and slipped out the wallet before discreetly dropping it on the ground.

"Oh, hey," she said, tapping it with her toe. "Is *that* your wallet?"

Dean ran his hands through his hair. "What am I going to do?"

Marlow shrugged. "I don't know, dude. Call a tow truck?"

He pulled out his phone and looked at it like it was a useless brick. "Fine." He tapped away on it and then blew air through his nostrils. "I can't find anyone in Paradise. I can't find Paradise at all."

"Did you spell the name right?"

He gave her a droll, tired look. "I know how to spell."

"Well, I don't know," she said with another shrug. "Try the guy in the motel office?"

"Fine," he grumbled.

"Fine," she replied, somehow leading the way. All she wanted to do was ditch this dead weight date, go back to her room, and put the night behind her. Tomorrow, she would get in her car and drive for as long as she could keep her eyes open. No more stops, no more encounters with strangers—not until she figured out her next plan of attack.

She opened the door to the office and ushered Dean inside. "There."

"Thanks."

Marlow lingered by the door while Dean marched up to the counter. Half asleep in the middle of a *Hustler*, Billy rested on his knuckles.

"Uh, hello?"

Impatient already, Marlow abandoned her post by the door and strode up next to Dean. She slammed her palm down on the bell, startling Billy back to reality. He didn't bother to cover up the naked lady he had drooled on.

"What?"

Marlow stuck a thumb at Dean. "This guy needs help."

"So?"

"Can he use your phone?"

Billy shook his head. "No."

"Why not?"

"Is he a customer?"

"No."

"So, no." He picked up his magazine.

Marlow pushed it back down. "Really?"

Billy glowered at her. "Yes, really, Miss..." He scanned the guest book on his desk. "Miss *Dixie Normous.*"

Dean grinned. "Nice."

"Shut up. Look, there was an earthquake and his car fell into a hole—can you call him a tow truck or something?"

"Don't think I will."

"Why not?" Now Dean was getting hot under the collar. "I'll pay for the call."

Billy raised the receiver off its hook. "Phone doesn't work. Only calls out to the police station."

"That doesn't make any sense," Dean said.

"Come on," Marlow said, hooking her arm around Dean's. "You can try in my room." She fired a cold glare at Billy. *"Useless."*

Billy scowled, exchanging his magazine for the phone.

Back outside, in the hot, stifling air, Dean frowned. "You could've handled that better."

"What do you mean?"

"Do you always give attitude to people in the service industry?"

"If some dumb hick is asking for it, then yes."

"And stealing someone's wallet—Is that also something you do regularly?"

"I didn't take it—I found it," she said, committing to the lie. She stuck out her chin, staring at him.

He stared back.

Finally, when she decided he wasn't going to back down, she pointed to the only unit in the entire lot that had a car parked in front. "I'm over there. It's got a phone, or you could try mine." She opened her purse, which had only her phone and a pack of gum.

"No, I should go back to the diner and pay Delores."

"Who?"

"The waitress—the one we dine-and-dashed on. We should go back and apologize."

A laugh burst out of her. "You do that. I'm good."

"I don't want to get into any more trouble."

She stared at him like he was crazy, and maybe he was. She had a way of attracting nutcases. "What trouble? There's nobody around for miles. Who cares? Live a little." She tugged on the end of his tie.

"I've lived enough, thank you." He swept the tie away from her, tucking it back in his jacket. "And besides, I can't get into any trouble. *At all.*"

She grinned at him. "Oh, sure you can."

"If I can't get that car fixed or if Delores decided to call the cops on us for that stunt you pulled—"

"Who would you be in trouble with?"

"Well, that's class—"

"Classified," she finished for him. "Okay, fine. Don't ask, don't tell, is that it?"

He cleared his throat. "Something like that."

"How about this... Come back to my room, call a tow truck, have a drink while you wait. That waitress isn't going to freak out over a $30 tab."

"She might."

"You worry too much."

"I never used to."

"Then take a break and come have a drink. I know you've got nothing better to do." She held up a warning finger. "But don't think this is because I like you or anything. I just feel bad that you lost your car *and* your wallet. And no offense—you're just not my type."

He shook his head, an amused smile on his face.

"What's funny?" she asked, leading the way.

"Nothing. I was just thinking the same thing about you."

5.

THE MOTEL

MARLOW SHUT THE door, leaving the chain dangling and the deadbolt off. Dean went straight to the phone, fussing around with the rotary dial like he had never seen an old movie before.

She left him to it, retreating to the closet for the bag that was just a bag. She sneaked out her stash of sample-sized booze bottles swiped from nicer establishments.

Crawling back out, she caught Dean staring at her. She wasn't surprised. Men were always admiring her backside when she wasn't looking. Some of the bold ones admired her even when she was.

"No signal," he complained, hanging up. She was still on her knees as he spoke, and he quickly averted his eyes and pretended to be interested in the gaudy, pastel painting hanging askew on the wall. "Nice place you got here."

"Home sweet shithole." She tossed him the bag.

He almost fumbled the catch, which made her

smirk. Recovering, he pointed to the painting. "What do you think about this one?"

Crossing her arms, she wandered closer to him. She stayed out of reach, because even though she had invited him in, she wasn't naïve. Inviting strangers—correction: strange *men*, because the few women she had hooked up with in motels never tried to threaten her with a switchblade—was not a smart thing to do, especially with a bag full of cash hidden in the closet.

But there was something about this Dean guy that was different. And sure, she had said the same thing about Tony up until the first time he knocked her around. But again, she maintained that she was a pretty good judge of character.

Dean may have carried a gun, but he wasn't a bad guy.

Probably.

"I don't know," she said, slipping one of the bottles out of the bag he held. She cracked it open—an itty-bitty Smirnoff—and downed it with one toss of her head.

"Funny," he said. "You had a bunch of opinions about stuff back at the restaurant."

Her eyes narrowed. He was obviously baiting her, but she couldn't help it. "I've got lots of opinions. I'm just not gonna waste them on an ugly-ass painting in a shitty motel."

"Then why are you here?" he asked. "Was the Ritz fully booked this evening?"

"Are you gonna make me drink alone?"

He selected a teeny bottle of Jose Cuervo, eyes trailing down her arm. "What's that on your wrist?"

"Tattoo."

"I *know* that. What's it say?"

She held it out, expecting him to read it, but it was upside down from his point of view. "It says, 'what the hell.'"

"That your motto?"

"My motto?"

"You know, a credo? A statement you live by? Like the Marines have *semper fi*. Always loyal."

She took another bottle and downed it, hoping his ego would try to catch up to her.

"You only live twice," she told him. "That's my motto."

"You mean, you only live *once*."

"No, it's twice."

"You don't die and come back. That's not how life works."

"Well, the expression *I* know is you only live twice."

"That doesn't make any sense."

She wanted to smooth out the two dark frown lines that pinched his face together. Maybe it would loosen him up enough for the stick to drop out of his ass.

"You gonna drink with me or what?"

He looked down at her tattoo, considering it. "What the hell, right?" Then he cracked open the Cuervo and knocked it back.

She smirked at him and he smirked right back.

They downed another drink together. Whatever Dean swallowed had burned him up on the way down. He bent over, exhaling like a dragon.

Snickering, Marlow plopped down in a chair. "You new at this?" she teased. "No, wait—don't tell me you're a *Virgo?*"

"I haven't been a Virgo since high school. What's this?" He picked up the brochure she had flung aside earlier. "'Whatever your heart's desire... Find it in Paradise...' Hey, did you know this place was voted the Best Roadside Destination for Honeymooners in 1960 by the State Hoteliers Commission?"

"Neato," she deadpanned, folding one of her legs under her butt and hugging the other one to her chest.

"Guess that explains the giant cupid."

"There's no explaining whatever the hell that's about."

"So if you didn't come here for the tourism, why are you here? There's nothing around for miles and even a major highway was built as if to help people circumvent this place."

"That's a big word," she teased, another bottle at her lips.

"No, seriously," he said. "Why *are* you here?"

This time he didn't shy away when they locked eyes. She kept her chin up, holding his stare. "I could ask you the same thing, but we both know that's classified, right?"

She hoped that was enough to deflect his interest. Why she was holed up in Paradise was none of his business. The only reason she was talking to him at all was because she had thought she wanted to get laid. Fortunately, she didn't have to make up any lies because he resumed studying the brochure.

It didn't occur to her that he let her off the hook.

"Says this was the world's most romantic town." He nodded at the bathroom. "Bet you've got a heart-shaped tub and everything."

"I wish," she muttered. "Would make this place *a lot* less boring."

"You're bored?"

"Aren't you?" Jumping out of her seat like a curious cat, she snatched the brochure from him and flapped it in his face. "You're reading a goddamn pamphlet *from the sixties*, for fuck's sake."

"Do you want me to go?"

She shrugged.

He pointed at the TV. "We could watch something."

"Cable's out."

"Well, I don't know what else to do," he said.

She tossed the brochure into the trash and perched on the edge of the bed. One leg crossed slowly over the other. "You're in a motel room with a stranger and you don't know what to do? You really are a Virgo."

The jab at his manhood got his attention. "I thought I wasn't your type."

Sitting with her back arched, all prim and proper, she tipped her head up to look at him. Most of her exes preferred a submissive woman. Playing meek put her in charge, shifting the power dynamics until the man was on his knees and then—

Red and blue lights flashed through the parted curtains, splashing the bland walls with explosive color. Her heart beat to their urgent, colorful rhythm.

As she leapt to her feet, the earth shook. She wobbled. The walls groaned and drywall dust sprinkled down from the ceiling. She reached out for something steady—and found Dean, tall and rooted to the ground like a tree. She fell against him, knocking him off balance. He overcorrected his stance and toppled over her. They crash-landed on the bed, Marlow caught between him and the spongy mattress. He tried to push himself up, but the quaking forced him back down, their bodies pressed together.

"You alright?" he asked.

"Get off of me," she grunted, pushing him.

"I'm *trying.*"

"*Try harder!*"

As the quaking ceased, the door banged open. Marlow shrieked—a police officer stood in the doorway. His expression was hidden behind a pair of mirrored sunglasses. His gun was drawn, aiming for someone to shoot.

"I'm gonna have to ask you both to disengage," said the officer. "You're coming with me."

6.

THE LAW

AT FIRST, DEAN thought the ceiling fell down and clobbered him, or that Marlow flipped out and head-butted him, and that's why, out of the blue, he was seeing a cop straight out of a seventies porno flick at the foot of the bed. In reality, he must have barged in after hearing Marlow scream, thinking someone was in peril.

Marlow shoved Dean aside and he rolled off the bed, landing on his elbow. The hit sent a shiver of silly pain down his arm and he guffawed. Marlow and the cop stared at him like he was a madman.

"It's alright," she said, fixing her hair. "I'm fine. It was an accident. The earthquake caught us off guard. I didn't even know you could get earthquakes this far inland. I mean, the ocean isn't even a thought out here, is it? Did I scream too loud or something?"

"Ma'am, I need you to calm down."

Dean sat up, stunned by the sight of the officer's uniform. Clad head to toe in *leather*, he squeaked with every small movement. His shoulders were bulked up with leather epaulettes with leather tassels. Even the buttons on his jacket were bound in leather. He looked like the personification of night and shadows.

His name tag said, "Officer Friendly."

This had to be a joke, though it wasn't funny in the least because if Director ███████████ caught whiff of this news, Dean was going to be so fucked.

"Officer—" When Dean tried to stand, the cop stuck a gun in his face.

"Don't move, sir, or it *will* be hazardous to your health."

Dean decided he was better off getting on his knees and keeping his hands where the cop could see them. But if he could just get to his badge... He dipped down toward his inside breast pocket and—

"He's got a gun!" Marlow blurted, diving to the floor.

Without warning, the officer fired. A chunk of wood exploded from the doorframe. Dean ducked down. Fuck the badge. The cop would see it when he searched him. Then this would all be over.

The cop's knee rammed into his back. Dean's stomach flattened against the floor as his arms were yanked behind his back and his wrists handcuffed.

Hauling Dean off the floor, Officer Friendly growled, "That was a warning shot. Next time I won't miss."

The leather cop shoved Dean into the back of his police cruiser while Marlow leaned in the doorway of her motel room. As soon as she could see the cop's taillights, she was going to grab her cash and slip away into the night. The evening would serve as a reminder to never stay in one place for too long and to be more thoughtful about the men she met online.

Tough luck for Dean though.

She ducked back inside the room to grab her bags when Officer Friendly re-entered.

"You need my statement or something?" she asked.

"Or something." He held out a pair of handcuffs that were definitely her size but not her color, and said, "It'll be a lot easier if you—"

A lot of things in life would be a lot easier *if only* Marlow had done what others expected of her. She wouldn't have had to leach off of dangerous men to make money if only she had finished beauty school, if only she had learned not to question authority, if only she hadn't been attracted to bad boy types. She wouldn't have been drawn to a life of crime if her crazy mother hadn't left her alone in front of the TV her whole childhood to romanticize *Bonnie and Clyde* and, worse, *Natural Born Killers*.

So, yes, it would have been a lot easier to walk up to Officer Friendly and let him cuff her and take her to the police station and book her and run her information until they found out that she was a suspect in several convenience store robberies, culminating in a bank job two states over, before running out on Tony with all their hard-earned cash.

But Marlow did everything the hard way.

She darted into the closet and grabbed the black duffle bag, running for the bathroom and slamming the door. She didn't bother with the lock; the cheap metal wouldn't hold for long.

She scrambled into the tub—not heart-shaped—and pried open the window above. She had just enough room to shove the bag through, and as she began to worry how she would squeeze out after it, Officer Friendly barged through the door and nabbed her.

She kicked and screamed out of the motel room—until he threw her down on the hot, ragged pavement. She spat on his boot and he gave her a swift kick to the gut, a stern message to stay down.

Once the cuffs were on her, Officer Friendly stuffed her into the back of his cruiser alongside Dean, who shook his head.

"What the hell were you thinking, running from a cop?"

"I wasn't," she lied, because she had been thinking very clearly.

What am I going to do if Tony finds me?

Alone with Marlow in the back of the cruiser, Dean fired dirty looks in her direction. He blamed her for everything and wished he could have been the one to arrest her.

The pisser was that neither of them had done anything wrong—unless this was about the accidental dine and dash. In that case, he hadn't done anything wrong. He had intended to return to the diner and pay the waitress ... until Marlow distracted him. Officer Friendly needed to be made aware of that fact so Dean could extricate himself from the situation. If the cop didn't believe him or decided to put him behind bars anyway, Dean was going to be in deep trouble with his director and the agency. He could get fired or worse.

Then it would be another fail in his long list of screwups.

His gun and wallet (with the badge inside) were on the cruiser's hood, their presence mocking Dean.

He twisted around to see where the hell the damn cop had gone. *Let's go already, and get this over with.*

"Will you stop it?" Marlow snapped.

He frowned. "Stop what?"

"Rubbing up against me like a lovesick puppy."

He pressed his back against the door, trying to put as much space between them as possible. Moments ago, when he was on top of her, squeezed between her thighs, something stirred inside him. But there was no way in hell he wanted her to know that.

He turned to glare out the window, but his simmering rage bubbled up and he spun back around. "Why'd you have to say something about my gun?"

"Because you were gonna shoot him! And me too probably."

"I'm not out to shoot people and I'm especially not going to shoot a cop," he said. "I'm a federal agent."

Marlow snorted. "Oh, right. Those guys *never* shoot people."

"If you hadn't opened your big mouth, we wouldn't be in this mess."

"No, you're right. I'd be covered in that cop's brains and you'd probably shoot me too."

He shook his head. "I wasn't reaching for my gun. I was trying to show the man my badge. Now he thinks I'm a criminal, like you."

"Moi?" She laughed. "I am *not* a criminal."

Officer Friendly reappeared. He dropped Marlow's duffle bag on the hood and unzipped it. It was bursting with cash.

"Not a criminal, huh?"

"I'm not," she pouted.

"Then lemme guess—inheritance from a dead uncle?"

"I want a lawyer."

Dean's stomach clenched. Lawyers meant records and paper trails, which meant his director would hear all about this. Pressing his head against the window, he called out to the cop. "Excuse me, officer? What are the charges?"

Dutifully bagging their possessions, Officer Friendly glanced at his two captives. They couldn't read his expression through his mirrored lenses. Only their sorry reflections stared back at them. "You are under arrest for breaking the law under Section 3A: Illegal consumption of a prohibited beverage; Section 2B: Unlawful copulation and cohabitation; and Section 4C: Defrauding a business owner."

"What does that mean?" Marlow asked.

Officer Friendly drew a deep breath and sidled up next to Marlow's window. He planted his fists on his hips, leather gloves squeaking against his leather pants, and leaned in until they were face to face. "Means you've been caught drinkin', fuckin', and stealin', and Judge DeVille is gonna have a field day."

7.

THE ORDER

ON THE UNLUCKIEST day of her life, Marlow was in luck. Officer Friendly promised that the public defender was already waiting for them. But when he hauled them through the double doors of the police station/ courthouse, the only other person around was a small man crumpled up in the far corner of a jail cell.

The station was just as small and sad and worn out as the lone prisoner. A huge crack disrupted the checker-patterned floor. Everything else was dusty oak: walls, counters, furniture, and the swinging, saloon-style door that separated a single workstation and two jail cells from the rest of the public space.

Burnt coffee and rotten eggs stank up the air, and with her hands cuffed behind her back, Marlow couldn't plug her nose. She stifled the urge to gag, noting it wasn't just her—Dean's nose twitched the entire time they were booked and marched into their cells.

"*Separate* cells," noted Officer Friendly, removing their handcuffs. "Can't have you two pawin' at each other like a couple of horn dogs."

Marlow didn't know what a "horn dog" was, but the cop had it all wrong. She wasn't interested in Dean. Although, she probably would have slept with him had their timing not been so out of whack. Earthquakes in the middle of the desert? What was this, the end times? She knew that once they were brought before the judge, she could explain that it was all a misunderstanding.

Still, it was pretty strange to be arrested for having sex in the privacy of her motel room. *Isn't that exactly what motel rooms are for?* It was all the more ludicrous because she and Dean hadn't even done the deed.

Instead of arguing her case to the cop, she entered the cell and plopped down next to the pitiful man on the cot, making sure to keep her distance of course. *You can't trust strange men*, her mother used to say—before bringing one home from the roadhouse.

Once the bars slammed shut, Dean started making demands. "If you'd just look in my wallet there, you'd see that I'm in law enforcement myself and I've never heard of those laws you say we've broken. Are you sure—?"

Officer Friendly said nothing and helped himself to a mug of coffee. The liquid dampened his mustache.

"They're real," mumbled the little man.

Marlow paid him closer attention. He was a paunchy, old guy. Fifties or sixties. Wiry, grey strands peppered his cardboard brown hair. A pair of thick frames pinched his button nose, battling for facial dominance over his wet, fishy lips.

His brown suit was the same sad color as his hair

and glasses, offset by his sickly pale skin. He rolled the end of his tie around his fingers until they turned purplish red, then unraveled it and started over.

"We weren't drinking in public and we weren't engaged in any sort of ... sexual congress," said Dean. "If anyone did anything wrong—"

The man waved his hand, cutting him off. "I don't need to hear it."

"That's right," Marlow said. "Save it for the lawyer."

"Oh," squeaked the man. "I *am* the lawyer."

"What?" Marlow spun around. "Then, yeah, you do need to listen, but listen to me first because—"

With another flick of his wrist, he cut her off too. "It doesn't matter."

"Yes, it does," she insisted. "I want my fair trial."

He scoffed. "Fair, yeah, sure."

"Are you saying we're not going to get a trial?" Dean asked.

"Oh, you'll get a trial. But don't expect it to be *fair.*"

Dean sighed. "I don't like this." He stomped back to the bars. "Excuse me? Officer Friendly? Could you please just look in my wallet?"

"Bribery won't work either," said the little man. "I tried it, and it got me another ten."

"Another ten what?" Marlow asked, dread creeping through her body.

"Ten years—and he still took my money."

"Who?"

"Judge DeVille, who else? He's the big cheese around here. Normally, I would never have tried such a thing, but I was desperate, you see, and—"

"And who are you?" asked Dean, giving up on Officer Friendly for the moment.

"I'm your lawyer— Well, public defender," the man said, meekly reaching through the bars to shake hands. "Arnold Martin, but you can call me Arnie."

Marlow rolled her eyes. *Christ on a cracker. I'm never going to beat this with a lawyer named Arnie.*

"So this Judge DeVille guy, I take it he's a hard ass?" Dean asked.

Arnie frantically shushed them, though Marlow hadn't said a word. "Quiet! You didn't say that! Don't say anything of the sort. His Honor is a good, benevolent man." His eyes darted around the station, as if they were being watched.

Dean puffed up his chest. "Don't we get some privacy to go over our strategy?"

Arnie chuckled weakly. All humor had drained out of him like every ounce of melanin in his skin tone. "We'll be lucky if we even get a *second* to talk strat—"

The phone on Officer Friendly's desk rang, startling the trio with its shrill, urgent ring. Marlow put a hand over her chest, feeling her heart banging around. She caught Dean looking her way and dropped her hand, fixed her hair, and tried to look composed. Inside, she was terrified, but didn't want anyone to know it.

Officer Friendly answered the phone. He never spoke, just listened to the tinny voice on the other end. Then as quickly as the call came in, he hung up.

"The judge is ready to see you now," he stated.

He downed the rest of his coffee on route to the cells. He flipped through his keyring until he found the right one. As he opened the first cell, he ordered Marlow and Arnie to stand back. When they did as they were told, he led them out and lined them up on a crooked piece of duct tape stuck to the floor.

"Don't step one foot off this line."

He went to Dean's cell next, but Dean refused to step back. He gripped the bars, pressing his face through. "Do we *really* need to get the judge involved in this? If you would just check my badge, you'll see—"

Officer Friendly reached through the bars and hooked Dean by the back of his neck. In one swift motion, he bashed Dean's face against the cold, hard metal. Dean stumbled back, groaning. He futilely tried to catch the blood gushing from his nose.

"That's enough of you," said Officer Friendly. "And because your lawyer is a useless sack of shit, I'll advise you to watch your mouth and your attitude around the judge."

Marlow resisted the urge to step off the line and help the hopeless dope out of his cell. But after experiencing Officer Friendly in full force back at the motel, she didn't want to get into it with the cop right before seeing the judge.

As it was, she had watched enough *Judge Judy* with her mom to know she wasn't wearing appropriate courtroom attire. Adjusting her shorts and brushing off her shirt, she hoped for the best.

"Time to go," Officer Friendly announced as Dean, holding his nose, shuffled onto the line.

Once they were again handcuffed, the cop led them through another door and into the courtroom. It looked straight out of a movie set, but older and dustier. Cobwebs lingered in the corners. The faded checkerboard tiles continued throughout, some cracked or completely missing. Rows of benches led to the attorney tables where Marlow, Dean, and Arnie were ordered to stand. There didn't appear to be a prosecutor, but after meeting Arnie in a cell, Marlow wouldn't have been surprised if some random guy dropped down from the ceiling.

Marlow looked up at the statue of Lady Justice behind the judge's bench. The arm holding the scales was gone, leaving her a blind, one-armed bitch with a sword.

A few people trickled in behind them, taking their seats. She recognized Billy the motel clerk and the waitress from the diner. There was an old-timer in a MAGA hat and a gaunt man in a sweaty line cook's t-shirt and apron. They all appeared exhausted, harried, and jittery. Tony gave off that same energy when he was popping caffeine pills so he could drive all night.

That feeling of dread, that she was trapped and things were about to go from bad to worse, was over-whelming. With nowhere to run, she held onto Dean's hand and squeezed him hard. He glanced down, concerned, but didn't shake her off or say anything snarky.

Thank god. She felt foolish enough without his snide comments about it.

Officer Friendly stepped in front of the judge's bench and cleared his throat. His thumbs tucked into his belt loops as he called the courtroom to order. "All rise."

The straggly crowd of spectators stood up. Marlow let go of Dean to adjust her outfit. Dean wiped his bloody nose on his sleeve, wincing.

The door behind the bench creaked open. The man who walked out wore a flowing black gown and a powdered wig—literally (and freshly) powdered. Talc particles floated in his wake. It sprinkled across his shoulders and chest like dandruff. The sight of it made Marlow's nose itch and her eyes water.

"The Honorable Judge Stanley DeVille is now presiding," Officer Friendly called out. He shifted aside, hands clasped together, and assumed the courtroom duties of a bailiff.

Marlow and Dean exchanged bewildered looks.

Taking his place at the bench, the judge zeroed in on them immediately. He brought his gavel crashing down. "Don't be making googly eyes at each other," Judge DeVille said. He tapped his gavel against his chest. "I want all eyes on me *or heads are gonna roll.*"

8.

THE JUDGE

JUDGE STANLEY DEVILLE spread his arms wide. The sleeves of his gown billowed as he motioned for everyone to sit. Arnie remained standing, staring in frozen, silent horror as Dean and Marlow settled.

The judge hollered at them. "What in the world do you two think you're doing?" he demanded. "You think you get to kick up your feet and relax? Oh, no—not in my courtroom. *On your feet*. And eyes on me."

Easier said than done. The judge was ancient. His flesh was the same pallid color as dust, except for the purple pigmentation of his lips and the dark circles under his squinty pig eyes, the corners of which branched out in a frenzy of crow's feet. His forehead was an accordion of deep, angry lines. What kinds of incredulous cases must he have witnessed as the judge of a small roadside town that wasn't even on the map?

His cheeks and jowls drooped down in a hound dog glower, jiggling with every motion of his head. "Now,

Officer Friendly, will you kindly read the charges before the court?"

The cop stepped up and without referring to any notes, he loudly and confidently listed off Dean and Marlow's alleged crimes.

"One count of illegal consumption of prohibited beverages. One count of unlawful copulation and co-habitation. One count of defrauding a business owner. And one count of armed robbery in a foreign territory."

"Ah, drinkin', fuckin', and stealin'."

Dean couldn't stay silent another second. He knew how the court system worked (more or less) and he couldn't stand there any longer and be accused of some ridiculous crimes that he had never heard of and also get roped into Marlow's transgressions.

"Your Honor," he began.

Arnie elbowed him.

Rubbing his arm and frowning at his lawyer, Dean tried again. "Your Honor?"

The judge sighed wearily, shifting ever so slightly in his direction. A rumble sounded from the spectator seats.

"Did I give you permission to speak, son?"

"No, sir, but—"

"Then zip the lip until I ask you a question. Or I will have it zipped for you."

Dean acquiesced, scowling.

"Mr. Martin? How would your clients like to plead?"

"Guilty, Your Honor."

"What?!" Dean and Marlow turned on him.

"Trust me," Arnie whispered. "It's easier this way."

"*Easier?*" Marlow cried. "We didn't do anything!"

The judge banged his gavel. "Order in the court!"

"We're not guilty, Your Honor," Dean said. "This is all a big misunderstanding. We didn't do anything wrong. If you'll please just listen—"

His pleas fell on unsympathetic ears, chocked full of thick clumps of white hair. "Officer Friendly, I will need you to restrain Mr., uh… What's your name, son?"

"Dean Dilton. *Agent* Dean Dilton."

A cold shadow fell over the judge's face. "A federal agent?"

"Yes, sir." He prayed to the highest office of the United States of America that his position, even on the lowest rungs of the government, would hold some sway with the man holding court. Hell, he would have prayed to the goddamn bird on the Froot Loops box.

"You work for the government then?" The judge's voice dropped down to a near whisper. He stared intently, waiting for Dean's answer.

"Yes."

The spectators murmured.

With a loud guffaw, the judge leaned back in his chair and slapped his knee. The chair squeaked under his surprisingly spry body. "Well, gosh. Why didn't you say so?"

Dean sighed. His stomach unclenched. Now that he had the judge's ear, he would try to help Marlow. She wasn't so bad, and maybe her bag full of money was legit and everything was just like he said, a big misunderstanding. He threw a smile her way to let her know everything was going to be alright.

Her grimace said she strongly disagreed.

Judge DeVille wiped his eyes. "Well, *Agent* Dilton, I appreciate your honesty. Takes a big man to admit the truth. For that, I'm only gonna give you five years' hard labor. You'll be outta here before you know it."

Dean whipped around so fast the room spun. "*What?*"

"That's right," the judge confirmed. The shadow on his face was even darker than before. "Five years for being a sleazy, sneaky, no-good, chicken-hearted toady for the U.S. government."

"What? No! Wait! Hey!"

The judge banged his gavel. "Officer Friendly, help Agent Dilton zip his lip."

Officer Friendly moved in swiftly. He unbuttoned his stiff jacket and reached in, pulling out a leather gimp mask. It had two mesh eye holes and a zipper across the mouth.

Dean put his fists up, but the cop was on him in an instant and punched him in the gut. Dean doubled over, struggling to breathe as Officer Friendly masked him. Everything went black. The cop tightened the neck restraint. Dean panicked. Flailing, he bumped into Marlow.

Officer Friendly put an arm around Dean's chest, holding him close, and patted his cheek. "Calm down, sir. You'll get used to it."

Doubtful, but what choice did he have?

The cop let go, then quietly adjusted the mask so Dean could see through the eye holes. Everything looked the way it had before. The rest of the court waited on him to stop freaking out so the trial could continue.

Officer Friendly returned to his post.

"Now, Mr. Martin," said the judge, "if you can't keep your clients in line, I'm going to have the whole lot of you thrown back in your cells—without supper—and

I'm gonna add ten years to all your sentences."

"No!" Arnie yelped. He covered his mouth, nodding. Quickly composing himself, he ran a shaky hand through his messy hair. "Y-yes, sir. Sorry, sir. There won't be any more outbursts. I promise."

I want a new lawyer, Dean thought miserably.

"Alright, let's get this show on the road," the judge said. "So as Officer Friendly relayed to the court, one of the charges is related to *unlawful copulation*. What do you have to say for yourselves?"

Marlow looked around at the faces in the courtroom before tentatively speaking up. "Uh, it wasn't what it looked like."

The judge stared her down. Tension in the air reached a fever pitch, and just as Dean was about to step in to try to explain (because neither she nor Arnie were doing much to get them out of this hellish situation), the judge howled with laughter. The spectators chuckled along nervously.

"What is your name, missy?" the judge asked.

"Marlow."

"That sounds like a movie star's name."

"I guess?"

"Has anyone ever told you you're as beautiful as any movie star out there?" he wondered. "Why, I don't think I could keep my hands off you myself if we were left alone in an establishment as fine as the Shady Palms Motel."

Marlow shifted uncomfortably, looking everywhere but at the judge as he admired her.

"I don't blame Agent Dilton for what transpired in your room this evening," the judge continued. "A man couldn't possibly control himself around such beauty.

Isn't that right, Agent Dilton?"

Dean tried to answer, but the mask fit snugly over his mouth and the zipper pinched his lips. He tried working his tongue to unzip it, but the effort was for nothing. The judge didn't actually want his response.

"Here's the thing, Miss Marlow." Judge DeVille leaned forward on his elbows. "This is my town and these are my rules. Copulation of any kind between two unmarried persons without permission of the court is strictly prohibited. Even if you and Agent Dilton had come to me and requested a special permit for the act, I would not have granted it. You see, we have morals here. You may have rolled into our little town, thinking, 'Why, this is the most romantic destination I've ever visited! Of course, my nether regions are on fire for my paramour—even though he is a disgusting rat employed by the traitorous U.S. government...'" The judge took a deep breath. "But I digress. Whatever the reason for your attraction to this ... *individual*..." he sneered, "we simply cannot tolerate unmarried people sullying Paradise with their sinful behavior. That's not what Paradise is about, and I will not sit idly by and let you taint our reputation with your sweaty, lustful deeds."

"It wasn't like that—" Marlow tried to explain.

"I can just picture it!" The judge held up his hands, framing a scene only he could see. "Two nubile bodies befouling poor Billy's motel beds with your rusty trombones, Amish snow plows, angry pirates, Alabama mudslides..."

Oh, Jesus Christ. Dean feared he would pull a muscle in his tongue trying to open the zipper.

"We weren't doing any of that," Marlow protested.

"It was an accident. Yeah, we were drinking a little bit, but we weren't having sex. We were just talking and then the ground started shaking—"

"Ah, yes. We get the rumbles quite a bit around here. You'll get used to it."

Used to it? Oh, hell no.

"Well, the ground was shaking and we weren't used to it, and Dean—*Agent Dilton*—fell on me. I didn't even know he was a fed, honestly."

Stroking his neck, the judge mulled over her testimony. "Interesting. I believe what Officer Friendly reported was that he caught you in flagrante delicto."

Marlow snickered. "With *Dean?* God, no."

"Hey..." Dean muttered, muffled.

"I don't know you, Miss Marlow, but many women just like you have come through my court. Your charms can't convince me to believe your lies. I know a woman's number one priority is to protect her virtue, no matter the cost. But here's the thing: I'm willing to overlook the drinkin' and the fuckin'—"

Relief rushed through Dean like a flooded dam. Marlow faced him excitedly. He could have picked her up and hugged her, he was so overjoyed.

Until the judge finished what he was saying. "—as long as you give me the honor of officiating your marriage ceremony right here and now."

9.

THE VERDICT

EVER SINCE MARLOW had been a little girl playing with knock-off Barbie dolls outside her mom's trailer, she had dreamed of her perfect wedding day. She imagined friends filling every seat in the church and flowers overflowing from crystal vases. Petals would be delicately scattered on the rich, red carpet leading to her husband-to-be.

A marked-up Barbie served as her proxy. Its only white dress was short with lace trim around the hem, which only came down to the top of the doll's un-bending knee. Appropriate for the trailer park she and her mom lived in, but in Marlow's mind, the gown was a Disney-esque creation and her betrothed didn't need masking tape under his Malibu muscle shirt to hold his head on.

While she played out her dream wedding, her mother's latest boyfriend stomped out of the trailer and slammed the door, leaving her mom crying in his wake.

Their whole drama dispelled any notion of a romantic future for herself, but then Marlow never imagined she might one day be asked to marry a stranger in exchange for her freedom.

So she stood gobsmacked before Judge DeVille as he presented his deal.

Standing at his bench like a southern Baptist minister preaching from his pulpit, the judge waved his arms around. "You see, we are standing here today in the great sovereign nation of Paradise, the greatest destination for lovers in the *whole wide world*."

Sovereign? Marlow had heard the word before, but between dropping out of high school and running around in social circles that never uttered such a word, she had only a vague idea of what it meant. When the judge said something as ludicrous as the town being not just a destination for lovers, but *the greatest one*, Marlow just about lost it.

I have to get out of here.

Feeling lightheaded, as if none of this was real, she bumped against Dean. Bound up in that ridiculous (and scary) mask, he held his ground and let her lean on him. It was a kind gesture, but it wasn't enough to convince her to marry him. Marlow had made some awful mistakes in her twenty-nine years, but getting married at first sight wasn't going to be one of them.

"So what better time and place than here and now to begin your perfect union," said the judge. "What do you say?"

"Umm..." Marlow glanced at Dean, his brown eyes wide and pleading inside the mask. She got the gist. *No fucking way.* "Thank you, judge," she said. "I think I'll have to think about it."

A muffled cry erupted from Dean. The spasm of sound was short lived. Officer Friendly stepped in and cracked him over the back of the head with his nightstick. Dean dropped to the floor. The cop moved to hit him again, but the judge called him back with the flick of his wrist.

"No need for escalation, Officer Friendly," he said. "Cold feet is a common affliction for a young man about to wed, even to a young lady as fine as Miss Marlow. Isn't that right?"

The spectators nodded and hummed in agreement, heads bobbing as if on puppet strings.

"Now, Miss Marlow, since Agent Dilton is incapacitated, why don't you think *real* hard and give us your answer," he prodded. "Will you marry this man here today? Right now?"

Thinking hard, Marlow twisted her bound wrists. Dean groaned at her feet. "I don't think it's a good idea," she admitted. "So, no. No thanks."

"Are you *sure?*" he asked, looking down his bulbous, red nose. "I'm giving you one last opportunity—and I never give second chances, remember that."

Dean struggled to get up. Blood stained his white shirt. The stitches were loose and frayed from his jacket's shoulder. He looked monstrous—a gawky gimp in a rumpled business suit.

Addressing the judge, Marlow replied, "No, I'd rather not."

"You'd rather not *what?*"

"I'd rather not get married."

"Not today? Not ever?"

"Well..." The disappointment in the air was palpable. She had robbed the court of a public wedding.

"Just not ... now." *And definitely not here.*

Judge DeVille's face puckered as the atmosphere turned sour. He rapped the gavel sharply on his bench and collapsed in his seat. "Well then, the matter is settled. If you're both *too good* to be wed in Paradise, I hereby sentence you to forty years hard labor."

Dean's zippered mouth split open. *"What?"*

"What?" Marlow echoed, searching around for anyone else who looked more shocked than her or Dean. But the spectators were tired, unamused. None of this surprised them.

The gavel pounded again and again until Judge DeVille had Marlow's attention. He lowered his voice, forcing everyone to lean in too. Dean dragged himself onto his knees.

"Now listen here, you pair of ingrates," the judge began. His words hummed like a rattlesnake's tail. Coiled up, ready to strike. "I don't care at all for weak-spined G-men employed as tools to destroy small towns such as mine. And I certainly don't care for sloven hussies who think they can turn my town into a whore's nest. But I concede that you are human beings with families and values somewhere—*I hope*—and because of that, I will not have you put to death."

Arnie sighed audibly, but Marlow's heart stuck in her throat. Death? Since when was a *death sentence* on the table?

"I believe that every person on this green earth has a purpose in life," he continued. "And because our town's population decreases every year, I would really hate to lose two more so suddenly. We need all hands on deck if we're going to ensure Paradise maintains its fine reputation. So I need you, Miss Marlow and Agent

Dilton. I was happy to bless your union and let you go on your merry way, but I think it is in all our best interests that you now give back to the community—and your new home. After all, forty years is a long time... *Forty-five* for *you*, Agent Dilton." He winked. "I may be old, but I *never* forget."

Marlow began to vibrate. She had held her tongue during this entire farce. She had put her *Judge Judy* knowledge to good use, and didn't speak up or talk back, even when the judge spewed his load of bullshit. For once, she had behaved herself and acted like a proper lady, and what did that get her? *Forty fucking years in hell.*

"No," she stated before Judge DeVille dismissed the court.

The judge raised his bushy brows. "What did you say?"

"No," she repeated. "No fucking way. You can't make me. I'm not doing it."

Marlow wilted at the sight of Officer Friendly nearing her like a shadow, silent and smooth. But he merely passed by to approach the bench where he asked for permission to speak.

"Yes, you may, Officer Friendly," granted the judge, narrowed eyes set on Marlow.

"I apologize for interrupting," said the cop, "but I could sense you were about to dismiss the defendants."

"Very perceptive, Officer Friendly."

"Thank you, sir. There is one other matter that needs to be settled, and it has to do with the young woman and her bag of stolen currency."

"Ah, yes."

Marlow shifted uncomfortably. *Should've kept my big mouth shut.*

"I scanned all nearby bulletins and found out that a pair of armed robbers have been holding up convenience stores throughout the tri-state area. Their latest hit was a bank."

"One of the big boys?"

"No, sir. A small-town job, but the robbers got away with thirty grand."

The judge whistled and the spectators mumbled.

Dean frowned at Marlow. She frowned right back. Who was he to judge? Look at the mess he had gotten her into. If he hadn't fallen all over her like the big, clumsy dope that he was, they would never have been arrested. Probably.

"I saw the security footage, and the perpetrators are a near match for the defendants."

Dean shook his head. "Oh, no. It wasn't me. No way."

"Is that man Agent Dilton by any chance?" the judge asked. "Greedy government pest moonlighting as a criminal? Why am I not surprised?"

As Dean started to sputter in a panic, Marlow spoke up in his defence. "Um, that wasn't Agent Dilton. The guy you saw is my ex. He made me do those things. I didn't want to. I tried to stop him, but he said he would kill me and feed me to the dogs. I had no choice." She was surprised how quickly and easily tears sprang to her eyes along with the lies from her lips. How eagerly she got down on her knees and crawled forward, hands clasped together. "I'm so sorry for the evils I was forced to be a part of, and I beg your forgiveness, judge. I throw myself at the mercy of the court and—"

"Enough." The judge banged his gavel. "Where's this other man now, Miss Marlow?"

"Reno, maybe?"

"What's his name?"

"Tony."

"Tony what?"

Standing up, Marlow hesitated. "I..."

"Well, out with it. We need to know the man's name so we can put up wanted posters."

"I don't know," she said. "He never told me."

It was a terrible time to have a revelation about her relationship with Tony, but if he couldn't even trust her with his last name (whether real or fake), he was never going to trust her with the money. In that case, she was glad she took it.

The judge shook a finger at her. "I can't tell if you're lying to me or if you truly don't know, but if this Tony steps one foot in my town, I won't hesitate to prosecute him. In the meantime, you can get to work right away."

"Work?" She looked down at herself. She wasn't built for hard labor, and he was kidding himself if he thought she could do any such thing for *forty* years.

"Officer Friendly will set you to your tasks. Agent Dilton, you're going to clear away some of the ... sludge that's been seeping out of the road cracks. It won't be pretty, but it's honest work, and the last fella that did it made it to two years before he succumbed to illness. You look much younger and healthier than him, so I wager you'll last quite a bit longer. Maybe you'll even live long enough complete your sentence!" His face darkened as he turned to Marlow. "As for you, missy..."

She swallowed, holding her head up high.

"I can't have a beautiful thing like you wasting away with that underground sludge. No, no. I think I'll have you working up at the motel with Mr. Billy. We get a few truck drivers through here on the regular, and it sure would be nice to offer them a little 'nightcap,' if you catch my drift." He gave her a wink and laughed. "Billy, son?" he called out into the smattering of spectators. "Think you can break this one in tonight?"

Marlow whipped around and saw the greasy motel clerk grinning and rubbing his hands together like a cartoon villain. Turning away, she crossed her arms. "No fucking way."

"If you can act as filthy as you speak, I think you're going to be *very popular* at Shady Palms." He knocked the gavel one last time. "Dismissed!" he cried, breezing out of the courtroom.

10.

THE CELL

ANGER ROILING, MARLOW ran after the judge. She was not going to accept this punishment. It was unfair and wrong. At best, she should have gotten a slap on the wrist. At worst, *a fair trial*. The judge was a joke and this was all a bad dream—it had to be—but before she could confront him, Officer Friendly blocked her path.

"Going somewhere?" he asked, fist clenched around his nightstick.

Marlow trembled with rage and fear and helplessness. "I want to speak to the judge."

"You heard the judge. You had your chance. Now it's time for splittin' rocks and takin' cocks. Move along... Or do I have to move you myself?"

Dean stepped in between them. "We're going, we're going," he promised, nudging her along.

She shook him off as Officer Friendly corralled them out of the courthouse and back into their cells, where he removed Dean's mask.

When they were once again locked up, Arnie shook his useless head. "I'm sorry, guys. You really don't want to be here too long. Not with all the toxic waste underground."

"Toxic waste?" Dean gulped.

"Yeah, that's the sludge the judge is having you dig up."

"Are you fucking serious?"

"It's pretty bad, and I should know—I did it myself for a couple of months." He lifted up his shirt, twisting around to show them a large patch of black, bubbled skin. Marlow gasped. "That's how I got this before they moved me back here. How's it looking?"

"No, no, no, no," muttered Marlow, hands up to block the sight. "No fucking way. I'm not sticking around for forty years to die of seven million different cancers. Nuh-uh."

"Don't be so callous," said Dean, but his horrified grimace meant it was bad. Really bad.

"She's probably right," said Arnie. "I haven't felt very good in a long time."

"Isn't there a doctor you can see?" he asked, sitting down. "Someone with a medical background? They can't keep you locked up like this."

"But they can," said Arnie, wincing as he tucked his shirt back in. "And besides, we don't get many doctors through here. When we do, they always try to escape and then don't get far, so I've never had a chance to get a professional opinion. But that's okay, I guess."

"*You guess?*" Marlow repeated incredulously.

Dean clasped his hands between his knees. "How long have you been here, Arnie?"

"Hmm, good question." He checked his cracked

watch. "Um, thirty-six years, six months, and eight days. I think."

"Oh, my god." Marlow collapsed on her cot like a crestfallen Disney princess and covered her eyes with her forearm.

Dean continued his line of questioning, even though Marlow didn't want to hear another word. "Why are you here?"

"I'm serving out my sentence," Arnie replied, as if Dean's question were the dumbest one he had ever heard.

"So you don't live here?"

"Oh, no. I was just passing through, just like you folks. Officer Friendly—er, the *previous* Officer Friendly—caught me speeding. I was trying to get back home to my wife and son. Oh, here..." He dipped into his suit jacket to retrieve a wrinkled and folded family photo of a husband, wife, and a young boy. He sighed longingly at the photo that Marlow could only spare a cursory glance. "Little Jamie's probably all grown up now. But I'll get to see him soon. Just a few more years."

"Jesus Christ," muttered Dean.

"Jesus Christ is right," Marlow agreed. *Forty years.* She couldn't live like that. She couldn't be Arnie. No way. Then she had a terrible thought at the same time Dean asked the question. "Does anyone actually *live here?*"

Arnie mulled it over. "Well, the judge does. I mean, we all do—we're all living and breathing, aren't we?"

"I'm not so sure," said Marlow. "Feels like I'm in hell."

"No, I mean— Where did the others come from? The motel clerk and Delores and those folks?"

Marlow rolled her eyes. "Not Delores again."

"Oh," said Arnie, thinking. "They're from out of town like you. Billy was a trucker. We usually let those guys come and go if they drop us supplies, but Billy refused, so the judge put him to work. Sludge at first, but when Billy got sick and too weak to fight, he was reassigned to the motel. And Delores and her husband disturbed the peace because of a domestic violence incident, so the judge says they have to learn to work together at the restaurant. If they can cook and serve five thousand orders, they can leave."

"And if they don't?"

Arnie scratched his chin. "No one leaves until they complete their sentence."

"What if they leave anyway?" Marlow pressed.

"They can't..." His eyes darted to Officer Friendly. "They'll get caught ... or worse."

"What about him?" Dean asked. "You said there was a previous Friendly."

"That's right. When one dies, the judge replaces him. Always give him the same name, you know, to keep the welcoming feel of the town."

"I guess it's not hard to recruit a power-hungry wannabe cop, huh?" Dean remarked.

"Not at all," Arnie said. Then he sighed deeply, skulking around Marlow for a place to rest.

"*What?*" she snapped.

"I-I just—"

"*Don't fucking touch me.*" A rush of tears clogged her throat, almost betraying her brassiness. *I'm not open for business. Not now, not ever!*"

"No, no," Arnie stammered, backing up against the wall. "I-I-I just wanted to sit." She sneered at him and he shook his head, planting himself criss-cross applesauce on the cold concrete floor. "Here's fine. I'm fine. This is fine."

Marlow turned away from the pathetic sight, only to look at Dean's stupid knees as he knelt down beside her.

"It's going to be okay," he said, with a shiny, hopeful gleam in his eyes. "If I can just get hold of my director, he can clear this right up and we'll be on our way."

She groaned, rolling onto her back. The ceiling above was cracked, probably from the town's "rumbles," as the judge had described them.

"Hey." Dean reached through the bars, gently touching her wrist. She gave him a curious look, but didn't slough him off or attempt to slap him. She studied his face. His jaw was set and his gaze was laser focused. "Listen to me: I'm not going to let anything happen to you."

"Oh, gee, thanks," she grumbled, breaking contact. She needed time to think and these stupid men were making her crazy.

Dean got back on his feet. "I mean it," he said. And he did. But the trouble with good intentions was that they didn't mean shit compared to action. Like her, Dean was stuck in a cell with an impossibly long sentence and certain death hanging over his head. Digging up toxic waste? Yikes. His hands were soft and he looked like he hadn't worked a hard job once in his soft, little life. He wasn't going to last two weeks.

"I can't stay here."

"And you won't have to," he insisted. "If I can just call—"

She stood up, cutting him off. "Yeah, yeah, yeah.

Your precious director. I heard you, but in case you blacked out back there under that stupid mask, they don't do things here the way they do on TV."

"Well, actually," Dean began, using the patriarchy's favorite two-word opener, "our court system has few similarities to its depictions in pop culture, and—"

"*I know*. What I'm saying is *that* was not normal. There is no court in the whole country that moves that fast. From pleading to sentencing in ten minutes—that's nuts, right?"

She could tell from the way Dean silently rubbed his chin that she was correctamundo.

"And for one thing, no prosecutor? And for another, I wouldn't have picked Arnie as a lawyer." She stuck her thumb in his direction. "No offence, dude."

"None taken," Arnie replied politely.

Marlow grabbed the bars that separated them. "I'm not sticking around waiting for your director to come to my rescue," she said. "'Cause here's the thing—he's gonna come for *you*. I don't work for your agency or whatever. I'm just a low-level crook who probably deserves to be locked up. That's what they're gonna say."

"You don't know—"

"*That's what they're gonna say*. So you can wait around for a slim chance of getting your hands on a phone, but I'm not. I'm leaving."

She stood in the middle of the cell and began to scrutinize every inch, every floor tile, every bar, every crack in the ceiling. She nudged Arnie out of the way with her foot until her eyes fell on Officer Friendly.

He sat straight as an arrow at his desk, typing on a keyboard. Periodically, he sipped his coffee. He was her only chance to get out. She just had to lure him over and get him to unhook the keys from his belt.

Dean laughed. "That guy? You really think he's going to spring ya?"

"Maybe."

"And then what? Ask him to call you a cab?"

"I'm a cab," she whispered. Disconnecting from her physical state of being trapped behind bars, she began manifesting a near future in which she was on the outside, free and running for her car, and driving far, far away.

Dean sighed. "Whatever you're thinking, it's not going to work."

"Ye of little faith." She pressed up against the bars. "Excuse me?" she called. "Officer Friendly? Can you help me? *Please?*" She put some beg into the last word and squeezed her breasts together.

Officer Friendly stopped typing. His head tipped up, watching and listening.

"Hi," she said. "Can I ask you a little question?"

"What?"

She glanced back at Dean and Arnie, observing curiously. Then she looked down at her breasts and pouted her lips. "It's private. I don't want them to hear."

Officer Friendly gave her a stern look, but got up from his desk. He marched over to the cell and stood in front of her with his hands on his hips. "What's your question?"

"Umm..." She bit her lip, gazing up at him through her lashes. Playing helpless damsel wasn't her usual shtick, but she could pretend for his sake. "I've been bad."

"I know," he said. "You're a convicted criminal."

Embarrassed heat warmed her face. She imagined

Dean snickering at her inability to seduce the cop, smug that her big declaration to get the hell out of dodge was going to fall short all because she was up against this human ice cube.

"No, I mean... I'm a *bad girl*... And I need a big, strong cop to punish me."

"I don't do that," he said. "I round up lawbreakers for the judge and he doles out the convictions. No one punishes anyone; the work you're assigned is the punishment."

Oh, my god, okay! Marlow swallowed a big fat frustrated groan and tried not to roll her eyes. "I *understand*. But what I'm *asking* is if I can help you *relieve* any stress you might be feeling after the trial. If you know what I mean..."

"No. I'm perfectly capable of managing my own stress levels, ma'am."

Ma'am? This asshole's really got it out for me!

"Is that all?" he asked.

This was it. Her time was up. All she had left was one terribly stupid idea.

She reached between the bars and put her hands around his neck, pulling him in close. She climbed up the bars, trying to mount him and keep him near, but his bristly, buzzed haircut and oily scalp gave her no grip. Her face closed in on his, and she caught a whiff of the coffee on his breath. But before she could plant a kiss on him, he shoved her off and whipped out his nightstick.

With a grunt, she hit the ground backbone first. Arnie rushed to her side, but she elbowed him back.

Officer Friendly smacked the baton against the bars. "Don't try that bullshit again."

Marlow glared at him as he stomped away. When

Arnie attempted to help her again, she swatted him away. "Leave me alone."

"Marlow—" Dean started but stopped when she fired a caustic glare in his direction.

"Don't."

She sat on the floor, hugging her knees to her chest. Dean and Arnie went to their corners, careful not to make the slightest sound. Officer Friendly resumed his desk work. After what felt like ten minutes, Dean started up again.

"I don't know what you were thinking," he said. "You could have gotten really hurt."

"Or more time added to your sentence," Arnie added softly.

"I'm going to fix this," Dean said. "I promise. Just as soon as I call my boss and..."

Marlow wasn't listening. With her chin nuzzled against her forearms and her head bowed, she watched Officer Friendly. Watched him type every goddamn letter. Watched him bring his mug to his lips and take a quick sip. Watched him down his whole drink and pour himself another, and then she watched him do it again.

He drank a cup and a half more before shifting back in his chair. When his gaze swept over the cells, Marlow averted her eyes to the floor.

He stood up and stretched, and Marlow hoped he didn't feel any different. Hoped he didn't feel any lighter. Hoped he didn't notice anything missing. And if he thought something was off, he didn't show it as he stoically passed them on his way to the bathroom.

As soon as he was out of sight, Marlow jumped up. She pulled the cop's pilfered keyring out of her shirt. Her hand shook as she tried to figure out which key opened the cell's lock.

"What are you doing?" Dean sprang forward from his cell's dark corner.

"I'm not going to be anyone's gross lot lizard," she told them. "Fuck that, and fuck you if you think I'm waiting for a rescue. *I'm leaving.*"

"Marlow—"

Arnie crowded behind her. "As your attorney, I'm strongly advising against this," he said.

The lock gave. She held her breath. *Oh, shit. This is it.* She pulled the winning key out, pinching it between her thumb and finger as an offering to Dean.

"You coming?"

11.

THE ESCAPE

MOUTH AGAPE, DEAN stared at the key. It glimmered under the migraine-inducing fluorescent lights, teasing him with a chance at freedom, however short-lived that would be. He had experienced first-hand Officer Friendly's swift and efficient iron fist. For Christ's sake, the man was only in the goddamn bathroom, and unless he was incapacitated from a vicious stomach bug, he wouldn't be gone long.

Besides, it was never a good idea to run from the law. Dean learned that lesson from his joyride back in high school—and that cop had been lenient when he mashed Dean's face into the pavement and screamed in his ear. Officer Friendly wouldn't be so kind.

Marlow shook the keys and asked again, "Are you coming or what?"

He couldn't say, *I can't. I'm a federal agent and my boring government assignment has broken my spirit. I'm a lawman now and I promised to be good.*

But a familiar, and not unwanted, fire warmed him from within. A mischievous sensation that stirred inside whenever he felt trapped or bored.

Mild anarchy.

It felt so fucking good to be bad, to push the boundaries of society and see what he could get away with. Not good—*instinctual.*

And now Marlow was literally giving him a key to unlock that part of himself he had tried to suppress, the part of him that his job, his parents, his therapist, and so many others tried to snuff out.

Naughty or nice—this was his moment. There wouldn't be any second chances.

He took the key, hand shaking. "We shouldn't," he told her, his voice strained.

She backed away from his cage. "Later then," she said, blowing him a kiss.

He could almost feel her breath shooting toward him like cupid's arrow, piercing through to release his fire.

And then she was just *gone.*

It all happened so fast. Dean blinked and from out of nowhere, Officer Friendly cut her down with a single blow.

Marlow groaned on the floor as the cop rolled her over. Jamming a knee into her spine, Officer Friendly drew his handcuffs and yanked her arms behind her back. She squirmed and swore and spat, but he had the upper hand.

"Lemme go, asshole!" she cried.

Arnie clung to the bars of the opened cell. His knees knocked together and his teeth chattered. There was no way in hell he was about to help her. The only person who could actually protect and serve (and who wasn't a leather-clad maniac) was Dean.

He twisted the key in the lock. With a snap, he was free. He ran up to Officer Friendly and kicked him in the ribs. The cop let out an *oof* and spun around. He clamped one of the handcuffs on Dean's wrist and punched him in the gut. Dean doubled over, not sure how much more abuse his guts could take.

Marlow pushed herself up and went into attack mode, punching and scratching at Officer Friendly's face. He simply shook her off and concentrated on subduing Dean.

Marlow wiped her nose and turned her back on them. She was going to cut and run, leaving Dean to deal with the cop.

Fine, he thought bitterly. *Just go. You're welcome.*

But what did he think was going to happen? He'd rescue her and they would ride off into the sunset together?

Newsflash: The sun was gone, the town smelled like toxic garbage, and they were all going to die of some nasty Paradise cancer. *No happy endings here.*

He balled up his anger and frustration into his fists and used that fire to wail on the cop. Grunting, Officer Friendly threw Dean over his shoulder and planted him on the floor.

Wind knocked out of him, all Dean could do was stare up at the cracked ceiling and wait for the final blow.

Officer Friendly's boot clamped down on his windpipe. As the cop added pressure, Dean flailed.

"Put the cuffs on or—"

Dean reached for the second cuff to snap on his

wrist. Anything to get his breath back.

Marlow appeared over Officer Friendly's shoulder. She struggled to lift a bulky computer monitor as she tiptoed behind the cop.

Gasping for air, Dean tried to tell her to put it down.

Too late. With a grunt, she raised the monitor up high enough to bash it over Officer Friendly's head.

The glass screen shattered. The cop's whole head vanished inside the box like magic—*ta da!* Then the rest of his body dropped down next to Dean.

"*Jesus Christ*," Dean whispered, rubbing his raw throat.

"You thought I ditched you," said Marlow.

"No," he lied, crawling over to check if Officer Friendly was dead. Handcuff dangling from his wrist, he touched the cop's hot neck and found a pulse. "He's still alive."

"Too bad," said Marlow.

"Oh, dear," whimpered Arnie, pacing inside the cell. "You're in real trouble now."

Dean stood up, prodding the cop with his shoe. "Nothing a little Tylenol can't fix."

"*No*," Arnie said. "I mean, Judge DeVille loves Officer Friendly like a son. Says he's the best policeman he's had in years, and you crushed his head! You're really gonna get it now."

"Get what?" Marlow's lip curled. "Another forty years? Fuck them, fuck you, and fuck this town." She stomped around, opening drawers and cabinets, searching for something.

Dean stared down at the unmoving cop. *This is not good.* It was one thing to escape from a podunk jail to avoid some trumped-up charges, but it was another to assault a cop in his own police station. Dean was going to have a lot of explaining to do to his director.

But Marlow was right—the whole trial had been a farce. It wasn't standard procedure. A forty-year sentence for fucking in a motel room when he didn't even have his dick out? *Another five years for being a federal agent?* Maybe beating up a cop wasn't the best way to make his case, but Marlow was right (how was such a ridiculous person so damn right?)—they couldn't wait around for someone to save them.

As Marlow snooped through the cop's desk, Dean picked up the phone, another old rotary dial model. He tried the number for the agency's after-hours line and waited, but no dial tone came.

He picked up the whole phone, studying it.

"You can't call out on that," said Arnie. "Local calls only."

Dean frowned. The thing was a glorified paper weight for a cop who still processed words on a cathode ray tube monitor from the '80s.

"Ah-ha!" Rising up from the desk, Marlow held up a keychain. "Found my keys. I knew he had to have kept them."

"What about our phones?" he asked, bumping her aside to see for himself.

"Hey!" She pushed him back until they finally settled for squeezing next to each other to dig around in a drawer filled with assorted keys and keychains. "I don't *know*. It's a *drawer* full of keys."

Dean dug around, picking out a *Welcome to Memphis!* keychain with an illustration of Graceland on it. The ring held several keys for assorted uses—house, shed, a Chrysler something or other, a gym locker. He dropped it and noticed others that all appeared to belong in the purse of some soccer mom or dangling off the belt of a truck driver.

"What the hell is all this?" he wondered aloud.

Marlow covered her mouth, whispering into her palm to stifle her unsettling revelation. "They do this to other people."

Their eyes met. Officer Friendly groaned. His body stirred and one of his boots squeaked on the tiles.

Marlow headed for the door. She didn't look back, but Dean did.

"We gotta lock him up."

"Why?"

"He won't stop. He'll call for backup. Help me out."

"How?"

"We'll move him into the cell."

Groaning, she ran back. Dean grabbed the cop under the arms and Marlow took his ankles. They shuffled him into Dean's open cell and slammed it shut.

"Ha!" Marlow snapped, giving him the finger as she marched back to the door.

Dean hung back, calling for Arnie. "Come on."

Arnie shook his head. "Oh, no. No, thanks."

"It's now or never," he said as Officer Friendly slowly lifted his head.

"I know," Arnie replied. "You didn't get the spare key."

"Spare...?"

"He always keeps an extra key on his person."

"Goddamn it. Are you coming with us or what?"

Arnie shrugged. "I guess I'll what."

Dean shook his head—*cowardly bastard*—and ran out the door. He jogged down the steps, catching up to

Marlow. "Hold up."

She wouldn't look back.

"Hey, hang on! I'm comin'." His nose started bleeding again and he wiped it away with the back of his hand, leaving a red smear, which he then wiped on his pants. His suit was a goddamn mess. "Just hold on. What's the plan?"

She spun around, but continued walking backwards just as quickly as she had been walking forwards. Her pretty face scrunched up as she sized him up. "The plan is to get the hell out of here before that cop wakes up and shoots me. *That's* the plan."

"And then what?" Dean noted they were heading back to the motel, toward her car. "You're just going to drive into the next town? You don't think Officer Friendly is going to call for backup or tell his buddies in the next county to be on the lookout for us?"

"Us?" She laughed. "There's no us, *Agent* Dilton. Just me and my car, and this time, I'm not stopping."

He caught up to her, blocking her path. "Sorry," he said when she huffed at him. "I just want you to stop and think about this."

Crossing her arms, she looked around for any sign that Officer Friendly was closing in on them. The town was quiet, and the surrounding buildings were dark and closed for the night. It wasn't particularly late, according to Dean's internal clock, but if it was a dry county, he doubted there was much to do after sundown but pray and go to sleep.

Which is what I should've done in the first place.

Marlow tapped her foot impatiently.

"We just did something very stupid, very illegal, and very dangerous," he said. "If we get caught, things are going to get really bad for us."

She grabbed his tie, pulling him along like a dog on a leash. "So let's not get caught. Come on."

He dug in his heels. "Wait, we have to think logically here."

She sighed dramatically and rolled her eyes. "There was *nothing* logical about that, that, that trial. Or this town. Or these *wackadoo people!* I saw *two dudes* wearing *MAGA hats* for shit's sake."

"I think that was the same guy, actually."

"Can you stop thinking?"

"What?"

"You keep telling me to stop and think. I'm telling you to stop thinking. What does your *gut* say? Mine says get the hell outta here right fucking now. Now you can come with me if you want, but I'm only taking you as far as the next town and you can call your bitch-ass boss from there. Otherwise, I'm not stopping 'til I see Canada or Mexico, and I don't care which."

Then she fled. His only chance was to follow her. Once they reached the Shady Palms parking lot, they kept low. They crept behind a row of dried-up bushes. Marlow didn't break her focus away from the Dodge Demon ahead, even when the door to the motel office swung open. Dean hung back, keeping his eye on Billy the motel clerk, as Marlow forged ahead.

Billy stepped out into the stifling hot air, summoned up a glob of phlegm from deep inside his sinus cavities and hocked it into the bushes, not far from where Dean hid.

Oblivious, Billy fished around in the pockets of his sagging jeans and pulled out a handful of quarters. He sauntered up to a condom dispenser and began shoving coins in. Each time, the machine spat out a packet. When he had about five or six, he crammed them into his pockets and started off in the direction of the courthouse.

Just going to break in the new lot lizard, Dean surmised in disgust.

Once Billy was down the road and out of sight, Dean raced after Marlow. She had gone inside the motel room, exiting just as Dean caught up with her. Her fingers ran through her messy hair.

"Fuck," she whimpered. Her big eyes watered, smearing her mascara.

"What's wrong?" he asked, standing by the car. "You didn't lose the keys, did you?"

"No. Everything's gone. My bags, the money..."

"It's all evidence," he explained. "Officer Friendly wasn't going to just leave it here."

"Yeah, but then where did it go? What did they do with it? It wasn't in the station and it's not here."

Dean held out his hand for the keys. "There are more important things than money right now, *Marlow.*"

"I just thought..." In a blink, her tears were gone, replaced by a stare that radiated hostility. "I *know* that, *Dean*. But it was $30,000."

He threw his hands up. "So? You're an accomplished criminal. I'm sure you can get more."

"It wasn't mine."

"*None* of it was yours," he replied. "You *stole* it."

"Yeah, but some of it belongs to Tony and—"

Headlights flashed across the parking lot. Dean and Marlow ducked down as a tow truck pulled in. The MAGA hat guy was behind the wheel and coming straight for them.

"Oh, shit," he muttered. *They're impounding the car.*

Marlow sneaked around the back and popped open the trunk. She bent over, pushing some things out of the way. Then she threw one leg inside.

"What're you doing?" he cried.

"They're gonna tow us somewhere. I've got the keys. I'm gonna wait until they dump the car, then wait 'til the coast is clear and drive away. Easy peasy, lemon squeezy." Once she was all the way in, she reached up to close the trunk. "You in?"

What other choice did he have?

Hunched down low to avoid being spotted, Dean was about to climb in after her when a horrendous sight stopped him in his tracks.

Jumping back, he bit down on a scream.

Surrounding Marlow in the trunk were half a dozen severed heads.

12.

THE TRUNK

DEAN HAD THOUGHT seeing a dead body would be no big deal. After all, it was just a lifeless, decomposing husk—but he always secretly harbored the morbid belief that death started the moment you were born. Some might call it growing, but Dean saw it as an eighty-year slog toward the grave. Eighty if you were *lucky*.

His training at the academy made it clear he would have to deal with a corpse eventually, but unlike being in the medical profession, handling the dead was not a requirement of his training.

So he put it out of his mind. He never imagined what would happen if he was ever on the other side of the law and might have to hide in the trunk of a Dodge Demon with an irksome stranger and a bunch of decapitated heads.

Holding onto the bumper, he leaned over and heaved.

Marlow popped up. "Move it or lose it."

He tried to compose himself, looking into the trunk with squinted eyes. He really didn't want to see, but perhaps it was better to get a glimpse now rather than let his imagination fuck with him in the dark.

The heads didn't have any faces or other identifying features. They were blank, white ovals.

Foam wig holders.

"Jesus fuck," he muttered, diving in after Marlow and shutting the trunk. Inside, he booted the heads out of his way. Marlow cried out when his elbow jabbed a warm, squishy part of her body. He rose up to give her space and banged his head on the metal interior.

"Ow, Christ!"

She grabbed his tie and yanked him back down. *"Shut up!"*

"You shut up!"

The trunk had barely enough room for the two of them to lie comfortably, forcing Dean to contort his tall, lanky frame around her smaller form. Her ass bumped snugly into his crotch, and he tried not to think of giving it a squeeze.

Then the whistling started, cutting through their annoyed huffs and crabby grumbles. The tow truck had come to a stop in front of the Demon and the driver climbed out. His boots knocked along the pavement as he dragged out his chains and hooks, beginning the work of hauling the car away. While he secured the Demon to the truck's brackets, he whistled contentedly —unaware that he had the two fugitives in a tight spot.

As the front of the car lifted up to a steady mechanical grinding sound, gravity rolled Marlow against Dean. The thought of grabbing her ass through those fishnet stockings dug into his brain like a tick, and his dick perked up, giving her a friendly nudge.

"Oh," she said, knowingly.

"Don't flatter yourself. It's just the friction."

"Ha, as if."

"Quiet. He might hear us."

Snickering, she began to rub against him.

"Stop it," he ordered, hating how good it felt.

"I'm not doing anything."

"Yes, you are. Now stop it." *Please.*

"Or what?"

"Do you want to get caught?"

That stopped her. They laid in silence, his heart pounding against her back. The tension in his private parts remained not so private. As the car was towed behind the truck, each bump and rut in the rocky road thrust her into him. On one nasty crater, she moaned as they rocked together.

"Stop it," he pleaded, gritting his teeth.

"I didn't do anything," she whispered, looking over her shoulder with those wide, bright eyes and those softly parted lips.

Fishnets, tiny shorts, pouty lips, running mascara. He couldn't stop the marathon Marlow was running inside his head. The horny tick preying on his tired brain dug in hard.

He reached up to wipe the sweat off his brow and his handcuffs smacked her in the nose.

"Ow!" she cried out.

He covered her mouth, drawing her closer. She arched her back, pressing against him. Her breath was hot against his palm as she shook him off.

"Get off me," she growled.

"Be quiet," he whispered.

"You're the one making all the noise," she replied. "Can't keep your hands—*or anything else*—to yourself."

Frustration seethed through his clenched teeth. "Trust me, I'm not trying anything. I just want you to shut the hell up."

She froze him out with a chilly silence. She hadn't been this quiet in almost the whole time they had known each other. Part of him was relieved. They needed to stay focused on their escape. But his words did come out a little harsh.

"Sorry," he muttered. "I'm just ... concerned."

"Because your boss is gonna fire you?"

"If you want to talk, let's talk about something else."

"Okay, fine," she mumbled. "What... what brought you to this shithole?"

He almost told her. At this point, did it matter? Dirt scientists taking soil samples in the middle of the desert didn't hold a candle to the shit they had seen tonight.

But eventually this night would be over and in the harsh light of day, he'd have to face his boss, who would ask if he revealed anything about the assignment. Dean needed something in his favor. "That's ... classified."

"Yeah, yeah, right. You keep saying that and I keep hearing 'boring government shit.'"

"It actually *is* boring government shit."

"Okay, fine. How about *you* tell me *your* secret and I tell you *my* secret and we promise not to tell anyone ever?"

Dean mulled that one over, doubting he could trust this weird stranger. But soon they would never have to see each other ever again, so what was the harm?

"Okay," he decided. "Ladies first."

"Why do I have to go first?"

"Christ. Don't then. We'll just sit here in silence. I don't care."

It was quiet for a few moments until Marlow said, "It's Tony's fault that I'm here."

Dean held his breath. Worried any sound might be enough to piss her off, he just listened.

"We met in a carjacking. I had just 'borrowed' some dude's car for a joyride, this gorgeous Mercedes, and no sooner than two blocks away, while I was getting a Starbucks, Tony threw open my door and stuck a knife in my face." She shook her head, reminiscing as if their meet-cute was actually cute. The slightest smile tugged on her lips. "It was one of those instant attractions."

As her smile faded, she curled up tighter, closer to Dean. "Trouble was we both love money so much. We tried getting regular jobs, but we're just not regular people, you know? And why do I have to slave at a desk or serve food to cheap bastards, breaking my back, just to eek above the poverty line every two weeks? It's bullshit. So we went to this seminar on how to get rich."

The session cost them each $500 and was led by a suit who claimed to be worth six figures. Dean surmised that those six figures came from scamming desperate people through false hope at $500 a session.

"The guy said if we repeat his special mantra, all our money problems would be gone and we'd be rolling in it. *And it worked.*"

"Bullshit," Dean blurted. "What were the magic words?"

"If you're gonna have that kind of attitude, I shouldn't tell you."

"Just tell me. I won't say anything. Your secret's safe with me, remember?"

"Fine," she sighed. "The magic words— I mean, the *mantra* is: *'I love money and money loves me.'*"

"Okay, and how rich are you now?"

"Well, I *was* up thirty grand before you got me arrested."

"Me? Oh, hell no, sweetheart. *You're* the one who ripped me off and brought the heat down on us. I knew I should've just stayed back at the trailer."

"Trailer, huh? Are you going to tell me your secret now?"

"Not yet, and don't change the subject. You said this magic mantra and got thirty grand—how'd that really happen?"

"Tony came up with this idea of sticking up convenience stores. Just dinky little gas stations in the middle of nowhere, but ones where a lot of trucks come through. He figured truckers have a lot more money and probably drop some big bills at their stops with gas being so expensive. I had nothing better to do..."

"That's a great reason to commit a crime."

She elbowed him, but continued. "So *anyway*, we started holding up convenience stores, but it was getting expensive to drive out to all these places, and I had to come up with a different look each time. That's why I have all these wigs—so the cops wouldn't always be on the lookout for a smokin' hot redhead."

"You're full of yourself," he muttered, but what he wanted to say was, *Damn right.*

"But then we were at a motel one night watching a movie. I don't remember what one. I don't really like movies, but there was a bank robbery in it. Something about a vault, maybe? I don't know. It was dumb and I fell asleep. But Tony was into it. He woke me up to tell me all about his big plan. We'd be set for life."

"Let me guess—a bank job."

"You didn't need to guess. It was pretty obvious that's where I was going."

"So then what? The job went wrong and Tony got busted?"

"Not exactly."

Tony targeted a small-town bank. For a week, while Marlow lounged around the motel pool, Tony cased the joint. He wandered around the neighborhood, watching for a pattern. He observed the people coming and going, noting the number of tellers each day (three) and security guards (one per shift).

But Tony was a take-action man, and he grew impatient with waiting and watching, so one night, he told Marlow to get ready—the job was going down the next day.

The robbery went off without a hitch. Tony overpowered the elderly security guard and subdued the tellers. By the time he jumped into Marlow's waiting getaway car, Tony had gotten his hands on thirty grand. They sped out of town without a single squad car on their ass. It was so much easier than Hollywood made it look—and Tony couldn't stop bragging about how incredible he was. He was a criminal mastermind and this one little job was only the beginning. He was going to be the richest man in America.

Dollar signs flashed in his eyes. The money was still hot and he was already talking about buying a fancy bomber jacket to go with his dream car—a 1950s Chevy Impala.

Money slipped through Tony's fingers faster than water.

At their first pit stop, Tony packed all the cash into his duffel bag while Marlow surveyed the parking lot for cops. Then she took the bag with her to the bathroom to change while Tony ordered breakfast.

Locked in a bathroom stall, Marlow rubbed two stacks of bills across her chest. *"I love money and money loves me,"* she chanted, as if asking the money gods to grant her clarity. And clarity she did get, whether it was her own brain reasoning out the situation or there really were money gods answering her prayers.

The answer that became apparent to her in that wet, graffitied bathroom stall was that if she left Tony in charge of the money, it would be gone in no time.

So after a quick change, she sneaked out with the stolen money and took off in the Demon.

"And I haven't seen him since," she concluded. "But I just know he's pissed."

"How do you know? Maybe he's heartbroken that you left him."

She snorted. "Yeah, right. Men love their money and toys, almost as much as they hate it when women take it all from them."

"That's not true... Not entirely..."

She snorted again. If she kept that up, she was going to give herself a nosebleed. "And how did you feel when you realized I took your wallet?"

"I ... see your point. Do you think he'd come after you?"

"Probably."

"Think he'll find you here?"

She shook her head. "No heckin' way. I'll be gone as soon as MAGA hat guy drops us off. Come on, it's your turn. What's your secret government detail all about?"

The warmth and comfort of being next to Marlow gave him a false sense of security and intimacy. The trunk was their own little confessional, keeping their secrets safe.

But it would be hard to follow Marlow's tale of money, love, and betrayal with what amounted to... "Dirt," he said. "My assignment was to monitor a couple of scientists while they sampled and tested dirt."

"Anything unusual about the dirt?"

"I don't know," he admitted. "I wasn't allowed to ask."

Pouting, she twisted around until they were face to face. "I told you about the worst thing I ever did to somebody and you tell me a story about *dirt*? And not even a story!"

"I never said it was storytime," he said. "And I didn't think you were gonna share that kind of secret."

"Well, I did and yours sucks. Tell me a better one."

"No, that was the secret I said I'd share." *No take-backsies.*

"I want a better one!"

"No!"

With that, the tow truck and the Demon came to a halt. Dean and Marlow stayed perfectly still, bracing themselves for all hell to break loose.

13.

THE HELLHOUNDS

THEY WAITED. NOTHING happened. Marlow's heart thundered in her ears. She wished Dean's gun hadn't been confiscated. They could've used it to surprise that MAGA hat-wearing trucker the second he found them—because he probably would, and being found at all cramped her escape plan.

But after several long minutes, nothing happened except for the car being dropped off and the truck's engine quitting. Somewhere in the distance a dog barked.

"Is it safe to come out now?" Marlow whispered. She found herself clinging to Dean.

His face was close to hers, his hand on her waist. She wanted to go back to being curled up next to him, feeling safe and snug and hopeful.

The trunk latch disengaged. Light peeked in. The old MAGA hat son of a bitch lifted the trunk, gasping at the sight of two bodies and half a dozen heads inside.

Dean pushed himself forward to shield Marlow, who grabbed for the closest weapon she could find. The trucker reached for his gun, secure in its side holster, but Marlow moved quicker. She hurled one of the wig holders at him. The man screamed, batting the head aside.

Dean leaped out, tackling him.

"No! Oh, god no! Please don't hurt me!" the man cried.

Equipped with a tire iron, better than any wig holder, Dean moved in as if to strike. Muscles clenched, he hesitated.

The man trembled. His fuzzy caterpillar eyebrows rose halfway up his wrinkled forehead. "Oh, dear god. Please don't hurt me!" From Dean's vantage point, the old man shivered. But Marlow could see his hand sneaking down to his holstered sidearm. She grabbed another wig holder and threw it, nailing the man's shoulder.

He hollered, more surprised than hurt.

"What did you do that for?" Dean asked.

"He was going for his gun!"

The man made another sneaky attempt.

"Don't touch the fucking gun!" Marlow screeched.

Dean waved the tire iron, handcuff dangling down his arm. "Don't move!"

Undeterred, the man drew on them anyway. A tremor wracked his body, throwing off his aim. The bullet hit the taillight. Marlow shrieked, ducking around the side of the car.

Dean slammed the tire iron down on the man's forearm. A bone cracked. The man cried out, dropping the gun. Dean kicked it away and it disappeared under a pile of junk. With the old man incapacitated, Marlow had a moment to catch her breath and look around.

"What is this dump?" she wondered, standing in the middle of a stinking junkyard surrounded by heaps of rancid trash several feet high. Mountains of garbage and scrap metal towered over them, threatening to topple. Shit and waste and rot stank up the air.

Marlow plugged her nose, trying not to gag.

"Looks like an actual garbage dump," said Dean. Swinging the tire iron, he turned to the man. "Who are you?"

The man spat on his shoe. "Piss off."

Marlow sensed that Dean was reluctant to beat the shit out of an old man, but he still wound up to hit him again. The bastard flinched, cradling his broken arm to his chest.

"Alright, alright! Name's Jessup. I'm the tow truck driver 'round here. I bring people's cars out here when the judge says they're done with 'em." He gazed at them with a pitiful look on his face. "You're not gonna hurt an old man, are ya?"

"No," said Dean.

"Aw, good, good." Jessup smiled, showing rows of white and gold teeth. Then he pursed his lips together and blew a long high-pitched whistle.

"What the hell was that?" Marlow asked.

"Oh, nothin'," he said, then started screaming to high heaven. *"Help me! Somebody, help! Officer Friendly! HELP! HELP! POLICE!"*

Marlow snatched the tire iron out of Dean's useless hand, cracking it over the old man's crown. His blood-shot eyeballs fluttered up as he fell face first into the sand. Part of his scalp split open, bleeding.

"What was that for?" Dean took the tire iron back.

"He was a squealer," she replied. "Snitches get stitches, old man."

"We ought to find that gun," he said, kicking himself for kicking it away.

"Let's just get out of here before someone else comes along," she said, heading to the car.

"You got the keys?" he asked.

Before she could give him an answer loaded with sarcasm, a lithe, black creature bounded over one of the mountains of trash. It had sharp, pointed ears and a narrow brown muzzle. It bared its yellowed teeth, froth oozing from its maw. Marlow would have guessed Doberman Pinscher, but like everything else in this town, something was slightly off—like the way raw, pink flesh bubbled up along its spine.

"Nice doggy," she said softly as the hellhound trod in between her and the Demon. "Nice mutant doggy..."

"That's not a dog," said Dean. "That's a fucking monster."

Jessup stirred, chuckling to himself as the hellhound herded Marlow and Dean away from the car.

"Call him off, Jessup," Dean ordered.

"Me? Oh, heck no. No one tells them what to do."

Them?

Jessup dabbed at his forehead, smearing blood across his fingers. His eyes bulged with an unspoken realization. "Oh, fiddlesticks."

Out of nowhere, a second hellhound appeared. In seconds, it launched at Jessup, sinking its teeth into his throat. Growling and tearing and scratching at the man's pleading body, the dog ripped out his trachea. In two swift crunches, the hellhound gobbled it up. Licking its bloodied mouth, it stared intently at the remaining humans.

Marlow ran. She had never been good with dogs. In fact, she was one of those despicable people that downright hated them. Too aggressive, too big, too loud, too yappy, too smelly, and now she had "incredibly violent" to add to her list of dislikes.

Turning sharply down a narrow trash corridor, Marlow looked back. Dean was trying to tame the dogs with his tire iron. *Good luck*. They snapped their slobbery teeth at him. One clamped down on the tool, yanking it out of his grasp. He changed his plan and ran, choosing a different route than the one Marlow took.

One hellhound raced after him, but the other—the first dog who wouldn't let them get near the car—tracked Marlow.

The toe of her boot snagged a piece of metal and she went flying. The gritty sand scraped her knees as she skidded across the ground. She pushed herself up and kept moving.

As she ducked and weaved through the towering piles of detritus, she lost track of Dean. The garbage subsided, replaced by crushed and cubed cars, trucks, and minivans.

Rusting shipping containers were stacked up to form a wall, and Marlow feared there was no way out of this dizzying maze. The only reprieve was a chain link fence that filled the gaps between the containers. She didn't even know what direction she had come from or how she was going to find her way back to the Demon.

She worried about Dean—that the other dog would catch up to him and tear him apart like lunch meat, leaving her alone to face *two* ferocious hellhounds.

Holding her side where a stitch stabbed her from the inside, Marlow hid behind a corroded station wagon. She rested her head against its wood paneling and stared up at the sky, listening for the hellhound's claws scraping through the sand. It made a soft whine.

In her heart, Marlow believed she could make it back to the Demon somehow. She had the keys and—

Or she'd *had* the keys. She patted herself down. Pockets were empty, bra was empty, palms were empty. The keys were gone. She peered around the station wagon's bumper. Laying on a clump of dirt, glinting under the moonlight, were the keys.

Oh, for shit's sake. She closed her eyes and breathed a sigh of relief—cut off by the hellhound's howl. When she dared to look back, she witnessed the dog scooping the keys up in its jaw, before trotting off toward a ragged gap in the chain link fence.

Marlow crept out of hiding to follow.

Like a knife through butter, the mongrel slid through the gap in the fence. Its smooth, black body vanished into the night. The only hint that it was there was the jangle of keys.

You little fucker.

Beyond the fence was a rocky hill and an old, dead tree. Long, gnarled branches nearly blocked her view of the old white house on the hill. Marlow recalled seeing it from the motel, but now she was really close.

Perhaps too close.

What kind of person lives next to a dump?

She rested her head against the fence, curling her fingers around the metal. The glowing windows of the house on top of the hill shed light on several smooth rocks jutting out of the grassy ground. Tombstones. The hellhound zigzagged around them on its way up to the house.

What kind of person lives on top of a cemetery?

Maybe the damn mutt lives there.

She peered down at the slit in the fence, wondering if she could squeeze through. Though she was proud of her physique, she had to admit she was a bit too buxom to fit.

She gazed up, then back down at her pointed-toe boots. She prodded one into one of the links and tried to pull herself up, but insecurity forced her back down. She was going to have to find another way out.

A loud panting erupted from somewhere beyond the station wagon. She stayed low, waiting, and peeked over the hood.

Dean ran toward her, exiting one of the trash corridors. His wide eyes darted in her direction, registering her presence, but she ducked back down upon seeing the other hellhound pounding the dirt behind him.

Just great, she thought. *I just got rid of my dog and now I have to deal with yours too. Thanks for nothing.*

If she stayed down, the dog (and Dean) would zoom right past and then she could sneak back in the direction of her car.

Which was a useless heap of metal without the keys.

Damn it. She would have to follow the dog up to the house. *Maybe it'll drop the keys along the way.*

"*Marlow!*" Dean blew past her, the dog snapping at his calves. "*Run!*"

Waiting until they had passed by, she ran for the fence. As she scrambled up and over the side, her stockings snagged on a sharp piece of metal. She tried to throw her other leg over to drop down, but got caught and fell upside down, swinging against the fence.

She scratched at her stockings, but her hands weren't strong enough. The netting cut into her fingers. And since she wore shorts over top, she couldn't slip out. Though, even if she managed that, she would probably land on her head and break her neck.

"Help..."

Just as the pathetic whimper escaped her, Dean reappeared. Rather than race to her rescue, he dove inside the station wagon and slammed the door in the hellhound's face.

Idiot, thought the woman snared upside down in her own undergarments.

But just as quickly as he darted inside, he slapped his palms against the smeared, greasy windows, luring the hellhound toward the back of the car. He pressed one of the fold-down seat buttons, looking inside the far back. As he climbed into the front, the dog stayed on him, snapping and barking and going full Cujo. Dean hit the trunk release lever, popping open the rear hatch. He scrambled over the seats for the back, reaching a long leg through to kick open the hatch.

The hellhound ran around to the back and jumped in after him. Already three steps ahead, Dean shoved the seat back in place and rolled out the rear passenger side door. He shut it. The dog yipped and scratched at the seat, and before it could attempt to go back the way it had come, Dean rounded to the back and shut the hatch too. Trapped like a rat, the hellhound threw itself against the window and howled.

Dean bent over, wheezing. Marlow didn't give him

another second to catch his breath.

"Get over here!" she shrieked.

Dean straightened up, head lolling back on his shoulders. His entire face burned beet red and his mouth gaped open like a suffocating fish. He shuffled toward her, loosening his tie. "Where's your dog?"

"He ran off."

"Where to?"

"Does it matter? He's gone."

"It *does* matter 'cause I don't want to get my ass chomped helping you." He pointed down—one of his feet was missing a shoe, leaving only a dirt-grey sock. "Bastard stole my shoe."

Inside the car, the dog tore into the dusty dress shoe. Dean was lucky it hadn't been his whole foot.

Marlow stuck her thumb in the general direction of the old house. "He went thataway, okay?"

"Good." Dean paused. Hands on his hips, he looked her up and down. "Uh, how'd you get like that?"

She sighed impatiently. "I didn't want to get my ass chomped either. Can you help or not?"

A grin spread slowly across his face. He rubbed his chin, studying the situation. "I don't know... Looks like you're in a real pickle."

"You're a pickle," she snapped. "Just get me down."

"What's in it for me?"

"Nothing."

He clicked his tongue. "You didn't even say the magic word."

"We don't have time for this."

He pretended to walk away, leaving her hanging. "You know, I'm sure there are *plenty* of people hanging from fences that could use my help. People who know how to say please. Maybe I'll go help one of them…"

"You're a real creep, you know that?" she sniffled.

He shook his head, coming back. "I'm just kidding. *Of course* I'll get you down. But … I can't figure out what's holding you up."

"It's my stupid stockings. They're caught…"

"Okay, well…" He neared the fence for a better look. "Stop swinging."

"I'm not doing anything!"

"Yeah, you're moving. Stop it."

"*I can't help it.*"

"I'll have to jump the fence for a better look."

She crossed her arms. "Fine. Just do whatever."

Dean took a running start at the fence. His weight shook the chains—and Marlow too. Her face banged against the metal and her fishnets dug defiantly into her thighs.

Come on, come on…

Dean jumped swiftly over and landed on the other side. *"Goddamn it,"* he groaned.

"Now what?"

"I stepped in something wet."

"I bet the dog pissed there on its way out," she teased, reveling in the disgusted look on his face. Her enjoyment was short-lived—all the blood in her body seemed to have drained into her head. She felt like a cherry tomato about to pop. "Will you *please* just get me down?"

"There's the magic word," he said. He planted his hands on her hips to steady her and began to tug. "Hang on, I got you." Her face smacked into his chest. "Huh."

"What's the matter?"

"You're really stuck."

A frustrated scream broke free. *"Oh my gawd! I know that! Just get me down!"*

"Can you take your shorts off?"

"No," she whined.

"Then I'll have to rip your stockings off."

"Whatever," she moaned.

"Okay, hold onto something," he said.

She grabbed onto the fence. "Ready."

He slid his fingers under the tight links of her stockings. His hands were warm and smooth. Using all his grip strength, he stretched the netting until the links snapped and Marlow came crashing toward the earth head first.

She cried out just as Dean caught her. "Gotcha!"

He gently lowered her to the ground. Cradled in his surprisingly strong arms, she gazed into his eyes.

For half a minute, it was like they were back in the trunk. Close together, blood rushing, skin ablaze.

She leaned in, gaze drifting to his lips—when he went and ruined the moment.

"You might want to stand up. I think that's where the dog pissed."

14.

THE TRAILER

IF MARLOW WANTED to be a stupid, fucking moron, that was fine by Dean. But he refused to go anywhere near the creepy old house on the hill, especially if there was a chance the hellhounds lived here. The dogs were deadly enough, but whoever owned them had to be much worse.

Marlow was adamant, however. "I have to get the keys. I want my car. How else are we gonna get out of here?"

"I'll take a fucking Pogo stick at this point," he replied.

They quibbled back and forth until it became clear that they were at an impasse and would have to part ways. Fine by Dean. He hated to see her march into the lion's den, but he wasn't about to follow. He was in enough trouble, and he hadn't even been dressed down by his superiors yet.

First things first, get out of Paradise.

When he was safe, he would send her some help. She was going to need it.

Marlow leaned against the fence with her arms crossed. "So you're just gonna walk off into the desert like Jesus?"

"Moses, sweetheart," he said. "*Moses* walked into the desert. And I only have to get as far as my trailer. Then I can use the satellite phone to call for help."

"Good luck with only one shoe."

She was right. It was going to be a rough slog, but he could worry about his foot later.

"And watch out for rattlesnakes," she added.

He wanted to tell her to shut up. Actually, he wanted to tell her shut up by pushing her up against the fence and taking her whole fucking tongue in his mouth, followed by any number of indecent acts that would surely add more time onto their sentences, but he had to get a move on. Officer Friendly must have been on the hunt for them by now.

"I'll be fine," he said, cutting around the cemetery. "Don't get caught on any more fences."

She stuck out her tongue before beginning her ascent to the house. He laughed to hide the terrible feeling in his gut.

Splitting up was a bad idea.

But he pushed forward, thinking about how he was going to explain everything to his boss. By the time he reached the trailer on the outskirts of town, he was convinced that there might be a way to not have to explain anything.

All I have to do is get to the airport. Once there, he could report his rental car stolen (not abandoned in a sinkhole at a lousy diner), send a taxi back for the scientists, and make an anonymous call to a police station in the nearest "normal" town to tip them off about what was going on in Paradise. Then someone else could save Marlow's ass and he could wash his hands of the whole ordeal.

Unfortunately, the airport was too far to get there on foot, so the next best solution was to hoof it to the trailer for that emergency satellite phone and prepare to take responsibility for everything.

Arriving at the dig site, he passed Dr. Burke and Dr. Gelman's trailer. All the lights were off. Dean presumed they had wisely gone to bed early and avoided the horrible, little town as per the director's orders.

Dean stopped at his trailer first. The door was unlocked; he never bothered locking it anyway because it was barebones. The only things of value he had with him on this assignment were his phone and his wallet. The soil scientists had everything else, including the satellite phone, but Dean didn't want to bang on their door at this time of night without wiping his face and getting a quick drink. No point alarming them when he had everything under control.

He hoped.

Away from the town and back in the safety of his trailer, he felt less urgency. He opened the mini fridge and helped himself to a cool bottle of water.

Inside the narrow bathroom, he used the toilet. As he washed his hands, he took a good look at himself—and it wasn't good. His nose had been bashed up, leaving a dark red waterfall from his nostrils down to his chin. Drips stained his shirt and tie. His jacket was torn up, and as he tried to take it off, the sleeve caught on the handcuffs still dangling from his wrist.

"Goddamn it."

He clumsily whipped off the jacket, ripping the shoulder seam completely. He threw it to the floor and kicked it out of his way.

Breath ragged, he stopped himself from a full-on tantrum. *It's just a jacket. Let it go. Just get the phone from Burke and Gelman and this will all be over.* Maybe he could convince them to call a cab and leave for the airport right away.

He splashed some water on his face, cleaning up as best he could. Then he slugged back half the water bottle and went back outside.

Climbing the steps to the neighboring trailer, he knocked on the door. "Hey, guys—"

With a whining creak, the door opened.

Dean peered inside. "Hello...?"

The smell hit him before he heard the flies buzzing. Old pennies and rotten meat.

Fuck. He had only been gone a couple of hours—*what the hell happened?*

He elbowed the door open and stepped inside the darkness. His socked foot squished down on a soggy rug. Cold wetness gushed between his toes, and that sensation, combined with the stuffy air and putrid rot doubled him over.

Blood. His eyes began to adjust. *Blood everywhere.*

He tried to put his head between his legs and breathe—*don't throw up, don't throw up, Jesus fucking Christ, don't throw up*—when he spotted Dr. Burke and Dr. Gelman, still in their lab coats from earlier that day, on the floor. Dead.

Someone had slit their throats, shot them execution style, and left them in a pile near their bunk bed.

Oh, fuck. Oh, fuck. Oh—

Three bodies in one day? It was too much for Dean. His first dead body should have been at a contained crime scene where a wizened, more experienced agent would guide him through the investigation process, while taking the piss out of Dean for being a crime scene virgin.

Now at the site of a double murder, he was beyond overwhelmed.

Done with everything, he was going to find the satellite phone, call Director ███████████, go straight back to his own trailer, and stay put until help arrived. The situation was officially above his paygrade.

Searching throughout Burke and Gelman's trailer, he had a jarring thought: *What if whoever killed them would've killed me too? I might have been asleep. Or worse, staring at my phone with my dick in one hand.*

Panic welled in his chest and rattled his concentration. He almost forgot what he was looking for, fearing that if he opened the bathroom door, a shadowy killer would strike.

Calm the fuck down, he tried to tell himself. *You're a government agent, for fuck's sake.*

But what did that really mean? He had a criminology degree and went through training, and then the agency handed him a badge and a gun, and said, "Get after it, boy!" But Dean hadn't *really* known what he was getting himself into. He didn't want to hunt bad guys or spy on mobsters or supervise a pair of nerdy dirt scientists who couldn't keep themselves alive for three hours without him. He had only wanted a job that could keep him on the straight and narrow.

But if I had been on the straight and narrow, if I had

gone to bed at a reasonable hour, I'd be dead now too.

So much for straight and narrow.

Spiraling, he sank to the floor and hugged himself. The floor creaked under his weight and he startled, again anticipating a shadowy killer. *Who killed Burke and Gelman? And why?* They were harmless geeks.

Maybe it wasn't about *them* but their work. Who really gave a shit about dirt, unless there was something else going on? Maybe the dirt was a coverup for something else, or they discovered some environmental trouble that would make Flint, Michigan look like a fucking waterpark.

It was the kind of crazy conspiracy theory that people online like to jaw about.

Dean picked himself back up and kept searching. This time he wanted notes and reports—anything about why they had been sent here. Maybe there was another reason why he had been arrested, not because he had broken some bullshit morality law with a stranger in a motel room—judges and politicians did that all the time. The murders—*the assassination*—had to be related to Dean's assignment.

Unfortunately, the two scientists were meticulous about keeping their information hidden away. Dean found nothing incriminating or useful—just takeout menus and several games of Tic Tac Toe scribbled on takeout napkins. All Burke and Gelman had done these past few weeks was eat, sleep, play games, and dig dirt.

He leaned against the sink, trying to think, when he spotted the satellite phone. Gelman clutched it in his cold, dead claw.

They knew they were in trouble, but they couldn't do anything about it in time.

Dean inched closer to the dead scientist. His socked foot sopped up more blood. Each step went squish. He reached out, as if he could will the phone out of Gelman's hand and into his. He didn't want to touch the dead body.

What if he wakes up?

Gelman's eyes were wide open, rolled up into his head. His fuzzy beard was dampened with blood, drawing his mouth down into a silent scream.

Dean stared at him, waiting for a blink, a nod, a gasp—any sign that Gelman was alive. Nothing.

He couldn't wait. A killer on the loose had compromised his assignment.

I *compromised the goddamn assignment. I should never have left.*

He snatched the phone from Gelman and dashed outside. Gelman never flinched. Dead was dead.

The air outside felt lighter. Dean breathed easier, though he doubted he would ever get that rotting, coppery stench out of his memory.

Hurrying back to his own trailer, he kept a lookout for anything suspicious. The desert was quiet (*too quiet?*) and the sky was clear. A blanket of stars hung over him. The closer he got to his trailer, the safer he felt.

Lifting the phone to his ear, he dialed the first four digits. He almost didn't hear someone rushing up behind him.

As he turned, his head avoided the worst of the shovel swinging toward him. The metal blade struck the phone, sending it tumbling under the trailer.

Dean spun around.

The attacker whacked him with the shovel. Upon impact, darkness and shadows flooded his vision. He dropped off the steps, onto his hands and knees.

He wasn't thinking about the strange woman trying to kill him or why. He was focused on the phone. *Gotta call the director...*

Reaching under the trailer, he surprised a snake. Its bone-like tail perked up, twitching and rattling, as the scaly creature coiled around the phone.

Fuck, shit, fuck.

Dean backed away, bumping into the woman with the shovel. He twisted around to ask her for help, forgetting that she had struck him, when she landed another blow. This time he blacked out.

15.

THE HOUSE ON THE HILL

IT WAS A grueling climb up the cemetery hill toward the house—especially so because Marlow's red boots, while aesthetically pleasing, had no traction. To make her way, she was forced to grab onto broken tombstones and corners of exposed coffins. She concentrated on the house's glowing porchlights, rather than think about the dead bodies surrounding her.

She had no idea what she'd do when she finally found the vicious dog, but this was her only plan and she was determined to see it through. And if *Agent Dilton* wanted to waste their lead by going after a long shot, that was his choice. Marlow was getting the keys.

A tremor vibrated up her legs and the earth rumbled. Gasping, she held onto a dried-up tree trunk —all branches, no leaves—until the quake subsided.

I hate this town.

The tree cracked, splitting apart. The piece she clung to was ripped away, and she tumbled several feet back down the hill. A tombstone broke her fall.

While she leaned against the slab to catch her breath, she manifested a second wind. Rallied. Marlow never gave up on anything. Not on her hopes and dreams, not on her worst impulses, not even on toxic boyfriends. If she set her mind to something, she was going to see it through. Sometimes a person just needs to say, *This whole situation sucks, but what the hell? What have I got to lose by going a little farther?*

Staring up at the broken tree, Marlow almost lost her lunch. Inside the desiccated trunk, a toothy mummified creature sneered down at her. It was most likely another dog, and thankfully dead.

Earthquakes, mummified dogs, and unhinged judges—*what* is *this place?*

She trudged upward to the house. Once she made it to the porch, she grabbed onto the rickety wooden railing. This time the ground didn't betray her.

Dusting herself off, she took a moment to look around. The house was in the style of a rundown antebellum. Jagged fractures spread up from the cracked foundation like spider legs. The house shouldn't have been in this spot, precariously perched atop a hill, nor situated in this part of the world. It was as if a madman constructed it on another planet or it had randomly dropped out of the sky from god knows where.

Marlow didn't care about its origins, only that she badly needed to piss and there was no cover. No bushes or trees big enough. Maybe a tombstone, if she wanted to shuffle back down and try to balance herself on the rocky hill.

Just find the keys and go somewhere else.

Out of the shadows, the hellhound darted across her path like a bad omen. Marlow jumped back, rattling the loose boards of the wraparound porch. The dog didn't notice her, or didn't care, racing away from the house and back down the hill toward the junkyard.

Hand clasped over her mouth, Marlow watched the creature until she was certain it was gone and not coming back. At the same time, she wondered why it ran like a bat out of hell away from the house. It was a bad sign for sure, and if she had checked her horoscope that day, she might have read: *Mercury is in retrograde, girlfriend. Bad moon rising. Trouble ahead. Lock your doors and don't talk to strangers.*

Once the devilish pooch was out of sight, she peeked around to the front of the house. The porchlights cast a blazing spotlight on the keys, left on a wobbling wooden plank in front of the welcome mat.

Marlow almost laughed. *Dumb dog.*

Knowing she too could be spotlit under the porchlights, she stayed low as she sneaked closer. When she stepped on an adjacent plank, something mechanical grinded underfoot.

The plank on which the keys sat angled downward. The keys slid down a small incline and disappeared. The plank tipped back into place as if nothing had been there at all.

Oh, fuck, no!

Marlow pushed the little trapdoor open and peered into the dark hole. On her knees, praying, she reached inside. *They can't have gotten far. No way.* But the tiny tunnel stretched on and on, and she only had so much arm to squeeze down before she had the very troubling thought that something sharp and mechanical and unforgiving might clamp down and take her limb too.

She withdrew and sat back on her heels.

As she pondered her plight and need for a bathroom, a car sped up the winding dirt road that led to the house. Rust corroded its sun-damaged black exterior. Thick, grey smoke plumed out of the chrome tailpipe and the engine growled loudly.

Marlow had nowhere to go. The driver would see her any minute.

She dashed to the door. The ornate doorknob turned easily in her hand. With a soft click, it opened. Crouched down, she crept inside with plans to hide behind some floor-to-ceiling curtains or a person-sized Ming vase until the coast was clear.

But the old house offered little coverage in the brightly lit foyer.

An unstable coat rack stood guard near the door and a moth-eaten rug slumped in a corner. The hardwood floors it was meant to adorn were scuffed, chipped, scratched, and stained—with what, Marlow didn't want to know. A cobweb-riddled chandelier burned brightly above, illuminating a path up the stairs and deeper into the house.

With nowhere else to hide, Marlow hid on the stairs behind the thick, oak railings. *I just need to stay out of sight for a minute...*

Outside, the car stopped beside the porch. The driver lumbered out and slammed the door. Despite the heat, he was wrapped in a thick wool coat. A flat-brimmed fedora sat on his bloated, red face—Judge DeVille, sans wig and gavel.

And he was toting her duffle bag.

You greedy son of a...

He shuffled up the porch steps, stopping at the welcome mat. With a frown, he glanced down as if he sensed that someone had stood in that exact spot only seconds ago. He cleared his phlegmy throat and spat a glob of green onto his own porch before barreling into the house.

"Honey! I'm home!" he announced.

A lightning bolt shot through Marlow. *How the hell does he know I'm here?* She cowered, afraid to reveal herself. *What's he gonna do? Add another forty years? It can't get any worse.*

The judge hung his coat and hat on the rack. Without the powdered wig, he was simply a bald man with little tufts of white hair littering his skull.

"Valentina! Valentina? Where the ever-loving Jesus are you, woman?" he hollered.

Marlow let out a breath. So he was someone else's problem. Although, the state of the house suggested that this Valentina person (if she was lucky) might only exist in the judge's mind.

"You wouldn't *believe* the day I had!" he bellowed. "Couple of canoodlers thought they could get away with breaking our decency laws. Well, I shut them down without delay. They won't be causing any more unsavoriness in my town."

The judge moved about the house as if he were certain he would find Valentina in the next room. Regardless, Marlow checked over her shoulder to make sure a decrepit old woman was not lurking, about to strike.

No one was there, of course, but she couldn't shake the feeling of being watched.

She glanced at the crookedly hung portrait next to

her on the stairs. It was one of those freaky ones where the eyes seemed to follow you around.

"Valentina? Are you listening to me?"

The judge planted a foot on the staircase. The step creaked. Blood rushing in her ears, Marlow tiptoed quickly to the second-floor landing, hiding behind the wide balustrades.

"Valentina?" he called. "Is that you? What're you sneaking around for?" He chuckled, licking his lips. "You know you can't hide from me."

Marlow listened as the judge dragged his old bones up the stairs, each creaking step a countdown to the explosive moment when he would find her.

Keeping her head down, Marlow pushed against the first door she came to. It was stuck. She tried the next one, but it was "pull" only. She eased it open and came face to face with a brick wall.

Or a bricked-up room.

Valentina?

She didn't want to think about women being bricked up in drafty rooms. Too gothic. She moved swiftly, heading further into the house. The next room was a dead drop into nothing. A bat flapped its leathery wings as it burst out of the depths. Marlow waved her hands, shooing it away.

The judge's liver-spotted hand wrapped around the banister at the top of the stairs. He would see her any second.

Marlow dove through the next open door, even if it meant falling to her doom or squishing herself against a brick wall.

"Valentina!"

Marlow shut the door behind her, leaning against

it. She tried to hold her panting breath and calm her thundering heart.

Certainly the old judge couldn't cause her much physical harm, not at his age or in his decrepit condition, but the whole point of an escape plan was to not get caught, and if the judge thought she and Dean were still locked away, that meant Officer Friendly hadn't reported them yet.

Her head-start dwindled with every minute, every poor decision, every new conflict.

The door banged against her. She yelped, then quickly covered her mouth. *No, no, no.*

"Valentina?" purred the judge, knocking on the door. "What're doing in my room? Feeling frisky, are you?"

Marlow caught sight of her own revulsion in a gold-framed standing mirror.

She searched the room for a place to hide. Under the four-poster bed, with its cobwebbed canopy? She didn't dare pull back the gauzy panels for fear of seeing the skeleton of some long-dead woman once known as Valentina, or crawl under with the dust bunnies and creepy crawlies. Nor did she want to hide in the oak armoire and get snared by some mechanical boobytrap. She considered climbing up inside the fireplace, but with the way her day had been going, it would be just her luck that the judge would decide to light a fire on this terribly hot night.

The judge knocked again. "Valentina? Quit playing around..."

Ugghhh. What do I do?

"Don't make me shoot my way in, Valentina," he warned. "Remember what happened last time."

What happened last time? On second thought, I don't want to know.

Car tires crunched gravel on route to the house—the sound carried through an open window on the other side of the room. Red and blue lights flashed.

Officer Friendly.

She wouldn't be surprised if the cop shot her on sight. It happened all the time on the news—that's why Marlow preferred *Judge Judy* and the home shopping channel. No one ever got shot on those shows. *Maybe I* should *have gone with Dean. He's probably miles away by now.*

She waited for the megaphone, the warning shot, the SWAT guys, the negotiation, the siege. Whatever came next, she waited for it to happen and end swiftly.

Instead, the engine turned off and a car door slammed. Boots stomped up the steps and across the porch at a steady, determined pace. The doorbell rang. The judge stopped knocking and clicking his nails on the bedroom door.

"Now what in tarnation...?" he muttered, shuffling back down the hall.

Marlow rushed to the window, eager to hear what Officer Friendly had to say. A million, agonizing seconds ticked by as the judge hauled his ancient butt back down the long staircase.

"What?" he croaked, when he opened the front door.

"Sir, I have some unfortunate news to report," said Officer Friendly.

"And what's that, son?"

Leather squeaked and floorboards groaned. "I've been a very bad boy."

Marlow's skin crawled, and as much as she needed to find a way out of the house, she needed to know why a grown man would phrase his fuckup that way.

"Is that so?"

"Yes, sir. Agent Dilton and the woman escaped and I haven't been able to find them. I need to be punished."

"Alright, son," said the judge. "Better get in here."

With the cop inside the house, it was only a matter of time before they sniffed out Marlow. She had to give up on finding the keys and go along with Dean's plan—walking into the desert like Jesus.

At least out there, she could pee behind a cactus.

She wandered around the room and into the judge's ensuite bathroom. A clawfoot tub was attached to an antiquated plumbing system. Rust and hard water stains ruined what could have been a fine antique, wall-mounted sink. It was an otherwise ordinary bathroom—with old man eyebrow clippings peppered all over the porcelain. Ordinary, except for the dual toilets.

The one on the right was a modern toilet, but the one on the left was an old-fashioned job with a cherry wood seat and an exposed pipe leading up to what Marlow presumed was a wooden tank. The chain to flush it dangled down from above.

Bladder cramping, Marlow gave in and squatted down. *Oh, thank god.* Listening for anyone approaching, she pissed as quickly and quietly as she could. Relieved, she let out a sigh.

The seat shifted under her weight. The floor began to move. And then the wall.

And then the bathroom disappeared, swallowing her up inside the house.

16.

THE OTHER SIDE

DIZZY FROM SPINNING around on a toilet, Marlow sat in the dark with her shorts down. No longer was she in the judge's commode, but a narrow hallway. Crusty plaster held up planks of wood and drywall that formed the opening to a secret passageway.

Like the plank at the front door, the toilet must have activated some secret mechanism.

This is some real Hardy Boys shit, she thought.

A Hardy man is good to find.

Pulling up her shorts, Marlow explored the passageway. As she stepped away from the toilet, the wall began another rotation. She spun around just in time to watch the bathroom return to its original configuration —with her trapped inside the wall.

"No, no, no, no!"

Alone in the dark, she kicked herself. Dean was long gone and it was too late to change course now. She hoped he would send help—even if that help would probably arrest her and throw her into a *real* jail.

I'll burn that bridge when I get to it.

For the time being, she could either cower on the other side of the judge's bathroom or find another way out. And if Judge DeVille had the wherewithal to build a secret passageway, he must have planned for an emergency escape route.

Letting her eyes adjust to the dark, Marlow placed one hand on the wall to her right and another in front of her. Then she began to inch down the hallway.

Almost immediately, something scampered over her boot. She kicked it aside and it bounced off the wall with a feral squeak.

Oh my god. Gross.

She kept going, a little faster now. More cobwebs, more dust, more creepy crawlies crunching under her feet. She walked lightly to keep her boots from echoing, but still heard footsteps nearby.

She stopped to listen. But it wasn't her—someone was coming up the stairs on the other side of the wall. Two different sets of steps. Two people.

The judge's booming voice sounded like he was right next to her. "I tell you, son, you're one of my finest officers. I wish you wouldn't beat yourself up about this. I know you'll find those two troublemakers and then I'll make them pay."

"Yes, sir," said Officer Friendly.

They walked down the hall and into a different room, closer to Marlow's position. She hoped they weren't planning to stick around; or if they were, that she could find a way out.

"Take off your jacket, son."

What?

Marlow pressed her ear against the wall, scraping the plaster. A beam of light shot through a crack, startling her. Again, she feared she had just been caught.

But no—next to her was a peephole. She peered through to see a brightly lit room with a black massage chair in the center. It was one of those fold-up units that massage therapists used so a customer could get rubbed down in the mall or at a farmer's market.

As Officer Friendly entered, he stripped off his leather jacket and hung it on a hook on the back of the door. He was bare-chested, not a scrap of shirt or undershirt clung to his muscles. A patchwork of thick scars and inflamed welts covered his back.

He took a seat in the chair. Without removing his sunglasses, he rested his head in the cradle. As he settled in, he shivered in anticipation.

Judge DeVille laid a plastic tarp around the chair. He shuffled to an armoire, similar to the one in his bedroom, and opened the doors. Whips, chains, and a few other BDSM accoutrements that Marlow had perhaps tried once or twice hung inside. He removed a small cat-o'-nine-tails (leather, of course) and gave it a test crack.

It snapped the air by Officer Friendly's ear and he cried out, "Oh, god, yes!"

Holding herself tightly, Marlow watched as the judge swung the whip around.

"Letting those two boneheads give you the slip was terribly irresponsible of you, son," said the judge. "I'm afraid I'll have to punish you."

Trembling, Officer Friendly gripped the armrest. "Yes, sir. Please."

The judge spun around. The whip cracked, snapping the tension like a thunderbolt. Fresh, red marks bloomed on the cop's back. Officer Friendly moaned, knees bouncing.

Marlow stepped back, bumping against the wall behind her. Something crackled, sprinkling dust onto her head. On the adjacent beam, a creature squeaked, hopped down, and buried its prickly snout in her hair.

A strangled cry escaped her mouth as whiskers tickled her neck and tiny claws dug into her shoulder.

"What was that?" the judge asked, pausing.

"Hit me again, sir," pleaded Officer Friendly.

"I heard something in the walls... Something *big*."

Marlow couldn't go anywhere without dropping the rat with a loud thud and drawing more attention. She clamped her hands over her mouth and prayed the men would ignore the sound.

But the gravity of Judge DeVille's words awakened the dedicated lawman in Officer Friendly. "Where?"

"Over there."

Unable to see through the peephole from where she stood frozen, Marlow assumed he was pointing right at her. She pressed against the opposite wall. The rat nuzzled closer. She bit back a scream.

Officer Friendly touched the wall, fingering the hole. "I see..."

The rat let out a squeak. *Traitor!*

"Ah-ha." The cop stepped back. *Bang!*

An intense ringing deafened her—her ears almost numb to the rat's shriek as it flopped off her shoulder and hit the floor. The dying thing dragged its mutilated body around the corner to die.

On the other side of the wall, Officer Friendly holstered his gun. "Rats," he said. "Real sneaky ones."

"Good job, son." The judge clapped him on the back. "That almost makes up for your earlier blunder. But no more dilly-dallying—I want you to find those two troublemakers right now."

"Yes, sir."

"You know what to do—head out and circle back."

"They're close," said Officer Friendly. "I can feel it."

Manifesting a scenario where she escaped, Marlow hurried back the way she had come. She moved quietly as the judge and the cop parted aways. Pipes rattled and hissed through the corridor, covering her footfalls all the way back to the bathroom. Water came flooding toward her and crashed into the porcelain tub on the other side of the wall. The judge began to sing about being in the mood for love.

"Valentina! Get in here, woman! I'm ready for my bath! Valentina? I need my back scrubbed! *Valentina!*"

Through a slit in the wall, Marlow spied the judge undressing. The sight was troubling, and not just because he was naked.

His back was covered in a rippling, black mass like Arnie's, but somehow much more insidious. It looked like it was a part of him, that he was the mass. Thick boils bubbled along his shoulders and down his spine. The mass itself was scaly and the color of spilled gasoline.

The judge reached for his bath scrubber to scratch himself.

Nauseous, Marlow changed course again, back the other way. *What the fuck was that? Jesus! What the hell?* The passageway grew darker and narrower, winding around and around. A spiderweb blocked her path. She chopped it down with her bare hands and kept going. There had to be a way out.

A random doorknob stuck out of the wall ahead. Marlow began to wonder if anything was truly random in the DeVille house.

Before grabbing the knob and twisting it open, Marlow felt along the wall for any cracks or peepholes. Her fingers slipped into two, above her sightline, forcing her onto her tiptoes to look through.

On the other side was an office. So far, it was the cleanest room in the house. An antique desk and matching chair were the only major pieces of furniture. The walls were plastered in vibrant green wallpaper with a bold, swirling pattern. The opposite side of the room had an open balcony. Floor-length curtains swayed under the spinning ceiling fan.

A powdered wig rested on a wig holder at the corner of the desk.

It was the judge's home office.

No one was inside and it was a straight shot across the room to the balcony. Once outside, she could find a way to climb or jump down.

She pushed her way into the judge's office, careful to shut the door quietly. She noticed how well the wallpaper disguised the opening to the hidden hallway. Much like the judge's revolving door/toilet, his office door was another well-kept secret. The man had layers, and his need for all these hideaways and escape routes made Marlow curious.

On her way to the balcony, she passed a wall of vintage portraits, each featuring younger versions of the judge. One picture made her pause—a ribbon-cutting ceremony for that godawful giant cupid. The judge wielded a pair of novelty oversized scissors. Though he looked about the same age, the date on the photo said *February 1964.*

Quickly doing the math, she frowned. *That would make him ... over a hundred years old.*

How's that possible?

Again, she didn't know and didn't care. She didn't even care about the keys anymore. She didn't care about the snakes and scorpions waiting to strike in the desert. She only wanted to leave.

That was until she spotted a safe in the corner. Its door was open, tempting her with its contents.

Curiosity killed the cat, but to the victor go the spoils. *It wouldn't hurt to look inside,* she figured. *Maybe I can get my bag back, if not my keys.*

She ducked behind the desk and prodded the door open further.

A tiny light blinked on like an Easy Bake Oven, casting a sheen over piles upon piles of stacked cash. Each bundle contained denominations of twenties, fifties, and hundreds. The bills were wrinkled, discolored, and inconsistent, as if gathered from various sources over the years and stacked together by hand.

Whoa... Marlow flipped through one of the stacks. *I love money and money loves me.*

This was better than finding the duffle bag. She knew from her time with Tony that one stack of hundreds equaled ten grand, and since she was short about $30,000...

She stuffed three stacks into her bra.

Better make it four... Even things out.

She was about to take two more—compensation for

her pain and suffering—when she heard a man shout.

"*Hey! Get offa me!*"

Startled out of her greedy thoughts, Marlow broke for the window.

As she stepped onto the balcony, the front door slammed. She ducked down.

Officer Friendly, with his leather jacket zipped up over his scarred flesh, marched to the squad car. He wore the same expressionless glare on his chiseled face, but something about his stance said he was even less happy than before. Marlow and the rat had interrupted his "punishment," and he was hurting to take it out on someone.

Just go away, she pleaded.

Another loud sound erupted from the next room, drawing Officer Friendly's attention. Any minute now, he would spot her. She stayed completely still.

When nothing unusual happened after several long seconds, Officer Friendly kicked up some dirt with a grunt. Then he got in his car, giving one last hard look at the house.

Marlow watched and waited as he drove back down the winding road. When he was far enough away, she stood up.

The entire town was laid out in front of her. There wasn't much to see but she could see it all, from the giant cupid at the center to the motel's glowing VACANT sign. The only site missing was the junkyard, which was at the rear of the house.

Something went thump in the room next door.

Valentina? she wondered, then shook her head. *No, I don't care.*

She checked out the balcony for anything she could

use to climb down. The pillars were tall and smooth. Dead vines clung to the railing, but crumbled under her touch.

Jumping down was too dangerous—she couldn't risk a broken bone.

Thoughts spiralling, she rubbed her temples. Maybe she could massage a plan into her brain. But all rational thought went out the door when she glanced through the window into the next room.

Handcuffed to a bed, while a strange woman dug around in his pants, was Dean.

17.

THE BOUDOIR

DEAN WAS OUT cold when his attacker tied his ankles together and dragged him away from the trailer. He slid in and out of consciousness as he was carried through the dark, unaware that he was almost back where he'd started.

When he finally woke, sand dried his mouth and his teeth grit together. Struggling to swirl up enough saliva to spit it out, he realized he wasn't in the desert or anywhere near his trailer.

Propped up in a ridiculously soft bed, he was up to his chin in satin covers. The lace fringe tickled his chin, and when he went to scratch, he found himself cuffed to the headboard rails. Pins and needles trickled down his forearms.

How long was I out?

Where am I?

His tongue pushed the grit around. The room was too nice to spit on the floor, and he figured his "kidnapper" had taken him to some kind old lady's house where he wouldn't want to be an ungracious slob. He could eat dirt a little while longer until he could call the cops (the *real* cops).

And the handcuffs?

Maybe she was a kind old lady who didn't want any trouble from a stranger? She was only trying to protect herself. Besides, once Dean cleared the air, she would understand and let him go. Maybe even insist that he borrow her vehicle or phone.

"Hello?" he said, scanning the room for any sign of life. The space was big—it had to be to fit the king-sized, four-poster bed he was confined to. A gauzy, pink canopy hung over him. He felt like a fly caught in a very pretty spider's web.

This is not a bedroom, he concluded. *It's a* boudoir.

Across from where his long legs stuck out from the covers was a fireplace. A golden-framed mirror was mounted over it, giving him a view of his own dumbfounded, dirty face. Two accent chairs and a small coffee table sat empty. Adjacent to the fireplace was a large bureau, partially hidden behind a room divider. Japanese cherry blossoms were painted all over the panels.

A shadow on the other side stirred.

"Anyone there?" Dean asked.

The shadow moved again, followed by a muffled giggle.

Dean cleared his throat and used his big-boy-federal-agent voice. "Alright, that's enough hiding. I know you're there. Come out right now."

The stranger croaked. At this point in the evening, Dean wouldn't have been surprised if a mutant frog person hopped out and smacked him with a stretchy tongue.

"Look, this isn't a game," he said. "I'm a federal agent and this is an emergency. I need to call my boss."

Fuzzy, high-heeled sandals poked out from behind the screen. The feet within were long and narrow with dry, scaly skin and cracked, yellow nails.

The owner of those feet wore a pink dressing gown. Flimsy material spilled off the person's scrawny body like a waterfall, but couldn't conceal the hard black mass that covered her back and shoulders.

Dean gasped at the sight of her.

The hopeful, yearning look on her face cracked. With a sob, she ducked behind the screen.

Fuck. Dean banged his head against the headboard. *Nice job offending the only person who can possibly help.*

"Please come back," he said. "I'm sorry. I just... You surprised me, that's all."

She poked her head out, eyes red and lip quivering. Her skin was a sickly shade of pale, and though she was slim, she was sinewy like a scavenger. A creature who had to learn and do terrible things to survive.

"I need your help." Dean shifted. "I'm really thirsty. Do you have any water?"

She made a drinking gesture.

"That's right," he said, studying her face.

Her age confused him. She was either a young wo-man painted up to look older or a middle-aged woman trying in vain to conceal her true age. Looking at her was disorienting.

While she shuffled out of the room, dragging the heels of her shoes along the hardwood floor, Dean tried to get a better look out one of the windows. He couldn't see much beyond his ghostly reflection.

After a painfully long time, the woman reappeared with a glass of water filled to the brim. She stared intently at it as if willing it not to spill a single drop until she was at his bedside. Then she shoved the glass under his nose and forced him to drink.

The warm liquid dribbled down his lips, but he greedily slurped it. The water kept coming until he couldn't swallow fast enough. It had nowhere to go. He choked, spraying water across the bedding and in her face.

With a tight-lipped smile, she set the glass aside and wiped at herself.

Dean clenched up. "I'm so sorry. I didn't mean—"

Frowning, she shushed him as she cleaned up. Using her gown, she dabbed at the wet mess.

"It's my fault," he said. "You don't have to do that."

She gave him the rest to polish off. Settling down next to him, she stared eagerly, as if waiting for him to say something.

"I need your help," he said. "Can you get these handcuffs off?"

She shook her head.

"What about a phone? Do you have a phone? Could you call my boss for me? The police? Anyone?"

She looked away.

Sighing and muttering under his breath, he hit his head against the headboard rails again.

The woman rested a hand on his thigh, patting him until he looked at her. She pointed to his chest and lifted her shoulders.

"I don't understand," he said.

She did the same motion over and over.

"Look, miss..."

She nodded, smiling. She rolled her wrist as if she could direct him to finish the rest of the sentence, but he didn't know her name, so—

She tapped his chest and then her own.

"Name?" he asked. "You want to know my name?"

Clapping her hands, she nodded like a proud and patient teacher.

"Dean," he said. "Dean Dilton. I'm a federal agent. Two other government personnel have been killed and I need—"

She hopped off the bed, disappearing behind her privacy screen.

Oh, fuck. Now what did I do?

On the other side, she opened and closed drawers. Papers crumpled and a pen scratched.

When she returned, she held out a note. He squinted, leaning forward to read it.

VALENTINA

"It's nice to meet you, Valentina," he said. He strained against his restraints, trying to get the shy woman to look him in the eye. "But I don't think you understand the severity of my situation. I can't stick around here and chitchat with you."

Her face fell, settling into a pout, like a child who couldn't have the animal they fell in love with at the pet store. She turned, about to disappear behind the screen yet again.

Dean couldn't let her get away. "Wait!" he called. "I need you!"

She froze. When she slowly turned back around, her eyes were wide and her hands were clasped between her small breasts. Before Dean could plead for help, she jolted forward, diving lips first toward his face. He jerked back in confusion and her frantic kisses landed on his cheek and chin.

"Stop!" he protested.

She curled up against him. Her body was too hot, too clammy. She smelled of baby powder, rotten fruit, and ... death. Her cheeks burned redder as she gazed longingly at her captive, who stammered and shifted uncomfortably. She was small but heavy, and much stronger than she looked.

He kept twisting his head away to avoid her lips on his, so she nuzzled her open mouth against his neck.

Dean pressed against the headboard, trying to get away, but he had nowhere to run. "No! Stop!"

Her fingers trailed down his neck and chest, over his stomach, and down to his belt. She clutched the buckle, giving him *the look*.

Dean squeezed his thighs together. "Valentina, I don't think—"

She snapped the buckle apart and violently yanked the zipper down, the belt burning against his skin. She shoved her rough hand into his pants and grabbed hold of his frightened, shriveled member.

"Hey! No! Stop!"

Valentina was too enthralled in giving him the worst hand job of his life—maybe the worst in the history of hand jobs. Her palms were calloused and dry, and though her brow glistened with sweat, her hands had not a drop of moisture to save him. The longer she went on, the more it felt like a steel wool exfoliation.

He tried bucking her off. The headboard banged against the wall.

"Hey! Get offa me!" he cried.

Valentina stopped, holding up a finger. She climbed off him and raced around the screen.

Dean slumped, shutting his eyes. *Great. Just great.*

A vinyl record popped and crackled as music began to play. A woman's voice full of romance and longing promised that her day would come.

I have to get out of here.

"Valentina!" boomed a painfully familiar voice.

The judge? The judge is here? In this house?

Dean looked around—*really looked* this time. The judge was everywhere. On photos and portraits hung all around. On the nightstand, between stacks of dog-eared romance paperbacks, was a framed photo of Valentina and Judge DeVille—on their wedding day.

Oh, shit. Oh, fuck.

Valentina twirled out from behind the screen and seductively slipped off her gown.

She blew Dean a kiss, but before she could return to him, the judge pounded on the door.

"Valentina! I know you're in there, woman!"

In a desperate, hushed whisper, Dean called her over. Smiling shyly, she rushed to his side, about to climb into bed with him—dangerously unhinged husband be damned.

"No," he pleaded. "The judge— You have to get me out of here. He's gonna kill me."

She pressed a finger to his lips. *"Shhhh."*

"Valentina, please."

"VALENTINA!"

Instead of freeing him, she pulled one of the pillows from behind his back and smothered him with it. As he thrashed, she shushed him again. He held his breath, waiting as she added more and more pillows until he was buried.

He held his breath. Each scrap of satin and frill was tainted with her body's cloying scent. She threw a blanket over his legs before covering herself up and going to answer the door.

"There you are!" exclaimed the judge. "What've you been up to? I had to bathe *myself!* Didn't you hear me? Suppose not with all that music. Well, enough of that. Get me something to drink, will ya?"

When the door closed behind them, Dean released a breath. Something in the room tapped across the floor, until his pounding heart drowned it out.

He froze as the pillows around him shifted. One was lifted away, replaced by Marlow's curious face.

"Having fun?" she asked.

18.

THE ENTANGLEMENT

DEAN WAS A sight for sore eyes, but also Marlow's disappointment personified. If he was in the house, that meant *his* grand plan to get out of town had also been a complete bust. No one was coming to save them.

"What're you doing here?" they asked each other.

Marlow gave him a hard look. "I thought you were going to call your boss on your fancy phone."

Straining forward, Dean shook off the pillows and blankets. "Almost did. The trailer... Someone knocked me out... Valentina, I think? You have to get me outta here."

Marlow pointed her thumb behind her. "That chick was Valentina?"

"You know her?"

"I know *of* her. The judge has been screaming her name."

"We're in his house, aren't we?"

"Correctamundo."

"Shit."

"Yeah." Glancing down at his unzipped trousers, she snorted. "So *you're* what was occupying her."

Blushing, Dean scowled. "That woman almost tore my dick off."

"Well, the balcony's free and clear," she said. "We just have to find a way down."

Dean clanked his wrists against the headboard, drawing her attention to the handcuffs. He wasn't going anywhere.

"Oh."

"Yeah, *'oh,'*" he grumbled. "Can you look around and see if she has anything to pick this lock?"

"You think you can just pick a lock?"

TV and movies made it look so easy. Stick a bobby pin in and in two seconds, *click-click*, the cuffs give way. But lockpicking was an art. It was one of the many "life" skills Tony had taught her when they were together, like the importance of wearing disguises and having no identifiable marks (even though Tony was fond of dressing up like a rockabilly weirdo). But like most of the lessons Tony—and life—tried to teach her, Marlow cherry-picked the ones she liked best.

"Can *you?*" Dean fired back.

She harrumphed, stuffing one of the pillows in his face. With him mildly irked, she marched off behind Valentina's screen to snoop around. On the other side, bright, high-wattage bulbs framed a mirror and a vintage vanity desk, which was littered with expired makeup and clumps of baby powder.

Marlow wheezed. A sneeze threatened. She drew a loud breath through her mouth, but before it could come, she pinched her nose and folded into herself to muffle the sound. Her body hitched and her eyes watered. She groaned.

Dean bounced on the mattress, struggling to see. "What's wrong?"

"Nothing," she said, nose itching. "I'm allergic to talc. Who even uses baby powder anymore?"

"Did you find anything?"

The bedroom door opened. Marlow ducked behind the screen. *Fuck.*

Hoping the bright lights wouldn't cast a silhouette, Marlow eavesdropped on Dean and Valentina. It soon became apparent that Dean did all the talking. Didn't he know when to shut up?

"You're here!" Dean announced, unaware that Marlow wasn't stupid. She got the hint. "I, uh, was wondering when you'd come back. Good to see you." He rattled his handcuffs. "Do you think you could uncuff me now? I'm not going anywhere. I like it here."

Marlow rolled her eyes.

Valentina shuffled around the room, tending to Dean, while Marlow scanned the top of the desk and all the little containers that held assorted hair elastics and perfumes. Her eyes fell upon a box of bobby pins. *Yes!* She scooped out a couple before Valentina shuffle-stepped in her direction. A pin slipped out between her knuckles and hit the desk, but it was too late to sweep it away.

Dean begged Valentina to come back, giving Marlow a chance to crawl out from behind the screen and take cover behind various pieces of furniture. She was almost to the balcony door when Valentina went on the move again.

Dean kicked his legs, demanding attention, but

careful not to be too loud. The judge was still some-where in the house.

Marlow rolled under the bed—hiding next to the decayed, mummified body of a housecat. Its eyes were long gone, the black pits of its rotting sockets stared deep into Marlow's soul. She imagined hearing its silent yowl. And by god, did the dead thing ever reek.

Afraid to close her eyes and look away, she prayed for this nightmare to end.

A sneeze threatened.

Slamming the balcony door, Valentina clomped over to the bedside. Pinching her nose, Marlow dared a look at the long feet that poked under the frilly bedskirt. Lifting one foot off the ground, the woman leaned over the bed and with a loud, wet smooch, kissed Dean.

The mattress springs compressed as Valentina climbed onto the bed. "Uh, no, wait. I think we should take it slow, get to know each other…"

Marlow covered her mouth, breathing into her hand. The urge to sneeze faded.

"I-I'm thirsty!" Dean cried out. "I need something to drink if you're going to… If I have to… Oh, god—"

Marlow snickered, but his lame excuse worked. Valentina got up and left.

Marlow waited until the door closed again. The second Valentina was gone, Marlow scrambled out from under the bed and let out a sneeze.

"Bless you," said Dean.

"Thanks."

As she wiped off the dust and cobwebs clinging to her clothes, her fingers brushed against a piece of spaghetti.

Dean's face scrunched up. "What's that?"

The noodle was caught in her hair, dangling down her shoulder. She plucked it free, inspecting the strangest piece of spaghetti she had ever seen. It was long and pink. On one end was a clump of raw, red meat.

Marlow hadn't eaten in a while, but what little was in her stomach lurched up. "Ugh—" Heaving, she bent over and flicked the rat tail to the floor. She half expected a fuzzy undead cat arm to reach out for it, or for the damn thing to slither away on its own.

"What was that?" Dean asked again.

She held her stomach, willing it not to overreact. "I don't ... want to talk about it."

"Okay, but you gotta get me outta here," he said.

"Yeah, yeah. I'm on it."

Dean slid the cuffs as close to her as he could, though his mobility and reach were limited by the short chain. She would have to get next to him, as much as she wanted to avoid it. Back in the trunk, he felt and smelled too damn good for her own good. It was like the dorky fed's pheromones had cast a spell on her.

Propping a knee up on the bed, she leaned over him. Feeling around for the keyhole, she felt him watching her.

When she glanced his way, their eyes met. They both looked away. Their connection had been different in the trunk. It had been dark in there, for one thing. There had been something daring about grinding against him and getting him riled up, feeling in control and secure in the belief that they would never see each other again. Ships passing in the night, that kind of thing.

But then everything blew up and here they were, together again. Being face to face was very intimate, and vulnerability made her uncomfortable.

She caught a whiff of his musky scent, spied the stubble on his cheeks and chin, imagined the coarseness against her soft skin, between her legs. The thought made her heat up, made her palms sweat. The bobby pin slipped out of her fingers, disappearing behind the headboard.

"Shit," she muttered.

"Come on," he said. "We don't have all night."

"I'm trying."

"She'll be back any second," he continued, craning his neck to look over her shoulder. "Did you see the way she was looking at me? Like she's in love."

"I bet you think that..."

"Think what?"

She didn't expect him to call her out. Now he was giving her a long, hard look, which made it challenging to pick the damn cuffs.

"Nothing. Never mind."

"Tell me."

She sighed again. "'Tall, dark, and handsome. The end'?"

He turned pink, becoming defensive. "Yeah, so?"

"Yeah, so you think it's that simple to make women fall at your feet," she said.

"I don't have women falling at my feet. I wouldn't have needed that damn app if that were true."

"You were on that app because you were horny."

"So?"

"So, what's wrong with Valentina? Just because she doesn't meet your traditional beauty standards."

"I didn't say that!" His voice rose up, echoing. They exchanged a cautious look and checked the door. He lowered his voice to a near-whisper. *"I didn't say that.* All I meant was that I'm not attracted to her, I don't want her sandpaper hands to rip my dick off, and when I was on that dumb app, I wanted *you."*

She stared at him. Her sweaty fingers slipped and the pin tumbled out, making a tiny clatter as it hit the floor. "Fuck."

Twisting his wrists, he held out a hand. "Give it to me. *I'll* do it."

"I can do it," she insisted.

"Clearly you can't or we'd be out of here already."

"Geez, fine." She stabbed the bobby pin into his palm.

"Ouch!" he cried. "Hey, where're you going?"

"Away from *you."*

This time he sighed. It was obvious from the increased carbon dioxide levels in the room that they were quite done with each other. Marlow considered ditching him to get a head start (*I don't have to outrun Officer Friendly. I just have to outrun Dean Dilton*), but when she considered the difficulty of climbing down the pillars, she decided to hold her horses. She might still need his help.

"I'm sorry," he said. "I didn't mean to be such a dick. It's been one helluva night."

"Do you always apologize this much?" she asked, arms crossed. One of the stacks of cash in her bra had shifted, coming loose under her shirt.

"Maybe it's something only you bring out in me."

She rolled her eyes, but was slightly flattered.

"So I know I doubted your lockpicking skills, but honestly? I don't know what I'm doing." He clanked the cuffs against the rails. "Mind giving it another shot?"

She returned to his side and snatched the last pin from him.

"Make it count," he said.

This time she climbed up on the bed, straddling him. His brows raised sky high until he realized that the position gave her better access to the keyhole. She set to work twisting and turning the pin while he made awkward conversation.

"So, uh, sure looks a lot easier on TV, huh? Where'd you learn to do it? Er, do *that*. Pick locks, I mean."

"Tony."

"The boyfriend."

"The *ex*-boyfriend."

"Must've been a fun guy."

"They're all fun and games 'til they punch you in the face or slap ya on the tit."

"I'm sorry—"

"Can you stop with the sorries? I don't need anyone feeling sorry for me, okay?"

"I don't feel sorry for you. I don't feel anything. Can we just get out of here?"

The double lock bar inside the handcuffs shifted. Marlow rotated the bobby pin until the main lock gave in. Metal clicked.

As the cuffs released, the house moved. Another "rumble" snaked its way up from the foundation. Quiet at first, building to a crescendo that cracked the floors and split the drywall.

The bed shook violently, threatening to buck off Marlow and Dean. They held onto each other for dear life.

She squeezed her legs around him, pelvis rubbing against his open fly as they rode the quaking. She bit her lip, hating how good it felt—and how badly she wanted it, wanted him.

Soon enough, the rumbles settled and the house grew quiet. They stayed in each other's arms, not moving. Not wanting to move. Marlow wondered what he was waiting for.

He was staring at her chest.

"Marlow?" he finally whispered.

"Yeah?" she sighed.

"Why do you have hundreds of dollars in your shirt?"

A stack of ten grand had pushed its way out of her bra. "I love money...?"

"... and money loves me?" he finished.

Valentina rushed in with a glass of water. She stopped in the doorway, frozen by the sight of a strange blonde in her man's arms.

"It's not what it looks like," they said together.

Valentina dropped the glass. Water and shards sprayed in every direction. The cuckolded woman opened her mouth—a black cavern of rotten teeth and a mutilated tongue—and released a raspy, heartbroken wail.

19.

THE LONG WAY DOWN

PUSHING EACH OTHER away, Dean and Marlow rolled off the bed in opposite directions.

Throwing blankets and pillows aside, Dean tried to silence the bellowing Valentina who, up until two seconds ago, had been as quiet as a church mouse. So loud was her anguish that she must have woken the whole town.

"Shh," said Dean. "Please..."

"Just chill, okay?" said Marlow, stuffing the cash back in her shirt.

"We don't want any trouble," said Dean.

"I don't even *like* this dude," Marlow added.

Dean shot her a dirty look that she shrugged off.

Valentina widened her mouth, drawing a deep breath to wail even louder. Half her tongue was missing and the longer her mouth gaped open, the more Dean was sucked into the horror of it.

Who did this to you?

He tried to remember his brief training in hostage negotiation, and while fumbling over his words, he had a troubling, but poorly timed, thought: *What if she tried going down on me instead of giving me a handy?* He shuddered.

Valentina's cry escalated.

"Oh, my god—enough!" Marlow stormed over to the vanity and snatched a perfume bottle, hurling it at Valentina and hitting her right in the middle of her forehead. Valentina was stunned. Tears flooded her eyes.

"Oh, shit." Marlow covered her mouth. "Oh, my god. Shit. I didn't mean that. I didn't think—"

"What'd you do that for?" Dean snapped.

"I didn't—" Marlow reached out to the other woman.

Breaking out of her trance, Valentina slapped Marlow when she got too close. Marlow pulled back, but Valentina was on the attack and charged after her.

Marlow hoisted up the vanity's stool, wielding it lion tamer style. But Valentina could not be tamed. She grabbed one of the legs, yanking it away from Marlow.

Out of luck, Marlow ran for the bed, hopped up, and rolled over the rumpled covers before disappearing over the other side. It took Dean a second, enamored by the sight of her, to realize she was making a break for the window.

He jumped in front of Valentina, blocking her warpath. "Valentina, please. Let me explain."

She raised the stool about to strike.

"Forget it!" He ran after Marlow, bumping into her at the door. She shot him an icy look, but there was no time to bicker. Dean pushed her through. "Move it! Go!"

He glanced back as Valentina tumbled over the bed, clumsily copying Marlow's moves. The doorway behind her filled with two familiar bodies—Judge DeVille and Officer Friendly.

"I knew it!" cried the judge. "Stinking, slimy rats under my roof!"

Officer Friendly bullied past him, drawing his gun. Legs spread as wide as his leather pants would allow, he took aim and yelled "freeze!" But to hit Dean, the bullets would first have to go through Valentina's head.

"Get down!" Dean warned.

Valentina ducked just as Officer Friendly fired. The gun blasted, deafening everyone in the room. The bullet struck the window frame. Splinters exploded.

Dean shoved Marlow out. She skidded on her knees across the balcony, swearing at Dean, who picked her up by the elbow and dragged her away.

"Be mad at me later," he said, peering over the side. It was a long drop with many hazards—thorny bushes and vines, jagged rocks, broken tombstones butting up against the porch. There would be no soft landing. "How the fuck are we gonna get down?"

"This way." Marlow jerked out of Dean's grip and dove in through a separate door.

No, no, no—not back inside! He followed, intending to drag her back out and find a way down that wouldn't result in a broken neck.

"Marlow," he said, locking the door behind them. A lot of good that would do since it was glass.

"Dean..." she jeered, leading him through an office.

"This is a bad idea."

She threw her hands up. "Well, I'm all out of good ones!"

Bang, bang, bang!

They spun around. Officer Friendly pounded on the door. Dean backed away, colliding with the large desk in the center of the room.

"Agent Dilton!" The judge was inside the house, shouting from the hallway and blocking the only other way out. "Come out right this instant or I will authorize Officer Friendly to extract you both with extreme prejudice. Do you hear me?"

Marlow was feeling up the vibrant wallpaper, distracting Dean from coming up with a plan. "What're you doing?" Something clicked in his brain.

Green wallpaper + old house = poisonous walls.

"Don't touch that!" He pulled her away, and she looked at him like *he* was crazy. "Don't touch the walls," he said, remembering the headline of an article he had once skimmed. "See that green? Old wallpaper used to have arsenic in it to get green that bright."

Marlow blanched, studying her hands. "No..."

"Yes." He squeezed her wrists. "Now maybe if you give the money back, we can—"

"There was a secret passage in the wall," she said, frantically wiping her hands on her shorts. "That's how I got in here. I thought we could find a way out..."

"I've instructed Officer Friendly not to shoot through the windows," the judge informed them, "but you're testing my patience. I might change my mind..."

Dean pointed at the wall. "Find it," he ordered. "However the hell you got in here, just find it."

Nodding, she returned to scrutinizing the wall, hands-free this time.

He searched the desk for a gun or a letter opener— or anything that could be used as a weapon. Or something precious, like money or a treasured memento he could use as leverage.

The judge's desk was relatively neat. There was a place for everything and everything in its place. He cautiously opened the desk drawers, expecting a new nightmare to pop out and bite him. All he found were neatly stacked files. On the top of one pile was a dossier emblazoned with the seal of the President of the United States of America.

It didn't seem like something a small-time judge in a corrupt, podunk town would or should have.

"I-I-I can't find it," Marlow said, fretting. She wandered back to the desk. "How long do I have?"

Dean didn't quite hear her. He was flipping through the file. It was an inch thick with memos and clippings and formal letters addressed to Judge Stanley DeVille, dating back to the Eisenhower administration.

Dean was confused. *How old is this old bastard?*

It had to be DeVille's father. A family name passed down. The judge could have been Stanley DeVille III or something pompous, but dropped it later in life. That had to be it.

Or he'd somehow been a judge since his twenties? A real go-getter in his youth?

No wonder this town dried up. Who could stand to live under the sixty-year reign of a twisted madman?

He stumbled upon a letter signed by *Richard fucking Nixon* peppered with the phrase "sovereign state," when Marlow reached across the desk and slapped a hand on the file in front of him.

"What?"

"How long do I have?"

"What're you talking about?"

Her eyes were wide, her face drained of color. Her hands trembled. "I touched it. I touched the wall. What do I do? Am I gonna die?"

Glass broke. Officer Friendly shot a hole through the door's window. His leather fist punched through the opening, unlocking the door.

Dean grabbed for something sharp in the desk's fancy penholder. He'd poke out Officer Friendly's eyes if he had to.

The pen was stuck. He yanked on it. A loud grinding rumbled under his feet—and Marlow vanished. She just dropped out of existence. Erased, along with the small patch of flooring she had been standing on.

The ornamental pen set had activated a trapdoor.

"Hold it!" Officer Friendly yelled.

Dean didn't think. He stuffed the dossier into his pants (discovering that his fly was down) and jumped over the desk. Officer Friendly ran at him, but Dean dove after Marlow, falling, falling, falling down a long, black tunnel that had no right being there.

Marlow's screams echoed all around him. She had a head start, but he was picking up speed and getting closer, gaining on her. And just when her wild blonde hair came into view, she turned a corner and disappeared again.

"Grab onto something!" he shouted.

The slide was never ending. It reminded him of a crazy waterpark slide, except his friends wouldn't be cheering for him at the pool end. Speeding through the dark, he was on a one-way ride to hell.

"Watch out!" Marlow shrieked.

The slide came to an abrupt end. The ride was over. Marlow was almost out, but spread her arms and legs wide to stop her descent.

Dean slammed into her and together, they slid closer to the end. She cursed at him.

"Easy!" he told her.

Shooting out onto the floor below didn't seem so bad—until a gleaming guillotine blade dropped down with a whoosh, just inches away from Marlow's boots.

"Oh, shit!"

Taking a cue from Marlow, he propped his long legs up just in time. His feet braced against the guillotine's wooden posts. Marlow clung to his belt, scrabbling up the slide to keep away from the deadly blade.

"Now what?" she asked.

He thought for a moment. If they could pass through, they might land safely on the other side. Sure, they would be trapped in the judge's basement (or the bowels of hell), but at least they wouldn't be sliced and diced.

Catching his breath, he watched the blade crash down again. Then it rose back up. He matched it to his inhalation, counting the seconds.

"Well?" she pressed him.

"The blade's on a timer," he said. "All we gotta do is time it right and we can pass through."

"No," she said firmly. "I'm not doing that."

"What? Are you scared?" he challenged.

She tilted her head to look up at him. Desperation and fear were written all over her face.

Dean felt bad. Softening his approach, he said, "Look, it'll be real easy. We've got about eight seconds before it drops back down."

"Eight? That's not enough time."

"It's longer than you think." He counted out eight

seconds using the tried-and-true Mississippi system. "...six Mississippi, seven—"

The guillotine slammed down a second early. Marlow glared at him.

"It looks scarier than it is," he insisted. "And you're shorter than me. You won't need that much time."

"And what about you?"

Dean was a lean six feet and he didn't entirely trust himself to move as swiftly, but he didn't want to freak her out any more than she already was.

"I'll be okay. Let's do it."

She shivered. "I-I-I can't... *You* go first."

"Fine," he grumbled. He pried her hands off so he could reposition himself for the dead drop down between the blade and the chopping block—though he hoped "dead" was just an expression.

He looked her in the eye. "Here, watch. Easy."

He timed the blade once more, letting it drop down. As soon as it pulled back up again, he let go. The end of the slide angled up, shooting him upward. He couldn't land on his feet because the crazy slide, like everything else in the house, threw him off balance. After an abrupt freefall, he crash-landed on the cold, hard concrete floor. His elbow bore the brunt of the landing. Pain rocketed up his arm.

"*Fuuuuuuuuuck.*"

"Are you okay?" Marlow called down.

Gripping his funny bone, Dean tried to respond. A clipped "mm-hm" was the best he could do.

"I-I can't," she said. "I can't do it."

Just when Dean thought the situation couldn't get any worse, the judge called down from above. "I see you've found the trapdoor. Most of my uninvited guests don't get to use it voluntarily, so I hope you enjoyed yourselves. But my patience has worn thin with your antics, so I'm ending this unpleasantness right now. Spike! Come here, boy!"

A dog—no, one of the *hellhounds*—whined as the judge and Officer Friendly crammed the terrified, man-eating beast through the trapdoor. Its claws scraped, losing traction on the slide. Then the hellhound rocketed toward them, howling all the way.

Dean yelled at Marlow to let go at exactly the moment she came flying out of the tunnel with a banshee shriek. She crash-landed on top of him, taking his breath away.

Gasping, Dean feared they didn't have a chance to defend themselves against the snarling terror dog on its way to kill them both.

As the hellhound exited the tunnel, the guillotine dropped down, chopping the beast in half. Its tail end landed by Dean and Marlow with a sloppy entrail splat, while the front half oozed down with a wet thump when the blade went up again.

With a relieved sob, Marlow buried her face in Dean's shoulder. All he could do was lay there, patting her back and thinking the same words on repeat. *Too close, too fucking close...*

20.

THE BASEMENT

THE GROUND BENEATH Marlow shook again. She was lifted up and sliding. *No more sliding, no more falling...* But it was only Dean sitting up and wriggling out from under her.

He was splattered with blood, as was her shirt, shorts, and torn stockings. The hellhound's eviscerated corpse bled out nearby.

The judge hollered from above, calling for Spike. "Here, boy! Where are you, boy?!" But Spike split and went splat, and it soon dawned on the judge that his hellhound wasn't going to respond to its master. "If you mongrels did something to that dog...!"

Marlow stood up quickly to move away from the nasty mess and, feeling lightheaded, latched onto Dean to steady herself.

"I'm done," she said. "So fucking done."

"Well, I'm not done with you!" the judge shouted back.

Dean peered cautiously up the tunnel. "We didn't do anything wrong, judge, and you know it. Just let us go and we'll forget the whole thing."

"I forget nothing!" replied the judge. "My mind is a steel trap, just like this house. Rats get in but they never get out. You killed my dog and sullied my wife—now you can rot down there."

And with a mechanized grinding and a metallic clatter, the judge sealed them up in the basement.

Dean held Marlow as an eerie silence settled in.

"It's gonna be okay," he said.

She looked around. Exposed beams propped up an unnervingly low ceiling. A few flickering incandescent bulbs burned overhead. A mysterious stain from some long-ago incident—*a murder, someone was murdered down here, oh god, oh shit*—remained on the floor like an omen. And the only door was bricked up on the other side.

"This is not okay." She pushed him aside in search of a way out. But the more she searched, the worse their situation looked.

The basement would have been the perfect place for an underground exorcism except for all the junk. Rusted file cabinets were overfilled with papers and random personal items: baseball caps, backpacks, purses.

The collection was as strange as the drawer of keys in Officer Friendly's desk. Marlow picked up a blue cap that said World's Best Grandpa. She stuffed it away before it could break her heart. All around the room were buckets and boxes of hoarded, miscellaneous items.

In one corner, a narrow vent snaked down from

above and fed into a mop bucket of keys.

"Motherfucking bingo," she whispered.

She rushed over and sure enough, the keys to the Demon were right on top. She snatched them up, parading them in front of Dean.

"Look what I found!"

Dean's nose was stuck in the file folder he had pinched from the judge's office.

"*Look!*" She dangled the keys in his face.

"We gotta get out of here," he said.

"I *know* that," she said, stuffing the keys into her already overstuffed bra.

"No, I mean, we have to get as far away from this town as humanly possible." He showed her the file, anxiously flipping through pages so fast it made Marlow's head spin. She didn't have a second to read anything. When she raised an eyebrow, he tapped his finger on one page. "Remember what Arnie said?"

"He said a lot of things."

"The town wasn't built on a toxic waste dump. It *is* the dump."

"I could've told you that."

"I'm serious. According to all these memos and letters, Judge DeVille signed a deal allowing the government to dump its waste here, part of some research, I think? But it backfired on his honeymoon destination plans because the agency he was working with decided to build a highway to divert people *away* from town, and when the judge threatened to take action—"

"What kind of action?"

"Don't know. But the president stepped in to grant Paradise full sovereignty from the United States."

"What does that mean?"

"It means we're not in the States anymore. Paradise isn't just a town. It's its own goddamn country with its own laws. We are royally fucked if we don't get out of here because there's nothing you or I or even the goddamn president can do to save our asses."

"And that's if the toxic waste doesn't kill us first."

"Exactly."

Marlow held herself. "They should just nuke this awful place."

"Oh, yeah," Dean sniped. "Add another disaster on top of this fuck-up. Good thinking."

Remembering the arsenic tainting her fingers, she held out her hands. "What about me? How long do I have?"

"What?"

How could he forget? Her hands had been all over that awful wallpaper. "The *arsenic!* What do you think? I'm dying here!"

"You're fine."

"How do you know?" Her voice cracked.

He took her hands in his, holding them tightly when she tried to whip away from him. "Listen to me," he said. "You didn't *drink* it, did you? You didn't fucking drape yourself in it and parade around the town for months. You touched it for *two seconds.* It won't kill you." As she stared at him in disbelief, he shrugged. "And I... I maybe overreacted a little."

"*Overreacted?!*" She shoved him off.

"I was worried about you, okay? This whole place is a death trap."

Shaking her head as she walked away, Marlow wiped canine blood off her face and neck. *He was worried about me... Loser.* But then no one else had ever worried about her. Maybe Tony, once upon a time...

She inspected her fingers. Even if the arsenic didn't kill her, she had still wiped those same fingers on her face. Now she wiped them on the back of her shorts, aching to wash her hands with soap and water.

"So what's the plan?" she asked. "How do we get out of here?"

Dean buried his nose in the file, thinking aloud. "I should've known there was something off about my assignment."

She repressed the urge to roll her eyes. *Everything is always about the man, isn't it?* "The super-secret classified dirt? The most boring secret mission I've ever heard?"

"Like *you're* privy to any secret missions. Give me a break. The thing is, they must have been checking the toxin levels in the dirt or something. Maybe it's been seeping outside of the town's borders and into U.S. soil—literally. That would also explain why my director was adamant about staying away from this town."

"Gee, wish your precious director and president could have extended that courtesy to little, old me," she said. "A do-not-enter sign would've been great."

He bit his lip, thinking and fretting. "When I went back to the trailer, Burke and Gelman were dead."

"Who?"

"The dirt scientists I was watching over. Someone killed them."

"Oh, shit... But also, not surprised considering..." She wiped her hands on her shorts, pacing around helplessly.

Dean slumped down against one of the boxes, going through the file. A cloud fell over him.

Marlow felt bad. "I'm sorry about your dirt guys," she said softly.

"Yeah, me too."

"Hey, do you think the judge—?"

He nodded. "Either because they're 'rats' like me or they found something."

"Huh," said Marlow. "So if you hadn't shown up at the diner..."

He nodded again. "I'd be dead meat."

"Wow... So... I guess you owe me a big thanks."

Frowning, he looked up from his reading. "What're you talking about?"

She shrugged. "For saving your life."

He groaned.

"I did! Like three times now!"

"Three?" he said doubtfully.

"Yeah!" She counted off on her fingers. "When I got us out of jail, and when I stopped MAGA hat guy from shooting you, and I saved you from the clutches of Valentina—"

"I wouldn't say 'clutches'..."

"I *saw* what she was *clutching* and let's just say—"

"Okay, okay. Enough."

She stuck up four fingers. "Four times! I saved your life four times."

He gave her a defeated look. "What do you want, a medal?"

She stomped off in a huff, nowhere to go and nothing to do but, peruse the disturbing collection of personal effects and found a box of cell phones. Next-gen fancy models mingled with clunky Nokia brick phones, all the way back to the blocky Zack Morris phones of the neon '90s.

None of the ones she picked up worked, and if she had more patience, she would have dumped out the box to check each and every one, but her attention was drawn to the next box—a plastic tote filled with expired driver's licenses, passports, and school IDs. One belonged to a young boy. His chubby-cheeked face beamed proudly.

Probably not the face he made when the judge sentenced him to hard labor alongside his parents. Or worse. Unable to return the boy's card to the pile, she slipped him into her pocket.

All the ID cards, dead phones, and abandoned keychains had once belonged to someone. A person, just like her or Dean. Someone with a family, like Arnie. Kids, a spouse, a partner, a parent, a pet. These people were never seen again—their bodies now dog food, broken down by cruel and unusual punishments, or buried in the boneyard holding up the judge's house. These people mattered to someone somewhere.

Marlow mattered too, and she didn't want to become another sad face in a pile of forgotten plastic.

There has to be a way out.

But they were trapped underground in a concrete bunker. Maybe if they could stop the guillotine, they could climb up the slide. *And right back to the judge and Officer Friendly? No way.* Unless there was another secret passage, a hidden doorway they'd missed on the way down.

Peering up, she noticed a narrow gap in front of the slide's exterior. Several lengths of rebar led up to a narrow crack of light at the far end.

It could be the way out.

Marlow stepped back for a better look. "Hey."

Dean sat cross-legged, surrounded by the papers from the file. He was wasting time reading that shit. Just because the judge had a letter from the president didn't make him or this town any more important than their present situation.

She snapped her fingers by his ear and pointed up when she got his attention. "Look."

He frowned. "At what?"

She yanked the file out of his hands and tossed it aside.

"Hey!"

Crouching next to him, she put a finger to her lips. She didn't want to alert the ghouls above, in case they were listening. Then she grabbed Dean's head, steering him to see what she saw. "Get it?"

He stared at her—not at the exit she had discovered and now waited to be praised for.

"Do you get it?"

"Yes," he said. "You found a ladder—"

"SHHHHHH!" She hoped her loud shushing was enough to censor Dean.

"So? We can't reach it."

"Yes, we can." She wasn't about to let another negative man suppress her brilliance with his negative energy and negative attitude. *Virgo for sure.*

As she fluttered about putting her plan into action, he didn't lift a finger to help. Just watched her. She stacked boxes and totes into a pyramid. Then she climbed up and touched the top of the slide.

"Ta-da!" she announced with a grin.

His mouth twitched, fighting a smile. Hell, yeah, he was impressed—she was clever as fuck. A woman of action in a do-nothing man's world. She found their escape route—*yet again.*

"So what?" he said. "You still can't reach it."

She curled her finger, seductively drawing him in as she climbed back down. "I *can* if you get off your ass and help me."

Muttering under his breath, he caved in and followed her instructions. Kneeling down, he let Marlow sit on his shoulders and wrap her legs around his neck.

"This is the worst plan," he complained, beginning their shaky ascent. "You don't even know where we'll end up."

"Anywhere is better than this." She twirled her fingers through his hair. "And besides, you're just afraid you'll get another boner."

"More likely I'll drop your ass because you're so annoying."

"*You're* the annoying one... Moping around, reading some stupid letters. Who cares about dirt? Who cares about the president?"

"Can we fight about this later?"

The higher they climbed, the less stable the pile. One of the lower totes shifted. Marlow held her breath, digging her nails into Dean's scalp.

He winced. "Could you let up? Jesus..."

If she let up, she might fall. *He's right. This was a bad idea. What was I thinking?*

As he mounted the highest box, his foot slipped. Marlow cried out. The end was near.

Huffing against her thigh, he urged her to calm down. "Almost there... Can you reach it yet?"

Marlow let go, grasping the first rung. "Got it!"

Dean stretched taller, giving her more height to grab the next bar and the one after that. When she planted her foot on the rebar, she looked down and gave Dean her most sincere smile. "We did it!" Adding, "Told you."

He smiled back. "Okay, okay. But we're not out yet." He latched onto the first rung that her foot occupied. "Let's keep moving."

Her celebration was short-lived. The ladder came to a full stop. Her head hit a metal hatch. Banged it like a gong. The sound reverberated throughout the basement. Colors flashed before her eyes and she tasted metal and rage.

"*Son of a fucking bitch boy!*" she shrieked, pounding on the hatch. "*Lemme the fuck out!*"

"Yeah, that'll work," Dean said sarcastically. "Did you try 'open sesame'?"

"Real funny."

"Let *me* see it."

He squeezed up next to her on the narrow ladder, cramping what little space she had. He pressed on the latch, feeling around, when it suddenly cracked open. Air hissed.

Dean grinned, wiggling his fingers. "Guess I've got the magic touch."

She rolled her eyes. "Dude..."

In this house of horrors, one nightmare bled into the next. Climbing through, Marlow and Dean had found their way into a drafty library. A fire was lit in the hearth, heating a house that was much too dry, too hot, and too stuffy.

Officer Friendly stood at the fireplace, poking the flaming logs. He pulled out the poker, its tip glowing red hot.

Nearby, Arnie cowered on a small leather couch.

He gave them a sad smile.

And in a wingback chair the color of blood, as if he had been waiting for Marlow and Dean all along, sat Judge DeVille. He laced his fingers over his bulging stomach, showing off the ivory-handled gun tucked in his belt.

"I told you—no one gets out alive."

21.

THE RATS

OFFICER FRIENDLY LEAPED into action, hauling Marlow out by the crook of her arm. When she fought, he threatened her with the poker, nearly knocking Dean back down into the basement—which might have been for the best. So far, it had been the safest place in the house.

"Don't hurt her," he said when the cop yanked her arm behind her back.

The judge ho-ho-ho'd. "Agent Dilton, this is my house and you've both trespassed. I will do as I wish. Now climb outta there and take a seat."

There was no easy way out of this situation, but at least he wasn't handcuffed. He climbed out and sat down in a smaller, but no less dusty, wingback chair.

Officer Friendly shoved Marlow onto the couch next to Arnie. She leapt up and Officer Friendly jabbed the cool end of the poker against her sternum. "Down, girl."

Marlow scowled. "Fucking murderers—all of you. Fuck you."

Officer Friendly unzipped his jacket, reaching for his handy-dandy gimp mask.

Please, Marlow, just shut up, Dean thought. The mask had been insufferable. He didn't want her to go through the same torture.

"That won't be necessary, son," said the judge. "I trust Miss Marlow will be on her best behavior. Now let's all relax and talk this out. Maybe we can come to an arrangement of some sort."

"Might be a challenge to relax," said Dean. "Your town's a hazardous waste dump, poisoning people."

A bitter smile froze on the judge's lips. "You have it all wrong, Agent Dilton. The town is a victim, just like me. It's your slimy government goons who are the real villains here. I'm simply a man trying to protect his people."

"You signed that deal," said Dean. "You made a fortune turning your town into a toxic waste dump."

"That wasn't the deal," the judge replied. "I was grifted."

"*You*, judge? You're pretty sharp. How'd you let that happen?" Dean was about to adjust his tie, remembering it was long gone. Then he noticed his fly was still open. He couldn't reach down and zip it up with everyone's eyes on him, so he sat up straight and folded his hands in his lap.

"So you've been snooping through my private correspondence."

Dean held his tongue, unwilling to admit to anything that could add more time to his sentence.

The judge let it slide, though his hand rested on the

handle of his gun. "I don't normally make a habit of chit-chatting with convicted criminals."

"Then don't," said Marlow. "Let us go."

The judge held up a finger. "Miss Marlow, I need you to be seen and not heard. I am speaking to Agent Dilton. If you cannot comply, Officer Friendly will assist you. And if that doesn't shut you up, you can ask Valentina about what I do to chatterboxes."

As if on cue, Valentina breezed into the room and took a seat on the floor at her husband's feet. Hidden behind her garishly painted lips was a mutilated tongue.

Marlow looked away, wisely keeping quiet.

Dean picked up the end of the conversation. If he kept the judge talking, he could delay whatever horrible fate awaited them. Maybe he could even talk their way out of trouble or at least buy more time. Plus, he had questions about the town's history, and perhaps if he knew the whole story, maybe Burke and Gelman wouldn't have died in vain. There had to be some key piece of information he could bring to his director that could bring down the judge.

"A lot of powerful men have been feuding with the U.S. government a lot longer than you have," he said. "How's it possible you were granted this land as a sovereign state?"

The judge drew a heavy breath, positioning himself as a man about to tell a very long story.

"As I stated before, *I* am not the bad guy here, nor are the good people of Paradise," he began. "My daddy was the reeve of this good town for many years and it was his good thinking that we needed a gimmick, some-thing to bring in tourists with fat wallets. Mama always told him to pursue more practical matters. Tourism is a fickle business, after all.

"But he couldn't be dissuaded. Back then, we were called Paradise Delta, for the geographical situation we're in, but when my daddy sat down with a few of the town's most respected business owners, he pitched the idea of a honeymoon spot for newlyweds. Young love is a renewable resource, and as he was still so smitten with my mama after decades of marriage—and up until his dying day—and his investors couldn't agree more.

"They renamed the town Paradise and soon we had motels with heart-shaped beds and kidney-shaped pools. We turned this dried-up desert rest stop into an oasis for lovers. More diners sprang up. We even had a couple of jewellery stores competing for a while. Photography studios made piles of money. Our town's success meant everyone's success.

"Everyone loved my daddy for his vision—and for the money his big idea brought in. He was celebrated! And the deep pockets the tourists had soon became my daddy's own deep pockets. He was able to send me off to law school. But when I came back, his health was on the decline. Seems he made a bad investment here and there, and now he was paying for it with his health. I told him not to worry, I would take care of everything, but I had nothing but my name and the faith of my people. So I decided to roll the dice on a big opportunity.

"Giant roadside attractions were all the rage in those days, and I thought what could be better for our little burg than the World's Largest Cupid!" He threw his arms up high above his head. The fire in the hearth behind him extended his flickering shadow to the ceiling, turning an average-sized man into a colossus. "The god of love, right here in the middle of town, sent down from heaven to bless each happy union. What could be better than that?"

Dean could think of a thousand things, but he stayed mum.

"Trouble was, giant gods cost money." The judge rubbed his thumb and fingers together. "The bank was tapped out investing in new businesses, so I had to find some way to fund this venture—and as it was nearly complete, I had to hustle. I asked everyone I knew if they could spare some funds, and while I scraped together quite a bit, I was falling short.

"And then, in the Summer of Love, I met a man from the government. Said he was in the business of working with municipalities and might have an opportunity for us. He promised an unlimited influx of cash if I signed on the dotted line. A deal with the devil that was!

"That wretched son of a harlot turned our beautiful town into a dumping ground for vile chemical concoctions, courtesy of the U.S. of A.! Truckload after truckload poured in, drowning the outskirts in poison. All our livestock and wildlife died off as the waste seeped into the earth. Even if you weren't in the immediate vicinity, well, it got you anyway. People fled faster than you can say Jack Robinson! And the tourism dollars dried up along with every doggone swimming pool. No one wanted to get married in a town surrounded by stinking sludge.

"The government sent more of its nosy men in. They tested the soil and decided our town must be condemned. They bought out the remaining residents, even my own mama. She ran off with her tail between her legs, leaving me and my daddy to fix this mess ourselves. Well, good riddance, I said." Hand trembling, he pointed at a portrait on the wall of an old woman who looked vaguely like the sour old man now telling his story. "You better believe it was *she* who killed my daddy, not the cancer in his gut. *She* broke his heart. *She* crushed him."

Sighing, the judge gazed up at the ceiling. "A few of us lingered behind, the ones who wouldn't give up on our town. But the poison ate them up too. I lost so many good people. And in their stead came more government men, this time in puffy yellow suits so they wouldn't have to touch anything. They ordered us to get the hell out, that the town was condemned, that we couldn't live here. Well, I was living just fine, I told them. I had to use force, but I bum-rushed them right out and kept on with business as usual.

"Then just outside of town, the diggers and pavers and men in hardhats rolled in. They set about building a highway, *a detour*, around my town. Tourists bypassed us completely. Well, almost..."

He stroked Valentina's hair. "After my daddy died, it was just me for a time," the judge continued. "Occasionally, folks took a wrong turn or two and wound up here, hungry and thirsty, in need of a bed to rest their weary heads. With a bit of convincing, some folks wanted to stay, like my beautiful bride, Valentina."

She smiled lovingly at him and he patted the top of her head.

"But others tried to tell me they couldn't stay. Parting is such sweet sorrow, you know, and a man can't rebuild without fresh blood, so I made it my mission to carry on daddy's vision. As you've seen yourselves, Paradise is a town you'd never want to leave." He nodded at Officer Friendly. "And to ensure no one ever does, we have a friendly policeman to welcome out-of-towners and help them settle in."

"And force them into servitude," Dean added.

"Oh, no, Agent Dilton. Anyone is welcome to leave at any time. As long as you don't do any crime, you don't do any time. My approach with repopulating this town is like that of the good colony of Australia. We take the ne'er-do-wells and turn them into hardworking citizens. Once you've served your time, I welcome you to stay or you may move on, whichever you'd prefer. Isn't that right, Mr. Martin?"

Arnie stood up, as if in the courtroom. He brushed down his tie as he addressed the judge. "Yes, sir."

Marlow smacked his leg and he sat back down.

"Everyone is assigned work based on what they can best offer the town. Mr. Martin is a fine lawyer and every good court has a public defender."

"But initially you had him shoveling toxic waste," Dean pointed out.

"That was for his disrespectful attempt at bribing me." The judge's face darkened. "I'm not a monster—I believe in the sanctity of the justice system."

"And what about me and Marlow? Don't you think our punishment is a little harsh?"

The judge belly-laughed. "Heck, no!" He fluttered his hand at Marlow. "Miss Marlow here is a crook and a trollop! Welcoming strange men into her motel room? That's what a lady of the night does. The punishment fits the crime. As for you..." His eyes narrowed, bushy brows cramming together. "You're a stinking rat who belongs underground with the other rats. You should thank your lucky stars Officer Friendly didn't find you out in those trailers when he exterminated your little rat friends, or you too would be food for the vultures."

Burke and Gelman. Dean clasped his shaking hands together. "They didn't do anything. They weren't even within town limits. *Your* man crossed into U.S. territory on *your* orders."

The judge's brows relaxed. "Those men shouldn't have been there to begin with. Your lying government knows the deal about meddling around here. How many more of you are going to intrude on my town and get themselves killed, I wonder?" He stroked his chin, cold eyes on Dean. "One more, perhaps."

Heat burned under Dean's collar. His undershirt stuck to his sweaty skin. "Burke and Gelman were human beings. They were just doing their job."

"So were the Nazis once upon a time. Everyone is always 'just doing their job.' Unfortunately, your men's job involved sticking their noses where they didn't belong."

"Why not arrest them?" Dean asked. "Didn't they deserve a fair trial? Why not lock them up or send them to dig toxic sludge for forty years instead, huh? Why waste them with a bullet through the head?"

"You assume I didn't have plans for them, Agent?" said the judge. "That I'm not gonna box them up and ship them back to your president with a big red bow on top? They're a message to the big man in the White House. A reminder to keep his stickybeak out of my business. His predecessors signed this plot over to me when they messed up and I'll defend it to my last breath." He smirked at Officer Friendly. "Which won't be any time soon."

"I don't think the current guy in the White House

gives a shit about this place or what you're doing here," Dean replied. "In fact, he'd likely be on board with how you run things."

"Isn't that something?" said the judge. "Y'all finally voted in a man of good sense."

"So why don't you just let us go?" pleaded Dean. "We'll drive straight to the White House and the Capitol Building. I'll tell those fat cats not to bother you or Paradise ever again. I'll remind them all about the contract they signed, the one where they don't quite admit fault, but that for no better reason, they allotted this chunk of land to be your very own one nation under god."

The judge nodded along, mulling over Dean's proposition. It was looking good until he puffed up his chest and said, "That was a nice speech, Agent Dilton, but *I* make the deals around here."

He stood up and, pushing his unbuttoned waistcoat aside, flashed the ivory-handled hand cannon tucked in the front of his pants. It was a bold gesture that displayed the judge's complete disregard for his own genitals.

He strolled around the couch, stopping behind Marlow. She squirmed, straining to keep an eye on him. He gripped her seatback as he spoke to Dean. "And I have a deal for you, but first, I have a rat to take care of."

The judge drew his gun, aiming it right between Dean's bugged eyes. Dean's stomach dropped, and he was quite certain he was going to shit his pants. Bracing himself for the end, Dean sat perfectly still. Everyone waited for the judge to pull the trigger.

Everyone but Valentina who jumped up, shielding Dean with her own body.

"*No!*" she cried.

"I know why she brought you here," the judge said. "She's smitten. Hell, maybe she'd even say she was in love with you—if I hadn't cut out her tongue for talking back to me." His eyes studied the two. "But I also know my limitations. You're a lousy rat, but you have more youth and vigor than I can offer her. She wants to have a child, you know. It's something I can't give her no matter how hard we try." The judge's eyes glistened. "I can see how happy you make her. Just look at her. You deserve each other."

Dean couldn't imagine what this poor woman had been through all these years. He wished he had treated her better in the short time he'd been around her. But he couldn't be the one to father her baby.

It was just too weird.

He exchanged a look with Marlow. A new deal was coming, and Dean wasn't going to like it.

He was about to speak up and express his concerns, maybe find some way to bow out of this situation.

The judge cut him off. "Having said that... Paradise may be for lovers, but I don't traffic in happily-ever-afters." He adjusted his aim. "Not for goddamn rats."

He pulled the trigger, firing a bullet into Valentina's head.

2.

THE DEAL

MARLOW COULDN'T HEAR a damn thing. The gunshot blasted over the top of her head. It felt like her eardrums imploded and a constant ringing filled the void. She felt outside of her own body, disconnected from the library and the gory scene of Valentina's head slumped against Dean's body.

A warm wetness dripped down Marlow's face. *Brain matter*, her own brain told her. She wiped it away, looking at her contaminated fingertips.

Is this real? This can't be real...

The earth started shaking. The judge fell forward. His sour breath panted against her cheek. "Hold tight, everybody!" he hollered. "Here comes a big one!"

A painting fell off the wall, its frame cracking as it hit the fireplace mantel on its way down. The walls shuddered, split apart. Books tumbled off the shelves. Drywall sprinkled from the ceiling. The whole house was going to fall apart. It was now or never.

Marlow bolted. She passed Dean, caught under Valentina's body. He cried out an incomprehensible warning.

Officer Friendly threw the poker. The hot metal tangled in her legs, tripping her.

When she could move again, the front door appeared in her line of sight. *Almost there...*

As she pushed herself up, a warm gun barrel pressed into the back of her head. The judge cackled and pulled the trigger. Marlow's heart exploded.

The gun clicked. Empty. The nothingness was as deafening as a gunshot. She cried, sinking to the floor as her muscles turned to water.

"Next time you won't be so lucky, my dear," he said, corralling her back to the couch.

"I don't feel lucky," she mumbled.

With a snort, the judge tucked his gun back into his belt. "You're both rich with luck. Evading my best man and outrunning my loyal hounds—say, what happened to Spike down there?"

"The guillotine got him," answered Dean.

"Oh, right—I almost forgot I'd had that little security feature installed," said the judge. "Well, as I was about to say, I'm impressed with your cunning and ingenuity. When you stepped in my courtroom, I had severe reservations that either of you would make much of yourselves. That's just the way your generation has been going, I'm afraid. Lazy and worthless."

As the judge prattled on, Officer Friendly booted Dean out of the way so he could drag Valentina's body onto a rug and roll her up inside.

Marlow couldn't take her eyes away from the woman. It wasn't fair—she spent her best years married to the judge only to end up with her brains splattered across the floor. Another victim of the judge's cruelty.

"I do know one thing," the judge said. "I know when I've misjudged a person. For instance, Mr. Martin here. In all my time running this town, with all the different people I've encountered and had the pleasure, and *displeasure*, of dealing with, I never would have pegged Mr. Martin to be so steadfast in his loyalty. How long have you been with us, Mr. Martin?"

Arnie, who may as well have blended into the wall-paper to disappear completely, straightened up in his seat.

"Um, thirty-six years, six months, and eight days, Your Honor," Arnie replied. "Almost seven days in a couple of hours."

"Heck, that's incredible. You could've lied and said, 'It ended yesterday, Your Honor,' and I might've have said, 'Well, it was nice knowin' ya, Mr. Martin. You have a fine day and enjoy the rest of your life. Kiss little Jamie and that wife of yours for me.'"

Arnie's eyes bugged out behind his smudged glass-es. Every sad line etched into his face seemed to deepen. "I-I-I could do that?"

"But not Mr. Martin," the judge continued. "He is loyal, scrupulous. A real man of honor." He lowered his voice to a stage whisper and added, "But also, I never forget, so I would have caught him in a bit of a lie and that would've cost him." He slapped Arnie on the back. "I would truly hate to see him go, and I hope I never do. I hope one day soon I have the honor of burying him right here in our cemetery along with my daddy and all the other commendable citizens who have given their lives to make our town a better place."

Head in his hands, Arnie suppressed a sob.

"But you two are nothing like Mr. Martin. You're fighters. And so, I'd like to give you an opportunity to fight for your lives."

"No," said Marlow. "We're not playing your sick little make-a-deal games anymore."

Officer Friendly swept in, grabbing her by the throat. Dean jumped up—but the judge had his gun on him, ordering him to sit his behind back down or else he could join Valentina in her rolled-up rug.

The cop pulled the gimp mask over Marlow's head. Inside was dark and damp, reeking of sweat. She gasped for air. Officer Friendly pushed her down, pressing on her eyeballs. She squirmed, suffo-cating under his weight. But as soon as he unzipped the eyeholes, he backed off.

"I told you, not another word," the judge said. "Now have a seat."

He hooked her by the elbow, pulling her into his lap. The muzzle of his gun dug into her ribs.

"Now here's the deal," he said. "I want to see a fight. No holds barred. One round to the death—government rat Dilton versus the ever-loyal Officer Friendly!"

Dean's face was pale and tired. "I'm not gonna fight him."

"I'm not just asking you to fight—I'm asking you to *kill*, and if you *can't* or *won't* kill Officer Friendly, then Miss Marlow here is going to die."

Marlow froze.

"But if you succeed, if you can somehow best by best man, I'll reconsider my verdict."

"You'll just let me kill him?" Dean asked. "With no consequences?"

Marlow shook her head, trying to get Dean's attention. It had to be a trap, just like everything else in the old house.

"That's only if you *can,*" the judge replied. "I can always find a replacement, another lawman with a grudge against the U.S. system. I've managed to do so before." He grinned at the expressionless Officer Friendly. "Now, what do you say?"

Dean looked to their lawyer. "What do you think, Arnie?"

Arnie sniffled quietly into his palms.

Marlow kept shaking her head, but Dean wouldn't look her way. He had already decided what he needed to do.

Cracking his knuckles, he said, "Let's rock."

23.

THE FIGHT

AT THE JUDGE'S request, Arnie and Officer Friendly pushed all the furniture out of the way until a makeshift boxing ring could be imagined atop the dusty area rug, dampened with Valentina's blood.

Everything was cleared aside except for the judge's throne, upon which he sat, his arm tentacled around Marlow's waist.

Dean lingered in one corner, desperate for another way out. He didn't have it in him to kill someone. At least, he didn't think he did.

The judge cleared his throat. "Let's get this show on the road!"

Officer Friendly stuck out his chest as stepped onto the rug. Dean no longer felt ready to rock. Those were the words of a man with false bravado.

"We don't have to do this," he said to the cop. "I don't want to hurt you."

"The feeling's not mutual," Officer Friendly replied

through gritted teeth. He cracked his knuckles.

"No, seriously," Dean continued. "We don't have to fight. If we work together, we can—"

Officer Friendly charged in, fist flying. His first punch sent Dean's jaw in the opposite direction. Dean spun around after it, wobbling on his feet.

The judge laughed.

Officer Friendly remained stony-faced.

The fight paused while the cop waited for his opponent to straighten up and return to the match.

Dean's mouth started moving. "I came here to meet someone online." Rambling, clinging to a scrap of hope that he could still talk his way out of the situation, he kept his distance from Officer Friendly. They circled the space, one after the other, the other fleeing with nowhere to go.

"See, I've been living out of that hot, cramped trailer for weeks, watching a couple of nerds scoop dirt," he continued. "I was almost bored enough to put a bullet through my—"

He stopped himself, thinking of Valentina. Her body had been rolled up and thrown in the trunk of the squad car. Just one more lost soul for Officer Friendly to dispose of. And if Dean wasn't able to beat this mountain of a man, he and Marlow would be right alongside her.

"There's this dating app—Naughty or Nice. You ever try it?" *A silent no.* "You get to choose if you want a nice girl or a... Well, you get the point. So guess what? I went for a not nice girl.

"What are you prattling on about?" asked the judge. "I asked for a fight, not your life story."

"Smoking hot redhead..."

Officer Friendly lurched forward, throwing a punch. Dean dodged aside, still talking. "Instead, Marlow shows up. I mean, I guess it was her, but she was wearing a wig. And that's been the least of my disappointments all night."

Officer Friendly swooped in. His heavy hands clamped down on Dean's shoulders. He hefted up a knee into Dean's gut, folding him over.

"You don't have what it takes," he growled into Dean's ear. "Just like your weak little friends in their disgusting little trailer."

Even though he managed to stay on his feet, Dean felt like he had been kicked in the teeth. Of course it had been Officer Friendly—who else? He had been observing them the whole time.

For four weeks, nothing happened. No run-ins with any locals. No rumbles. No visits from local law enforcement. Only on the last day of their assignment did something happen—Dean left to meet up with Marlow, giving Officer Friendly the perfect moment to strike. Maybe he couldn't go up against three men (one trained with a gun), but he could handle two puny nerds.

Dean had left those poor bastards alone, unprotected and vulnerable, just so he could try to get lucky.

He was still just the same impulsive, selfish idiot he had always been. The military hadn't changed him, nor college or the agency. He was a hot-headed fool for life.

Either way—at the trailer in the dead of night or in a house of horrors—Dean was fated to die tonight.

Might as well go down swinging.

He thought back to his training at the academy. During a self-defence seminar, he was partnered with a cute brunette with a bouncy ponytail. They spent part of the morning throwing each other down on gym mats, surrounded by other recruits doing the same.

While Dean didn't remember exactly what they were supposed to be learning, he had vivid memories of ponytail girl pinning him down until finally they ditched the afternoon portion of the seminar to hook up in a broom closet.

The only thing Dean learned about self-defense that day was how to avoid getting a mop handle up his ass while yanking on a girl's ponytail.

He considered what his past therapist once said. *Mr. Dilton has a tendency toward mild anarchy and a level of impulsivity that can only be detrimental to his entire existence.*

Sinking down, Dean needed to tap into those instincts now more than ever.

He tried thinking back to the real lesson of that self-defense class, but he couldn't get that girl out of his head. She had grabbed onto his belt the second he closed the closet door and—

Officer Friendly came at him with another hook. This one didn't hit as hard as the first, but Dean spun into it until his back was to the others.

He laughed.

"What's the matter with him?" the judge asked. "Did you break his brain already? Worthless..."

Surreptitiously, Dean slid his belt from its loops, wrapping it around his fist. Because that was one thing he'd learned in that seminar: *Improvise.*

Officer Friendly came for him, boots pounding the floor. He grabbed Dean by the back of the collar. The shirt material tightened around Dean's chest, snapping off a button. The cop dragged him to the center of the room.

"Finish him off," the judge directed. "He just doesn't know how to put on a good show."

"I'm ending this," the cop growled, even as Dean slinked down to the ground. "What're you—?" Officer Friendly tried hoisting him up. "On your feet."

"What?" Dean hesitated.

Officer Friendly shook him. "I said *on your*—"

Dean launched up, swinging the belt. The metal buckle cracked Officer Friendly across the cheek. His aviators flew off his face. Though the hit was a stunner, the buckle was too light to cause much damage. The rest of the belt dangled limply from Dean's hand.

Shit.

Officer Friendly touched his cheek, chin quivering. Dean thought he was about to cry.

"That's all right, son," the judge said. The only thing preventing him from standing up to interfere was Marlow on his knee. "You'll get him! Don't give up!"

The cop sank to his knees, moaning.

Dean looked all around. *Did I win?*

Then Officer Friendly tilted his head up, pursing his lips. "Hit me again, daddy."

Keeping his distance, Dean studied the cop. *Is this a trick?*

"Please," Officer Friendly begged. His fingers laced together. "Hurt me good."

Certain he hadn't heard him correctly, Dean readied himself to run like hell.

Officer Friendly drew his gun, aiming it squarely at Dean's chest.

"Whoa!" Dean cried, holding up his hands.

Marlow jolted forward, shouting something along the lines of *not fair!*

"No one said anything about guns!" Dean yelled, hands in the air.

"No guns, Officer Friendly!" hollered the judge. "Put that down, son! I want a fair match."

The cop wasn't listening to anyone else. He stared intently at Dean. "I'm not fucking around," he said. "Hit me."

"You're gonna *shoot* me."

Officer Friendly shook his head. *"Hit me, please. I need* it. Give me your best shot."

"Hell, no."

The cop fired his gun. Dean flinched. With the slightest tilt of his hand, Officer Friendly fired next to Dean's foot. No harm done. Yet.

"If you don't hit me, I *will* shoot you," he promised.

Dean's stomach turned at the nasty thought of beating someone who was already on their knees in surrender. He didn't like punching down. It was sick, even if that was the nature of the game.

Officer Friendly aimed at Dean's head. *"Hit me."*

Rather than eat a bullet, Dean wound up his arm and cracked the belt. The metal buckle hit the cop's shoulder, stinging past his ear.

"Oh, god, yes," he moaned. His head rolled back. "Again."

Dean raised his arm and belted Officer Friendly across the mouth. This time the buckle broke skin, splitting the cop's lip open. Blood dribbled down his chin. He wiped it away with the back of his glove. His knees knocked together.

"Oh, yes..."

Not wanting the cop to enjoy it too much, Dean walloped him again. And again. The cop fell to his knees, arching his back in ecstasy. He thrust his crotch outward with each hit.

"*Again,*" he begged.

"No."

Without his sunglasses to conceal his gaze, Officer Friendly opened his pale blue eyes. Disappointment, anger, and rejection muddied his blank stoicism. He got back on his feet and adjusted his aim. "I said *hit me.* That's an order."

"No, this is getting ... weird."

"I won't make it weird, I *pwoooooomise.*"

Baby talk? The whole night had been a severe mindfuck and this encounter was the cherry on top.

He looked to the judge for a ruling.

"Officer Friendly, that's enough. We're not playing one of your games—we're playing mine. Now on your feet and—"

Blood rushing through his ears and head pounding, Dean didn't hear it at first—the rumbling engine of a metal dinosaur roaring up the long and winding path to the judge's house. But the sound drew everyone's attention away from the fight.

"What on god's green earth...?" The judge dumped Marlow to the floor so he could look out the window and see who or what was disturbing the peace.

Dean rushed to Marlow's side, helping her peel off the oppressive mask. She took a deep breath.

"Oh, my god, that thing is gross."

"Tell me about it." He steered her toward the door. "Let's make a break for it."

She nodded.

Before he could bolt, his legs were kicked out from under his body and he hit the ground hard. Officer Friendly had the upper hand again.

"We're not done."

Leaping up, Dean jabbed the cop's ribs. They grappled, shoes skidding on the rug, until Dean got his arms around Officer Friendly and forced him onto his stomach.

He tried to grab Officer Friendly's handcuffs, but they were sandwiched between his pelvis and the floor.

The cop thrashed, trying to buck him off, but Dean held on. He didn't have much time or energy left. All he had was the belt. He looped it around the cop's neck, cinching it tight. He felt sick to his stomach at what he was about to do, but his adrenaline sharpened his focus. This was fight or die.

Pressing his weight into Officer Friendly's back, Dean pulled the belt taut. His sweaty palms slipped, but he held on. Officer Friendly heaved, unable to break away, fighting to the end.

Dean's forearms shook. His teeth grinded. Sweat dripped off his brow. He didn't let go until the cop's purple face relaxed and his neck and body went limp.

Dean held tight a moment longer, until a new thought registered—*he's dead.*

He let go, scurrying away from Officer Friendly's body.

I killed a cop. I'm a cop killer. I'm a fucking murderer.

Panting, he tried to collect his thoughts. More than ever before, he needed to run. He needed to grab Marlow and get the hell out of town before anything worse could happen.

He got to his feet. Marlow was pressed against the

window next to the judge. They were dumbstruck by whatever was going on outside.

Dean had a sinking feeling that it wasn't safe to leave the house.

"Now what?" he asked, as Marlow looked forlornly over her shoulder.

"He's here... He found me..."

24.

THE GUEST

SOMETHING BIG AND flashy sped toward the house. At first, that meant nothing to Marlow but a convenient distraction so she and Dean could get away.

But the vehicle that approached had an aggressive engine and a loud presence that could only compare to another loud and aggressive presence she once knew.

She wandered to the window, drawn to the sound, like a moth to a bug zapper. She touched the glass, staring as a classic 1950s Chevy Impala in seafoam green climbed the crumbling hill toward the house.

Music blasted through the open windows—"Will You Love Me Tomorrow?" rang out, the singers in perfect harmony.

She knew the song all too well. It was *their* song.

The car's driver began honking madly. He drove much too fast on the narrow road and came to a screeching halt inches away from Officer Friendly's squad car.

The engine shut off. A tense silence sucked all the air out of the house.

She looked back at Dean, his hands sliding off the belt wrapped around Officer Friendly's throat. Dean asked a question, but she couldn't hear him.

"He's here... He found me..."

The driver got out and slammed the door.

"Who is that?" asked the judge, frowning. "What does he want?"

The driver mounted the Impala's hood. His patent leather dress shoes slipped but he managed to find his footing. Even without the song and the wheels, Marlow would have recognized the oil-slicked greaser hairstyle and the 1950s style. He was Elvis, Brando, and Jimmy Dean rolled up in a Marlboro.

Tony.

He cupped his hands around his mouth and began hollering.

"What's that fool doing out there?" the judge asked. "He's gonna break his damn neck and wake the whole town!"

Tony's face was slick with sweat and tears as he shouted her name into the night. *"Marlow! MARLOW!"*

"Friend of yours, I presume?" said the judge.

"MARLOW!"

"Let me guess," said Dean. "Tony?"

"I didn't think he'd find me here," she said, but in her heart, she knew he'd never let her go. Not that easily.

She swallowed. *Maybe if I give him the money I took from the safe, he'll take it and leave me alone. Maybe he won't hurt me again.*

She rubbed her cheek where a phantom pain from not too long ago flared.

Her mind did gymnastics, bending over backwards to make the situation work in her favor. Maybe Tony still had a purpose. He could take her away from this place.

The judge will have to let me go now. No one says no to Tony. No one denies him a goddamn thing.

And better the devil you know than the one who rules over a toxic town.

I got away before and I can do it again.

"MARLOW!" Sobs broke up his thundering words. "MARLOW? BABY, I NEED YOU!"

Marlow moved for the door, but the judge's gun poking her ribs was quick to remind her that she wasn't free to go.

"Hootin' and hollerin' and kickin' up a fuss like that?" he said, hooking her by the elbow. "Disturbing the peace? I won't have such a thing! Officer Friendly?"

Dean looked visibly ill, like he wouldn't be able to stand on his own for much longer. He gulped and said, "I'm sorry, judge—he's dead."

"What?" the old man croaked.

"You missed it. I-I killed him."

The judge barked out a laugh. "Oh, he's dead, is he? You'll have to do better than that! Don't you know anything? You can't keep a good lawman down."

Officer Friendly sat up. Coughing and wheezing, he unwrapped the belt from his neck and tossed it aside. Giving Dean a dirty look, he picked up his glasses and got to his feet.

"What the—?" Dean breathed.

"Don't move." His teeth clenched so tightly the molars could pop like popcorn. "I'll be back." Reaching for his handcuffs, he headed outside, straight for Tony.

Marlow stared at Dean. "I thought you said he was dead?"

"Officer Friendly is truly unstoppable," said the judge, beaming proudly. "You tried your best, Agent Dilton, but I suppose it just wasn't good enough. Looks like it's curtains for the two of you."

Tony continued shouting at the house, going full Brando, until Officer Friendly advanced and swept his legs out from under him. Tony dropped onto the hood with a bang.

The cop grabbed him by his ankles and dragged him off the car. Tony hit the dirt in a cloud of dust.

Watching her ex choke and sputter, Marlow didn't know if she should be relieved or terrified. *Either way, I'm so dead.*

While Officer Friendly cuffed Tony and loaded him into the back of the squad car, the judge gleefully escorted Marlow and Dean from the house.

"The hubris!" he cried. "The hubris that you could defeat my officer! How ridiculous you must feel!"

Neither said anything, just scowled at the ground as the judge prodded his gun barrel into their backs.

"I won't let that feeling fester for too long though—we'll make quick work of your executions, I promise."

They were almost to the squad car when Arnie slinked out the front door. His hands were stuffed in his pockets and his glasses were smudgier than before. He stared shyly down at his shoes. All this time, he had been hiding in the house, helpless to save them.

"Do something!" she snarled.

His neck curved downward. If he could have rolled

up inside himself to avoid confrontation, he would have contorted into a humanoid snail—another being that seemed eerily possible in Paradise.

"Arnie, come on." Dean pleaded. "You're supposed to be our lawyer, for Christ's sake."

The judge bullied them along. "Get moving."

Marlow stopped in her tracks, reaching into her pocket. The judge's finger tensed on the trigger, happy to blow her away to maintain control.

All Marlow had left was the dead boy's school ID. She flung it onto the porch, where it landed at Arnie's feet.

"No one gets out of here alive!"

The back of the squad car was a tight squeeze, and Dean was helpless to do anything but feel Marlow shivering next to him as Tony whispered his toxic words into her ear.

"Hey, baby girl." He rested his chin on her shoulder. The only things stopping him from snaking his arms around her were the handcuffs he wore behind his back. "I knew I'd find you sooner or later."

"How?" she croaked.

"Baby, I'd find you anywhere. Remember, like the song? I will follow you wherever you go."

"Really?" Dean snorted.

"Was I talking to you?" Tony elbowed Marlow. "Who's this piece of shit?"

"I'm a federal agent," he replied. "And if you want to make it out of here alive, you'll keep your mouth shut, pal."

"Don't," Marlow warned him.

"I'm not your pal, asshole," Tony fired back. "And I haven't done nothin'."

Dean shook his head, staring out the window. "You have no idea where you are or what you're up against."

"Shut up or I'll shut you up."

Officer Friendly got behind the wheel and slammed the door in time with Judge DeVille planting himself in the front passenger seat. The engine started and the car began to move.

"What a sorry sight," declared the judge, craning his neck to look back at the sad sack trio. "I'll be relieved once we're back in my courtroom. But believe me, I won't be so lenient this time."

Tony smirked. "I just stopped by to collect my girl. We'll be outta your hair in no time, old man."

A tight smile curved the judge's discolored lips. "Miss Marlow? Oh, no. She and Agent Dilton are on their way to the gallows. And you, young man, well... We'll see about you."

Tony twisted around to face Marlow. "What the fuck did you do?"

Marlow mumbled something.

"Just leave her alone," Dean said. "She's had a really bad night."

"I told you to shut it," Tony snapped. "I don't care if you're some bitch-ass fed or what—you look like a little boy. Bet your mommy still wipes your ass."

Dean, whose mother hadn't played any part in his personal hygiene since he was six years old, clenched his fists. He couldn't do anything with Marlow in the middle. He would have to bide his time and see what the judge had in mind for Tony, and hope it would be worse than his own fate.

Tony puffed up his chest and muttered, "Chicken-shit little bitch."

Blood pumping, Dean lost it. He drove his fist into Tony's big mouth. His knuckle split open against Tony's teeth. Tony gurgled, head rocking back.

Marlow ducked.

Tony snapped back, quick as a boxer. He pulled up his legs, working to get his handcuffed hands out in front of himself. Marlow tried to block him, to calm him down—and he headbutted her.

Her nose cracked. Blood flowed down her lips and chin, down her chest and soaking into her shirt. She groaned, slumping against Dean.

Blood turned Tony's toothy grin a sickly pink.

"Settle down back there!" the judge barked.

He was craning his neck to admonish the men when bright lights flooded the car. Everyone went blind—except for Officer Friendly in his sunglasses. Dean covered his eyes, unable to pinpoint the source of the light. Was it a long-awaited SWAT team? An alien spaceship? Fucking Santa Claus?

Squinting through the blinding glare, Dean saw the Chevy Impala. Revved up, the possessed car bolted forward and rear-ended them. Dean and Tony crashed against the cage.

The Impala rode their bumper, tapping and scraping paint. Officer Friendly tried to regain control. He lost the battle, hands slipping as the wheel jerked away. The Impala struck them again and they spun out, leaving the road. One side lifted off the uneven ground. They were going too fast—and with one final tap, the squad car began to roll.

25.

THE END OF HIS ROPE

[DIRECTOR ███████████: *Agent Dilton, must I remind you that I don't have a lot of time here?*]

[AGENT DILTON: *I understand, sir. But I thought this part was important.*]

[DIRECTOR ███████████: *Your rambling explanation has gone on long enough. Stick to the facts and spare me the conjecture.*]

[AGENT DILTON: *That's just it, sir. He's long gone, so I can only speculate what happened the night Arnie Martin finally grew a pair of balls.*]

MAYBE IT STARTED when Arnie took a wrong turn and found himself traveling in the opposite direction of home. He had promised his wife he wouldn't be late for their son's birthday dinner, and by his calculation, taking that supposed shortcut put him three hours behind schedule.

Maybe it was because he thought he could make up time by putting the pedal to the metal. Maybe he just didn't see the town limits sign or the dilapidated billboard that once promoted a romantic desert oasis. With his poor eyesight and outdated prescription, he certainly didn't notice the black squad car tailing, or for how long.

An earthquake struck and he stopped. He thought maybe he had fallen asleep at the wheel and rode over the rumble strips as he veered off the blacktop. When the cop tapped on his window and demanded he step out of the vehicle, Arnie knew it wasn't a dream.

He just didn't know he was caught in a nightmare.

Hauled into court, Arnie did a piss poor job of explaining he needed to get back home for his son's birthday. Judge DeVille merely laughed and joked, making him a spectacle in front of a gallery of dead-eyed locals. But when Arnie mentioned he was a lawyer, the judge grew serious. He wanted to see if Arnie could get himself off. He wanted to see how good of a public defender he was.

Arnie chuckled, tugging on his collar. It seemed like a joke, but also like an interview for a job he didn't need in a town he didn't want to stay in.

The judge refused to go easy on him and that didn't seem like a big deal. After all, he figured he could pay the fine.

Speeding in Paradise earned him forty years.

Stunned, Arnie thought it was a joke. But when the joke appeared to have no punchline, he became anxious and desperate. He offered a bribe. He had seen the town. He knew it wasn't worth much, so how much could the judge possibly be earning?

Incensed and offended by the offer, the judge ordered Arnie to dig toxic waste for the remainder of his sentence. Thankfully the judge had a change of heart when Arnie got sick. He decided to keep him around to serve as the town's public defender. "It'll be good for you, Mr. Martin," he said. "Imagine all the good people you'll help."

If Arnie hadn't been able to save himself, how was he supposed to help others? He couldn't even negotiate a phone call to tell his wife he was going to be late—*forty years late*—but he clung to one of the last things she had said to him before his business trip: "Do your best, dear! We love you no matter what!"

So Arnie did his best. Sometimes he got lucky and convinced the judge to let folks go, but that was a matter of managing the old man's mood swings. The people who got to leave scot-free had no idea how truly lucky they were. Arnie chose to remember those ones, rather than dwell on the hundreds of not-so-lucky people.

Maybe it was that after festering in Paradise for thirty-six years, six months, and almost seven days, Arnie was told that the judge wouldn't have noticed if he walked out of there yesterday. Even if it had only been yesterday, it would have been one day closer to reuniting with his family.

But Arnie was an excellent bottler. He spent nearly four decades of his miserable life bottling up all the shit that dumped on him for no good reason. He suffered in silence. So while it was likely that his bottle had filled and overflowed, that wasn't entirely it either.

If you put a gun to his head, Arnie might have admitted that it was the school ID card Marlow threw at him. Arnie stared at it as the rowdy bunch piled into the squad car for a trip back to the courthouse, back toward the gaudy cupid statue taking aim at the center of town.

Any other time, Arnie would have rushed after them to offer his legal advice, but he didn't bother. Just stared at the ID card.

He bent down and picked it up, rubbing his thumb over the worn picture of a gap-toothed child in a neon yellow shirt. He hadn't seen anyone wear neon for decades now. Had that been just another fashion trend? If so, that meant the kid in the picture was not a kid anymore.

Deep in his gut, Arnie knew the kid wasn't an adult either. He was dead.

He also couldn't say for certain if his own kid was grown up or dead—*his own goddamn son*—and that uncertainty shook him to his core. He snapped the ID card in half, slicing his thumb open, spilling blood.

The only other sign that Arnie was well and truly pissed off was the quiet grinding of his molars as he stepped off the porch and marched over to the abandoned Impala, the keys left in the ignition.

Arnie hadn't driven in years, so he expected to be a little rusty. What he didn't expect was instant road rage to fuel his muscles as he turned the engine over. He squeezed the wide steering wheel and put the pedal to the metal once more. The car transformed into a tank, and Arnie was going to drive it right up Judge DeVille's ass on his way out of town.

He raced after the squad car, flooring it until he was upon the others. Then he flicked the lights on, blinding himself in the process. The Impala's front end crashed into the squad car, and the other driver began to lose control.

Invincible in his seafoam-colored tank, Arnie didn't let up. He was the pedal *and* the metal. One good smash and the judge would be dead.

Arnie pushed all his weight down on the gas and the Impala roared. It flew over the fallen tombstones, shooting dust and debris in its wake. He struck the other car again and again, forcing it to roll over.

Upon final impact, he banged his head on the steering wheel and his glasses fell into his lap. He blacked out for a second—and the Impala rammed into a row of tombstones and came to a halt.

He slumped into the passenger seat, bleeding and aching all over, and wondering how many years he'd get for vehicular homicide.

26.

THE GETAWAY

EVERYTHING HURT. EVERYTHING was upside down. Marlow huddled against the car's up-turned roof, breathing in smoke and dust and Tony's cologne. She smelled blood, sniffling it back into her aching nose.

She tried to push herself up. Broken glass littered the ground under her palms. Exhaust wafted over flashing orange hazard lights.

In the front seat, the judge hacked out a lung.

Marlow grabbed Dean's shoulder, shaking him awake. He groaned, head rolling from side to side.

"We have to go," she whispered, looking over her shoulder. Tony's head turned toward her. The bastard's eyes were shut, blood trickling down his split-open eyebrow.

Marlow patted Dean's face. He coughed, slowly blinking back to life. She shushed him at the exact moment his eyes shot open as he remembered where they were.

She nodded at the broken window, mouthing the word *go!*

Rolling onto his side, he stifled a cough and began to crawl. Glass pricked his hands and he paused to tell her to be careful—as if the entire car wasn't a wasp's nest.

Once he was out, Dean reached in to help Marlow. He got her arms—but Tony snapped back to life and latched onto her ankle.

"Get back here, bitch."

She yelped, kicking at him. Her heel smashed into his teeth. More blood oozed in between, distorting his grin into a gory mess. The hit was enough to loosen his grip, and Dean pulled Marlow free. He yanked her to her feet and they ran.

She couldn't see through the smoke or the dirt tearing up her eyes. Fingers laced with Dean's, she followed him blindly through the graveyard, a hill of bones.

"MARLOW!" Tony screamed.

He was out of the squad car and coming after her.

"Just leave me alone," she panted.

They didn't run for long. There was another car just down the road. The Impala—its engine was running, both headlights were busted, and a fresh crack split across the windshield.

Arnie was collapsed across the bench seat.

Pushing Marlow into the front seat, Dean was hit from behind. He released Marlow's hand and she flew into the Impala, looking back as a bruised and bloodied Officer Friendly planted a boot on Dean's back.

"Freeze," he sneered, raising his nightstick to strike again.

Marlow slid in next to Arnie. She put her hands on the wheel, feeling around the steering column for the gear shift lever.

I'm gonna run you down, you son of a bitch.

But she couldn't run down the cop without running over Dean, who was belly down in the dirt. He shakily raised his head. Their eyes met.

"Go!" he yelled.

She hesitated. "I..."

Arnie groaned in the seat beside her. He had done a very brave, but very stupid thing, and if they stuck around any longer, he would be executed right alongside them. No chance to see his wife and kid ever again.

"Where am I?" he wondered.

"Still in hell," she said. "Trapped in Paradise."

At the utterance of the town's name, Arnie fumbled for his glasses, placing them crookedly on his nose. "What about the judge? Did I do it? Is he—?"

"Don't worry about it," she said, swallowing her own worries. "You did good. Time to go home."

She shifted into reverse, peeling away from the wreckage. Handling the Impala was like driving a boat; it ran smoothly but it was larger than anything she had ever tried to make a getaway in.

On top of that, her visibility was screwed up because she couldn't stop blinking away tears. She didn't want to leave Dean—the guilt was eating her up—but she couldn't stay another second. She'd have to escape to send help. There was no other way.

Shifting into drive as she aimed the Impala down the hill, she patted her chest. Finding the cash still wedged in her bra and pressed against her pounding heart, she breathed a little easier.

Before the Impala could pick up speed, the back door flew open. Tony leered at her in the rearview mirror.

Bang! Bang! Crack!

Two bullets cracked the back window. Tony ducked down and out of sight. Arnie cowered in the fetal position, sliding onto the floor mat.

Officer Friendly was distracted with subduing Dean, so the judge came out guns blazing, firing after the three escapees.

"Floor it, baby!" Tony squeezed her shoulders. He looked back, laughing at the old geezer and his one-man police force. His laughter sounded like breaking glass. "Fuckin' right!"

Once the car was free of the winding cemetery road and speeding through the streets of Paradise for the next exit out of town, Tony leaned in over the front seat and sighed.

"I gotta admit, it worked. It really worked."

Frowning, Marlow studied his reflection. Curiosity got the best of her. "What worked?"

"That whole prayer, chanting bullshit. Remember that thing you dragged me to?" He chuckled at her puzzled face. "Come on, I *know* you remember. It was about getting everything you could ever want if you just put your wishes out into the universe, or some shit. Well, guess what?"

Staying mum, she could probably guess.

"I said it just like they said to," he continued. "Right after you ditched me, I sat down and put it out into the universe. I said, 'I love Marlow and Marlow loves me.' And then guess what happened?"

Her eyes flickered back onto the road. She didn't

want to talk about this. She wanted to leave. She wanted to be free—first the town and later Tony.

But he wasn't going to let her go. His hand reached into her hair, digging his nails into her scalp. He pulled her head back, stretching her neck as far back as she could still drive.

"And you know what happened?" he asked again. "I *found* my lying, cheating, stealing, two-faced bitch of a girlfriend, and now I gotta make her pay."

27.

THE DEMON

TONY DIDN'T LIFT his hands from Marlow's neck and shoulders. "Go north," he directed. "Drive until I tell you to stop." He pursed his lips at Arnie, rocking himself in front of the bench seat. "What's his problem?"

"Leave him alone," Marlow told him. "He just wants to go home and see his kid."

"Well, tough titty for him. Next town, dump his ass. He can walk home for all I care."

"He's been gone forty years," she said.

"Good, then nobody remembers him and it's no big deal."

Arnie raised his head, puppy-dog eyes wet and blinking at Marlow. "They won't remember me?"

She tried giving him a reassuring smile, but she was all out of hope. "That's not true," she said, the words as hollow as she felt inside.

Tony snickered. "It's true. My old man ran out when I was a kid and I forgot all about his sorry ass right until you mentioned you're a shitty dad."

Moaning, Arnie hugged his stomach. "No..."

"It's true. Bet your brat thinks you walked out 'cause you didn't want him. So now he probably doesn't think shit about you." Smirking and shaking his head, Tony leaned back in his seat. His hands slipped off Marlow's shoulders.

"You're going home," Marlow told Arnie, keeping her voice low as if that would keep Tony from butting in. "You'll see your son and your wife." He nodded, but that wasn't enough. "Say it."

"Huh?"

"Say you'll see them."

"I-I'll see them?"

"That's right," she said, while Tony kept chuckling. "Keep saying it and it'll happen."

"Okay..."

"Say it."

"Uh... I'm going home?"

"Again."

"I'm going home."

"Fuckin' bullshit," Tony muttered.

She glared at him over her shoulder. "Why? Why's it bullshit for him but worked for you?"

Tony smiled, eyes narrowing without any trace of humor. "You talking back to me, baby girl?"

"Why's it bullshit?" she pressed.

"I'm going home," Arnie said.

"I didn't say he couldn't go home," Tony said. "I just said he's not getting a ride with us. He's on his own."

"I'm going home."

"That's right, dude," Marlow said. She gazed out at the black night turning dark blue, and hoped the universe could hear her heart's desire too. *I'm getting the hell out of this car.*

"I don't like this attitude of yours," Tony said, leaning forward again. He didn't touch her this time, but his dissatisfaction weighed heavily in the space behind her. "I think you'd better pull the fuck over."

She didn't slow down. She kept going, foot pressed down on the gas pedal.

"You still wanna go home, Arnie?" she asked.

"Y-yes."

"Good." She let off the gas and flung open the door. It lurched open slowly and heavily. The car began to swerve. She grabbed one of Arnie's sweaty hands and planted it on the steering wheel. "Better take over then."

Arnie bolted upright. The wheel spun out of control. The men started yelling, scrambling to take over.

"Go home, Arnie," she said, before Tony could snare her in a headlock.

As Arnie fumbled to take her place behind the wheel, Marlow scooted to the open door.

He tried to save her *and* find the brake pedal, but he couldn't do both at the same time.

But she didn't need anyone to save her.

The car coasted, slowing just enough for her to lean out. The rough blacktop raced by.

Tony roared, clawing after her, but as always, she was just out of his grasp. "Marlow!"

She gulped down a deep breath and before anyone could stop her, she threw herself out of the speeding car.

When Marlow woke up, it was still night but everything felt red.

She blinked her eyes, checking herself for any signs of life. Touching her chest, she found her heart where it always had been, beating away inside its cage. Nothing seemed to be broken but everything hurt like hell. An angry red rash prickled her left leg. She vaguely remembered trying to plant her feet on the ground as she exited the Impala, taking big running steps alongside the car, but ended up skidding along the road until her head struck the pavement.

One brief blackout later, her eyes fluttered awake. The Impala's blazing taillights were gone.

Though she hoped Arnie would make it home, she felt so alone—until a nearby groan alerted her that she wasn't.

She pushed herself up, arm muscles trembling. Her swollen ankle made her raw skin tighten. When she put her weight down, a sharp spasm fired through her ankle. She cried out, dropping to her knees.

"Marlow..."

She looked around, seeing a man's shape sprawled out in the middle of the road. Either Arnie managed to kick Tony out or—

He jumped out.

Arnie wouldn't stop and he jumped out after me.

An old, part of her might have found that gesture romantic, once upon a time. But it wasn't love that compelled Tony to make the leap—it was obsession and revenge and hate.

His banged-up shape peeled itself away from the blacktop. Teeth gleaming and face shiny with blood, he called to her.

"Marlow…"

"Ugh, fuck," she sobbed. She couldn't catch a break—except for maybe a broken bone.

She hooked two fingers inside her tattered shirt. Her bra clung to her feverish skin. When she touched the metal keyring, hope surged. There was still a chance.

I'll get the car, she thought. *I'll run back to that godawful town and get the Demon. Fuck Tony. The Demon is mine and I'll drive it right up his ass. The judge too. And I'll find Dean and we'll stick with the plan—get the hell out of this hell together.*

That was if Dean didn't already have a bullet fired into his brain.

Picking herself up, Marlow staggered along the side of the road. Her boots were wildly impractical now, tight around her swollen ankle. She was going nowhere fast and danger was everywhere, lurking just out of sight in the dark.

She pushed ahead, watching for flashing lights or the glint of moonlight on a silent, sneaking black squad car. She looked over her shoulder at Tony, grabbing his head as he slowly got to his feet.

"Marlow…" he moaned. *"Get back here…"*

Over one of the hills ahead, she spotted the judge's house. All the lights were on, casting a yellow spotlight on the tombstones littered across the property. She thought about the dead boy and all the others whose corpses filled up that plot of land. She had to hurry if she didn't want Dean to be among them.

Cutting across the desert toward the lights of Paradise, she followed the chain link fence back to the junkyard. By the time she rediscovered the opening, she was out of breath.

Tony wasn't far behind. He kept calling her name and she kept running.

Hauling ass with a messed-up leg was harder than she imagined, and her brain was in a constant battle between telling her to carry on and telling her she would never make it to the car and that Tony was going to kill her.

She squeezed through the fence. As she crossed to the other side, a dog howled. The last hellhound—the one Dean had trapped in the dead station wagon—had gotten free. The upholstery was chewed to shreds and the trunk was wide open. The damned beast must have triggered a switch and gotten loose.

Like Tony, the hellhound sounded far away—for now. Marlow backtracked in the direction of the Demon, hoping neither furious killer found her. She slid her middle finger through the ring, clutching the keys in her palm to silence their jingle.

Keeping low and moving quickly, she limped through the maze of junk. Her heartbeat and ragged breathing echoed in her ears, as she retraced her steps to where the Demon had been left.

In the dark, disorienting maze, she turned a corner. Her foot snagged on a soft, meaty log, and she landed on the tow truck driver's body. Chunky, black flies buzzed around his torn throat. Marlow rolled aside, gagging, and as she looked over, there was the Demon. Right where they'd left off.

Oh, thank god.

Before she could get up, an arm locked around her neck. "You fucking bitch," Tony snarled, dragging her around like a rag doll.

She dropped the keys, trying desperately to keep an

eye on where they landed.

"You think you're so fucking smart," he said. Spittle flew off his lips. He jerked her around, not giving her enough air to beg for her life. "Think you can leave me over and over again, steal my shit. My money! My fucking car! *Fuck you!*"

She elbowed him. He loosened his hold just long enough for her to slip away. But her boots tangled up with some junk and she fell again. *The keys!* Her hands frantically swept through the sand. *Where are they?*

Snatching the back of her shirt, Tony spun her around and slapped her. Her cheek stung white hot. Tears burned her eyes.

Then he spat in her face. "Fuck you."

He slammed her against the hood. She gasped for breath as his body pressed on top of hers. His hands found their way to her throat, thumbs adding pressure to her windpipe.

Searching all around, she wondered if she could run for it. As if reading her mind, he laughed. "Baby, you got nowhere to run."

"Tony—"

He let go for a second to wipe his bloodied face on with his palm. Red dribbled down his wrist, staining his jacket's sleeve.

Shaking his head, he looked forlorn. "First you wreck my car, then my goddamn jacket. Fuck..."

He cracked his knuckles again, then kissed each one. His babies. He stuck his fist in her face, rubbing her stinging cheek with his middle finger. "Shh. Don't you worry about a thing. It'll all be over soon. Now gimme a little goodbye kiss."

He was dead serious. He offered his knuckles to her.

Jaw trembling, she kissed his fist. A smug grin crept over his lips.

"See? That wasn't so bad. Maybe if you just shut up and do what I tell—"

Before he could finish, she sucker punched him.

Blood burst from his nose. His jaw dropped, a roar building up in the back of his throat.

Rolling aside, Marlow stuck two fingers between her lips and blew. A sharp, shrill whistle cut through the night.

He clocked her. The impact knocked her back against the hood. As the world faded in and out, she slid off the car.

He kicked her aching leg. *"Get up, bitch."*

A hellhound darted out of the junk maze. Its nose twitched, picking up the scent of fresh blood. It rushed at Tony. There was no stopping it. Its front paws coasted through the air, leaping toward its prey.

Marlow ducked, covering herself.

Tony held up his forearm, blocking the dog's attack. Its slobbery teeth snapped and ripped through his fancy clothes to get at his flesh. It growled and grumbled and gnawed down to the bone.

Tony punched it, but the hellhound was relentless. Tony's fancy shoes slipped. The hound had him on his back. Man versus beast.

"Fucking do something!" he screamed.

He was right. She did have something to do.

She grabbed the keys and ran around to the car. Doors unlocked, she climbed inside and locked both monsters out.

She started the ignition. The Demon came to life. The radio crackled and a woman's buttery smooth voice crooned a love song through the speakers. One of Tony's favorite golden oldies.

His screams intensified. Marlow couldn't stand to hear it—it was bad enough he was laid out in front of the headlights as the hellhound tore onto his throat and shook the life out of him.

Marlow reached for the volume knob, drowning out Tony's cries, and then helpless gurgles, and then his final death rattle.

It was a good song. Maybe one of her favorites now.

28.

THE GOD OF LOVE

FROM THE JUDGE'S house, the road, rough and riddled with potholes, widened into a two-lane street. In handcuffs, Dean was marched down that road toward the center of town. The gimp mask impaired his vision, so Officer Friendly's nightstick forcefully guided him along.

When the nightstick jabbed into his gut, he knew he had arrived at his final destination.

Officer Friendly pulled off the mask and Dean sucked in the fresh air, gazing up at the diapered rear-end of the giant cupid.

He hadn't given the statue much thought when he first drove into town, other than, *Damn, that's a big fucking cupid.* All small towns had the "World's Largest…" something or other—ball of twine, cheese wheel … a crumbling ode to a half-naked symbol of love.

The judge sidled up next to Dean, flashing his gun. "You're about to meet your maker, Agent Dilton," he said, nodding up at the cupid's big arrow. "With a little help from our mighty friend here."

"Swell," muttered Dean.

"We are going to tie a rope around your neck and hang you until you die."

"Can't you just shoot me and get it over with?"

The judge barked out a *ha!* "What would be the fun in that?"

"All this was never about justice or sovereignty or any of that," said Dean. "Killing innocent people is all fun and games to you, and the U.S. government signed your permission slip."

The judge leaned in, lowering his voice so the gathering onlookers couldn't hear. "Let's get two things straight here, Agent Dilton. *You* are *not* an innocent person. The moment you put on that badge you became as guilty as the rest of those scum suckers. Secondly, putting people to death is part of the job. Plain and simple. It's hard work, but there's no harm in taking pride and pleasure in one's efforts."

Dean didn't bother to reply, just stared sullenly at cupid's lumpy ass.

A decent-sized crowd gathered, made up of motel clerk Billy and Delores the waitress and the few others from the courthouse (minus one tow truck driver and one public defender). They yawned, rubbing the sleep from their eyes. The judge had summoned them not just to have an audience, but to remind everyone who was in charge.

Officer Friendly set down a small crate for the judge to stand on. Towering a mere foot above the townsfolk, the judge called everyone to order.

"Thank you all for being here," he said, his voice a

mighty, bellowing spirit that carried down main street. "Unfortunate circumstances have brought us to this moment, and I'm calling on all of you to act as witnesses to the end of this cold-hearted criminal's miserable life. It is not a death sentence granted but rather a hope that Agent Dilton will be taken into the arms of our lord and granted some sweet serenity in his afterlife, whatever that may be."

The judge's words fused together into meandering nothingness as soon as Officer Friendly lassoed a noose over cupid's arrow. The thick rope dangled down next to Dean, who swallowed with great difficulty, unable to look away.

So this is the end.

Officer Friendly looped the noose around Dean's neck. The rope scratched his skin, tightening under his Adam's apple. Dean gulped as it choked him. He thought about shaking it off and making a break for it. But Officer Friendly watched him like a hawk, rendering the plan next to impossible.

Fine, Dean thought. *I'll think of something else.*

But he couldn't concentrate. There were a million ways he could try to escape and they all ended with him dead. *And no one will know what happened to me. I'll be another missing person on some bullshit TV show, or I'll get swept under the rug to save face for the agency.*

He thought about his parents. His friends back home. The girls who rejected him. The girls who slept with him. The redheaded archivist with the velvet heels. And Marlow.

God, I hope she made it.

Officer Friendly grabbed the end of the rope and gave it a tug, hoisting Dean onto his tiptoes. The line slackened. Dean caught his breath. The cop sneered—*just testing.*

Judge DeVille wrapped up his blowhard sermon about good, decent people and how government devils like Dean had no place in the world. "It won't taint our souls to be rid of this demon tonight," he explained. Then he addressed Dean. "Any last requests?"

"Yeah—*let me go.*"

The judge turned back to the audience and laughed, like their repartee was all part of the show and not capital punishment on grand display for a bunch of dead-eyed, broken prisoners.

"Agent Dilton, you are a barrel of laughs," he said, with ice in his eyes.

"Can't blame a man for trying."

"No, you cannot," the judge had to admit. "But now it's time to say goodnight, farewell, au revoir, and all that cow dung."

"Goodnight, judge," Dean replied, as coolly as he could. His insides turned to ice and his legs melted into a gelatinous goo. He felt the need to puke, piss, and shit himself all at once, but he wanted to go out like a man. He wanted to be as cool as Paul Newman in *Cool Hand Luke* or Steve McQueen in anything. He didn't want to die in front of a bunch of people like a chickenshit.

He didn't want to die.

As the rope tightened, Dean shut his eyes.

"Officer Friendly," said the judge. "It's your duty to help expedite Agent Dilton into the great beyond. You may now begin. See that he hangs until his last breath."

"Yessir," said the cop.

Winding the rope around his fist, Officer Friendly stepped up to his mark. His breath huffed in Dean's ear.

Dean expected him to ask forgiveness or pray for his soul (as executioners sometimes did). Instead, he whispered breathily, "Let me show you how it's done."

He gave the line a jerk, lifting Dean off the ground.

Gritting his teeth, Dean tried to focus on something positive. And no matter how hard he tried, he couldn't *not* think of Marlow. The way she sauntered into the diner in her red-hot boots. The heat of her body pressed against him in the dark trunk, driving him wild, or clinging desperately to him in Valentina's boudoir.

He started choking. The rope dug in, cutting off his air. Officer Friendly heave-ho'd, hoisting him higher and higher.

Dean opened his eyes, searching the small crowd for anyone who might help him.

Was it too much to ask for a revolt?

Beyond the crowd, a car sped straight down the one road through the center of town—and coming right for them. A Dodge Demon with its headlights off. The maniac behind the wheel had a shock of wild blonde hair.

Marlow, you beautiful, freakin' moron.

He would have smiled if he weren't fighting for his life, legs kicking frantically.

The car careened down main street. By the time the judge saw it and pointed, the crowd broke apart and people scattered—everyone but Officer Friendly and the judge, who held their ground.

Dean twisted, trying to get anywhere and going nowhere fast. The Demon was upon them.

"Don't you dare let go!" screamed the judge, diving out of the way.

Officer Friendly held onto the rope, even when three thousand pounds of metal crashed into him, pinning his body to the statue's chubby leg.

Only then did he let go.

Gasping, Dean fell onto the car's roof. He raised his head, searching for Marlow as the smoke cleared. He pulled off the noose. *Live to die another day...*

The door swung open, busted and bent. The horn wailed, then died on a flat note.

Traversing the Demon's cracked windshield on his knees, Dean slid down beside the driver's side door. "Marlow...?"

A cold metal cylinder dug into the back of his head.

"Hold it," ordered the judge.

Dean ignored him, reaching his cuffed hands inside the car. Tears stinging his eyes, he touched her lifeless hand.

Her big, hairy, masculine hand.

What the hell? He brushed the hair away from her face. A blonde wig slid off Tony's bloody scalp. His throat was torn out and his glassy eyes stared into oblivion. On the floor, a rotten two-by-four and a brick had dislodged from holding down the gas pedal.

Dean cackled so sharply and suddenly that he startled the judge.

She's still alive.

"What's so funny?" the judge asked, prodding him. "Get up."

Dean couldn't—he was laughing too hard. All the stress and fear and unreleased tension from the last several hours was working itself out in the worst way, at the worst time.

"Sir..." groaned Officer Friendly.

"What now?" snapped the judge, spinning around. "Oh, no..."

Officer Friendly wasn't going to make it. His pelvis and both legs were crushed, the internal injuries too severe to do anything other than put the poor bastard out of his misery.

The judge stood by his side. "No, no, no, no..."

"S-sorry, sir..." he wheezed. "I-I think I need to take a personal day."

The judge patted his cold hand. "Take all the time you need, son."

When Officer Friendly tried to speak, he spewed up blood instead. He coughed, spraying the judge who stepped back in disgust. "S-sorry..." The cop slumped over the hood. His cracked sunglasses slipped off his nose.

The judge picked up the mirrored shades and tucked them in his breast pocket. Hand trembling, he turned on Dean. But the agent was gone.

"Get back here, you cowardly rat!"

Dean sneaked up behind him, hooking his handcuff chain around the judge's throat. He twisted and tightened, strangling the son of a bitch.

The judge fired into the night sky. He tried to shoot the man behind him, but his arms were too inflexible to bend that way, and every shot went wide, disappearing into the darkness. All he had was his bulk, which he used to push Dean backwards, forcing him off balance. Together, they landed on the ground, rolling back and forth.

Dean refused to let go and the judge refused to give in—until the earth began to shake. More rumbles.

Wide-eyed, the judge stopped to see his town turning to dust. "It's the big one!" he cried.

Around them, shops and buildings wobbled as if

built with popsicle sticks. Foundations crumbled and roofs belted under.

Every window at the Shady Palms exploded, spraying glass across the parking lot that cratered open, sucking all the motel units down into a deep, dark pit.

The art deco bank with its beautiful columns split apart, cracked open like a child's piggy bank. Across town, the diner quivered like a jelly mold, collapsing in on itself as steam erupted all around.

And atop the cemetery hill, the judge's house shuddered, breaking apart. Large chunks of the structure slid down the hill. As the judge screamed for his home, the road next to him burst open. More hot, rancid steam shot up from the ground.

Cupid groaned and tilted. One leg bent, the other snapped. The rumbles freed the leaning cupid from its rusty, warped base. As it leaned downward, the statue's arrow pointed right between Dean's eyes.

Dean released the judge and rolled aside, narrowly getting crushed. He sat up, dazed and anxious.

The judge screamed.

Dean scrambled to his feet. He ran around the fallen statue until he found the judge, speared through the heart by cupid's arrow. Black blood pumped out of his chest, and still the old codger fought to break free.

"You just don't quit, do you?" Dean remarked.

The judge grunted. "You're still ... not getting out ... alive, Agent Dilton."

"Oh, no? Just watch me."

He walked away, leaving the judge to die slowly and painfully as a human shish kabob.

He returned to Officer Friendly's body and dug through the dead man's pockets for the handcuff keys.

Once he freed himself, he tossed the cuffs aside and looked around.

The town was in shambles and only a few confused stragglers remained—Marlow among them. She limped toward him with a sly smile.

"I saw that dumb statue falling and I thought—"

He pulled her into his arms, breathing her in. "Jesus Christ, why'd you come back? I mean, I'm glad you did, but—"

She pushed him off, poking him with a ragged fingernail. "A *thank you* would be nice."

"Excuse me?"

"For saving your sorry ass *again*. *Five times!*"

He sighed. "You know, just when I thought we were starting to get along..."

"Wait," she said. "Where's the judge?"

29.

THE PIT

JUDGE DEVILLE SHOULD have been right there. He was as good as dead. An arrow literally staked him through the heart.

But when Dean took Marlow to see for herself, the judge was gone. Blood smeared the arrow. They followed a trail of dark droplets away from the cupid and Officer Friendly's for-sure-dead corpse.

"Why weren't you watching him?"

Dean didn't appreciate the accusation in her tone. *"I don't know, Marlow.* I guess I figured there was no way he was gonna make it."

She groaned. "I swear these people are zombies."

They didn't search for long. As Dean suspected, the judge was in bad shape.

He clutched his chest, stumbling around the statue. Cupid's arm had punched through the earth. The judge gasped as Dean and Marlow approached.

"Stay back! Stay away from me!"

"It's over, judge," Dean said.

"I-I suppose it is…" The old man collapsed against cupid's elbow. Mopping his brow, he chuckled to himself. "Just give me a minute."

Dean wasn't in the mood to give him anything, least of all a minute to collect himself. *Why the hell aren't you dead, old man?*

"I don't like this," Marlow grumbled.

Dean didn't either—and it got even worse when the judge ripped open his shirt. Buttons flew in every direction. His chest spasmed. His body contorted. A thick black mass—bigger than, but almost exactly like the one killing Arnie—spread across his body. It moved like a serpent, wrapping around his back to his chest wound.

"Oh, Jesus," Dean whispered.

Neither of them could look away. The horrible, creeping mass engulfed most of the judge's body. As it reached his chest, it plugged the wound that should have killed him.

"What is it…?" Marlow asked. "What is it *doing?*"

Dean was too stunned to speak, too revolted to scream.

The poison that had run all the other residents out of town and killed most everyone else who stayed behind was now the one thing keeping the judge alive. It was one helluva symbiotic relationship—if the judge lived, the town survived, and if the town survived, the poison continued spreading through the soil, taking more lives.

That was what Burke and Gelman were studying. Not the dirt, but the poison.

Dean's mouth opened and closed.

The judge sneered. "What's the matter? Cat got yer tongues?"

Dean couldn't believe what he was seeing. The judge had gone from death's door to fully healed in a matter of minutes. No wonder the agency had been routinely monitoring Paradise. The government had inadvertently turned the town into a research experiment for immortality, and the judge was their guinea pig. That was why he had his own country, his own rules, and why generations of presidents bent over backwards for him—they wanted his secret.

And it was also why he was so impossibly old, so impossible to kill—because something even more impossible made it so.

Flexing his arms, the judge laughed. He was reinvigorated. "What doesn't kill you makes you stronger, Agent Dilton."

The earth began rumbling again. The cupid plunged deeper into the ground. A blast of hot, rancid air burst up around the sinking statue. The judge wobbled backward as the land behind him crumbled away. One second, he was there and the next he was gone, along with the statue.

As the earthquake intensified, the cupid was swallowed up by the hole it had made. The hole expanded; more of the town fell into its deep pit. Green flames burst upward and neon liquid bubbled and churned, dissolving the statue until nothing remained.

The few townspeople who hadn't run away were sucked in, screaming all the way down. Billy the motel clerk and Delores the waitress—they tried running away, but they couldn't trust the ground they walked on and fell to their doom.

Dean reached for Marlow's arm, but the earth between them broke in two. He fell away from the pit as she pinwheeled toward it—landing in the arms of Judge DeVille.

He wrapped around her like a boa constrictor. She fought against him, but he was stronger than before. He laughed, full of vigor and good humor, despite standing at the edge of oblivion.

The quaking subsided, but the currents of poison rushing and whirling behind them grew louder. It burned through the earth that had concealed it for decades, and it wanted flesh and blood.

"Let her go," Dean ordered. He crouched, keeping his center of gravity low in fear of another tremor, and held out a hand.

"I don't think so, Agent Dilton," said the judge. "I'd like to see if she can swim!" He swung her over the edge and she screamed, splitting Dean's heart in two.

"No!" He charged forward.

The judge held on tight. "Not so fast there, son. You take another step and I'll surely feed her to the pit."

Dean stopped, body vibrating with the compulsion to act. He had to do something. It couldn't end like this. "What do you want?"

"I want my town back," replied the judge.

Dean looked around. The town was gone. "I don't think I can—"

"Oh, yes, you can," the judge insisted. "You can help me rebuild. Me and you, side by side. You'll round up the lost and directionless. The drunk and disorderly. You'll bring them here and they'll help too. We'll start from scratch. We'll make it better than before. People will be *dying* to visit Paradise. I'll carry on as the

Honorable Judge DeVille and you'll be my right-hand man, my *new* Officer Friendly."

"You're crazy!" Marlow cried.

The judge shook her. "Am I? Was I crazy when I took that terrible deal from the government? Maybe! But look what it's done for me. I'm not about to turn tail on a good thing—*on my home*—just because no one else can see it. Does that make me crazy? Nuh-uh. I've always been a dreamer, Miss Marlow. A big-picture thinker!" He addressed Dean, letting Marlow squirm. "You see, I can make Paradise great again. Restore her to her former glory. But I need people, and you can help me get them."

"You killed innocent people."

"I've seen enough in my long life to know that no man is truly innocent."

"And the kids?" he asked. "You killed children, for fuck's sake. What did they ever do?"

The judge squinted. "Sadly, some folks, even the young ones, are dealt a poor hand in life."

Dean shook his head. Whether or not the judge believed his own bullshit, he had still imprisoned and killed people for his own amusement.

But because he couldn't let Marlow be flung to her death, he was willing to do or say anything to get her back on solid ground.

He had to make a deal with a monster.

Dean inched closer, extending his hand.

"Don't!" Marlow cried. "If he doesn't kill us, the town will!"

"It's just as bad out there, if not worse," said the judge, staring off into the great unknown. "The world is dying. There's poison everywhere, not just here. But at least here in Paradise, there's no crime, no pollution. We're neighbors. We're like the good old days. We're apple pie and church on Sundays. We're bobby socks and malt shops. We're romance and honeymoons and new beginnings. Who wouldn't want any of those things? So what do you say? Will you join me, *Officer Friendly?*"

He really didn't care what the old man had to say. It was just another speech, more words that had no effect on him whatsoever. He only cared about saving Marlow —not some awful town, not some cruel bastard's dream.

He lurched forward to make a handshake deal. "I'll do it."

"Really?" The judge's eyes gleamed and he flashed a twisted smile. "Just kidding!" And he swung Marlow over the cliff.

This time he let go.

Marlow disappeared over the edge, screaming all the way down.

Dean scrambled after her, too late and too slow to do anything. *"MARLOW!"*

"Going somewhere?" The judge blocked him with his belly, pushing him toward the widening pit of eyeball-scorching toxic ooze. All around, cracks vented poisonous steam.

"MARLOW!"

"She's gone, Agent Dilton. And that's for the best. You know, my very first Officer Friendly had been married to a lovely—"

Dean punched him. The judge whirled around, grabbing onto Dean's shirt. The two men fell toward the ooze, their final descent stopped by the edge of a rocky cliff. Toxic sludge lurched upward.

Somehow the judge got to his feet faster than Dean could think and he punted him in the ribs. Starting another long speech about loyalty and duty, he dug his nails Dean's scalp and shoved his face into the dirt.

"I'd never make another deal with a lying, no-good rat," he said. "Not on my life."

"Fuck ... your ... deal," Dean grunted.

"When I finally get my new Officer Friendly, I'm gonna have him drain this swamp and pull up dear Miss Marlow's corpse so I can fuck it over your grave, you slimy piece of rat shit."

Dean roared, headbutting the judge. He threw punches and kicked until the judge dropped onto his rear end. As he raised a leg to stomp the judge's face in, the old man rolled aside. Dean fell forward—the pit closing in.

He caught himself just in time, but with the poison rising rapidly, he had no way to climb up without help, and he wasn't going to get it from the judge.

"It's time to say goodbye, Agent Dilton," he said. "You've certainly overstayed your welcome."

"You too," said Marlow, standing above them.

Her motto was true after all—*you only live twice.*

The judge whipped around and she drove a boot into his nose once, twice, three times. Stunned, he stumbled backward. As he grasped for something to hold onto. She kicked him again until his eyes crossed and he fell.

He desperately grabbed onto everything in sight. The sand and rocks and crumbling earth slipped through his greedy fingers. He plummeted past Dean. And then in a splash, he was gone. The toxic swells below swallowed him up.

Dean watched the ripples until a pebble hit his head. Marlow tapped her foot impatiently, cupping a handful of dirt and rocks. "Can we go now?"

He was so glad to see her—relieved—that a goofy smile stretched foolishly across his face. "Yeah."

She dumped the dirt and offered her hand to help him up. Ascending the rocky cliff, he looked back at the murky ooze. With a bubbly belch, a skeletal hand burst upward.

Dean and Marlow froze, watching it claw the air. It soon went limp, sinking back down.

"Enough of this shit," Marlow growled, reefing on Dean's arm.

He made it to higher ground, falling into her arms. For a few long seconds, he said nothing. Just admired her. He was about to spill his guts about how upset he was when he thought the judge had thrown her over— but she slapped him, breaking the spell and reminding him that he was in the real world, not a fairy tale.

He rubbed his cheek. "What the hell?"

"I almost died!"

"I'm sorry?"

"You let him throw me down there!"

"The hell I did! Besides, you got out!"

"Like, *just barely!* I was this close." She pinched her thumb and index finger together.

"If you had just agreed to marry me, none of this would have happened."

"That's not fair! I didn't even know you and I sure as hell didn't know any of *this* would happen!"

"Well, fuck me then."

"Yeah, fuck you."

Before she could stomp off in a huff, he grabbed her

hand. *Isn't that what we met up to do? Isn't that why we both opened that stupid app?*

Thunder roared and the earth rippled again. More rumbling—yet different. Bright, blinding lights flashed all around and from above. Man-sized spiders swung down from the sky, shoving Dean to the ground and tearing him away from Marlow.

Now what? he wondered as his face scraped the pavement. The spiders turned into men, sliding down ropes from a swarm of helicopters. They shouted all kinds of SWAT guy lingo into crackling shoulder radios.

Sand blew into Dean's eyes and mouth. He couldn't see Marlow. She vanished amid the black uniforms and loud men. Pulled away into the chaos, she cried out and called his name.

"Marlow?!"

When he could see clearly again, an SUV pulled up and the rear door swung open. Director ████████ exited, straightening the lapels of his suit and adjusting his watch.

"Agent Dilton," he said, approaching.

"Sir," replied Dean, kissing distance from his boss's shoes.

"Just couldn't stay out of trouble, could you?"

30.

THE MORNING AFTER

(Reprise)

DEAN DILTON'S COLD, bloody hands are cuffed to the steel table. He's tired, sore, and anxious all over. His only comfort is that he's not in Paradise any longer.

"After everything that occurred in the last twelve hours, what do you have to say for yourself, Agent?" asks Director ███████████ from across the table.

"What happened to Marlow?"

The director sighs. "That's what you're concerned about?"

Dean sheepishly meets the director's eyes. "I fucked up, I know that. Everything I do… I just… I can't change what happened, but maybe everything happened exactly the way it was supposed to? And so, if that's how it all happened, then it's out of my hands now, and all I want to know—need to know—is where she is."

Lines deepen on the director's tired face. "I see." With a frown, he gets up and leaves. Dean is alone again, staring at his reflection.

He taps his feet. He wishes he wasn't handcuffed—*again*—but at least his head isn't crammed into a gimp mask. He taps his fingers on the table, orchestrating a cacophony of anxious sounds as he tries not to imagine Marlow thrown into a jail cell or a million other much worse scenarios.

When the director finally returns, he's got Marlow in handcuffs. Dark, tired circles ring her eyes, but she lights up as she enters the room.

"Holy shit," she mutters. "I thought you'd be long gone."

"Hell no," he says. "Where were you? I was—" *Worried about you? Thinking about you?*

"In the next room." She cocks her head to the left. "They wanted my side of the story, whatever that means."

"I think it means they think I'm full of shit."

Director ██████████ clears his throat. "I needed to make sure we're all on the same page here," he says. "About the Paradise incident."

"Ooh," says Marlow. "That'll be a great name for the Netflix documentary they'll definitely do about this fuck-up."

Dean grins at her. "I'd watch it."

The director pulls out his chair, making the metal legs screech on the floor to get their attention. He waits a beat to make sure they're listening, then summons a deputy to uncuff them. Once they're freed, they both instinctively rub their wrists.

"Does this mean we're free to go?" Marlow asks. "Because I don't know where I am and I probably don't wanna be here."

"Not quite," says the director. He stands over them

like an exasperated teacher. "My superiors have asked me to extend a thank you on behalf of the agency and the current administration."

Dean leaned back. "Someone's *happy* Paradise is gone?"

"Yes. A *lot* of people—*very important people*—are relieved to see an end to what amounted to a bureaucratic nightmare."

"So we did a good thing?" Marlow asks, quickly adding, "Allegedly?"

"*We* didn't do anything," says Dean with an edge to his voice. "*The government* did. Maybe it was our agency, I don't know. Pumped that town full of ... whatever that stuff was and just abdicated all responsibility. Now there's a bigger mess than before."

"A mess we can contain ourselves without that hotheaded lunatic DeVille inserting himself," says the director. "Reclamation work has already begun."

Marlow looked back and forth between Dean and his boss. "If the judge was such a pest, why didn't you guys just off him? Isn't that what you do?"

"Honestly? He wasn't worth the expense or the risk."

"So you let all those poor people and families and little kids die out there?" Marlow's jaw hangs askew, like she can't stand the taste in her mouth. "You let that creep get away with everything, like *literal* murder."

"It's ... complicated," the director says. "We were monitoring the perimeter, but with DeVille in place, he could oversee the situation from the inside, even if he didn't completely understand what he was seeing."

"He didn't seem too cooperative either," Dean notes.

"No, he certainly wasn't."

"Is that why you gave him his own country?" Marlow wonders.

"The sovereignty stuff?" Dean adds. "The country sold its soul to cover its ass. We've gone to war over less."

The director waves dismissively. "It was all just paperwork. A cheap certificate we reprinted under every administration to placate the old bastard. It meant nothing. But you two traipsing into town screwed it all up. At least the outcome has been somewhat positive."

"*Positive?*" Dean chokes on the word. "We were beaten, arrested, chased by hellhounds—"

"Hellhounds?"

"—locked in a basement, forced to participate in the judge's fight club, hanged to die—"

"That was just you," Marlow interjected.

"—and a lot of other stuff that's kinda fuzzy now 'cause I've been hit in the head a bunch of times. And then we almost got drowned in a pit of toxic waste—"

Marlow holds up her hands. "Don't forget arsenic poisoning!"

"And you say it's all *fine?*" he finishes.

"I think what my dude here is trying to say," says Marlow, "is that we may be entitled to some financial compensation."

The director crosses his arms and releases a long, deep breath through his nose.

"Agent Dilton," he says, voice low and steady, placidly calm, "if I'd known you'd entered that town—stepped one foot on that land—I would have ordered a drone strike to take you out. Consider yourself lucky you made it as far as you did, for as long as you did." He turns to Marlow and adds, "As for your 'financial compensation'—no."

Marlow pouts.

Dean's heart pounds so loudly and steadily he can feel it in his throat. "Sir, and I say this with the utmost respect, the people we work for have fucked this up for the past sixty years. Isn't it time *someone* takes responsibility for *something?*"

The director scoffs. "Who, me? You? Uncle Sam? The moron in the White House? Agent Dilton, you're kidding yourself if you think—"

Dean stands abruptly. "I'm *not* kidding. I'm done. I quit. Consider this my formal resignation." If he had either his gun or badge, he would slam it down on the table and spit on it. "This job... It isn't for me."

"Clearly," the director says drolly. "But sit your ass down because I haven't dismissed you."

Dean reluctantly returns to his seat.

"I still have a problem here." Director ▮▮▮▮▮▮▮ points two fingers at them. "You two are my last loose ends. I can fix that mess out in Paradise, but I can't contain it without your cooperation."

"You need *our* help?" Dean chuckles. "The tables have turned."

"Careful." The director points at him. "Dr. Burke and Dr. Gelman might still be alive had you followed orders. Instead, you abandoned your post for this ... *woman*—"

"Hey...?" Marlow mumbles, uncertain if she should be offended.

"—And they were killed. Both fireable offenses, if left to me. But if you hadn't just quit as part of your little tantrum, you would have found out that your job is protected as a thanks from the head of this organization. Someone up there likes you."

"Huh," Dean says, finding it hard to swallow.

"I saw your personnel file," he continues. "You think the agency doesn't conduct thorough background checks—well, you're wrong. We know all about your 'tendencies toward mild anarchy.' But I saw potential in you, and I'd hoped this assignment would straighten you out. Keep you away from our archivist before you dipped your pen in the company ink."

Marlow smirks, raising an eyebrow at him.

"So when I say I need your help with containing the problem out in Paradise, it's because I need you to promise you'll keep your idiot mouths shut about it. Because if you don't, the only alternative is that I take you out behind the Dumpster and put two rounds in the back of *both* of your heads. Do you understand?"

Staring his boss dead in the eye, Dean asks, "So why don't you?"

"Trust me, it would be so much easier for all of us," he says. "But as I mentioned, my superiors are satisfied with the outcome of your ... 'work.' They're offering you an opportunity to leave this situation with your lives. Consider it a thank you for your ongoing cooperation and discretion. However, you both need to agree—*in writing.*"

He removes two folded papers from inside his jacket and slides them across the table. He hands each of them a pen.

Dean reads over what they'd be agreeing to. "Another goddamn deal," he says.

Marlow's already scribbling her name across the bottom. "It's better than getting shot in the head or going to jail." She slides the signed paper back to the director, before shooting a warning look at Dean.

Which is Marlow's way of saying "take the deal."

Dean returns to reading the paper. He doesn't like what he's seeing. He wanted the chance to sing like a canary to another government body or even a reporter at the *New York Times*. He wanted a chance to bring down the men responsible for the stinking shit they pumped into the earth. A town was destroyed, people got sick and died, and others were murdered just to appease some megalomaniac in the desert whose accidental exposure to chemical waste unlocked the secret to never-ending life.

Scowling, he signs it and shoves the paper back. He should take comfort in knowing that with the stroke of a cheap pen, he saved both their lives. Instead, he feels empty, exhausted, and hungry.

Marlow reaches over and places her hand on his. "It sucks, but that's life."

"Another one of your mottos?" he asks.

Instead of a snarky reply, she tips her head to one side and asks, "What's that sound?"

Both Dean and Director ███████████ listen. A vibration snakes up through the table before the room starts to shake. The mirrored glass rattles. It's not a rumble—*it can't be.*

They're nowhere near Paradise. The town is *gone.*

The director runs into the hallway, shouting questions at the deputies wobbling around the station. He narrowly avoids being crushed as the interrogation room's wall caves in after him.

An old black car embeds itself in the wall from outside. It stalls out, filling the interrogation room with plumes of smoke.

Dean and Marlow are separated by rubble, broken drywall, and a fluorescent light fixture swinging between them. He can't tell if she's okay.

"Marlow?" He crawls through the detritus to find her. They have to get out before they choke to death.

As he nears the idling behemoth, the horn blasts. Dean turns, facing the driver—and of course, it's the judge.

The cruel bastard somehow survived, dragged himself out of the pit, and hunted them down. True to his word, he's never going to let them leave. Never.

The judge roars like the monster he's become. The massive black tumor on his body has spread, consumed him. He's more cancer cell than human.

He oozes out of the car. Crispy, bubbled flesh ripples all over him, stinking of barbecued skunk. An eyeball dangles from its socket.

"It's over, judge," Dean says. "The town's gone."

The judge grins. A long, black tendril whips out from behind his back, wrapping around Dean's ankle. As it tightens, Dean trips and lands on his back. The tendril reels him in.

Once again, he's brought before the judge. *Judge, jury, and executioner.* The sentence this time is death by undead mutant.

The judge plants a foot over Dean's heart, testing the give of his ribs.

"I told you, you little shit," the judge gurgles. *"You're not getting out alive."*

Dean pushes back, but the judge is stronger and bigger. He digs his heel into Dean's caving chest, grinding him up like a nasty cockroach.

"I want to hear your bones crack, Agent Dilton."

Marlow jumps on the judge's back, wielding a wooden hammer. The monstrous man releases Dean, tumbling backwards until he pins Marlow against the one remaining wall.

More tendrils split off from his back, each grabbing one of Marlow's limbs, eager to tear her apart.

She screams through gritted teeth and tosses the hammer—no, not a hammer, *a gavel*—to Dean.

He picks it up. He doesn't think. He raises the gavel up high, high over his head and—

ORDER IN THE COURT!

—brings it crashing down, smashing through the judge's skull. Rotten brain matter oozes out like yolk. Dean doesn't stop hammering until the monster releases Marlow.

She crawls to his side and lends her fists. They don't stop until he's truly dead.

When the dust settles, Dean buries the gavel in the splattered remains of the judge's head. Marlow shakes the brain matter off her hands, flicking slimy chunks at the director as he returns to the scene.

He groans, undecided about how to handle the gore on his suit, the judge's corpse, and his two loose ends.

"I think we got him this time, sir," Dean says. "Can we go now?"

Marlow links arms with Dean while Director ███████████ remains speechless. "We should go," she says. "He's got a big mess to clean up."

Dean shrugs, letting her guide him out the door as deputies and firefighters rush into the station.

"By the way..." She looks down at Dean's pants. "Your 'mild anarchy' is showing."

He follows her line of sight down to his open fly and

zips up. "Oh, shit. How long have you left me hanging like that?"

"Oh, it's *my fault* you've been strutting around like that since the judge's house?"

He stops, turning her to look at him. He strokes her dirty face, runs a hand through her frizzed hair. "I don't wanna fight anymore," he tells her.

"So what then?" she wonders, sticking out her chin.

"Let's try something else."

He kisses her. She kisses him back. And they don't let go until the decontamination crew arrives.

31.

THE END

THE SUN HANGS low in the sky by the time Dean and Marlow are decontaminated, medically examined, and patched up.

Director ████████████ assigns them separate motel rooms and tells them in no uncertain terms not to skip town until he completes his investigation.

They rummage through a lost-and-found box for clean clothes before a pair of deputies escort them to their living quarters for the time being, however long that might be.

Later, Dean sits on the edge of his bed, staring at the ugly motel art on the walls and pondering his future.

What future? He has no job, nowhere to go. His folks will be disappointed—again. What does an ex-agent do after uncovering a government conspiracy?

For a lark, he imagines running off with Marlow and robbing convenience stores to survive. He shakes his head. *Talk about disappointing the family.*

And yet, it'd be on brand.

His phone rings, startling him out of his thoughts.

"You hungry?" Marlow asks on the other line.

"Starved. Uh, but my wallet is somewhere in a deep, dark, toxic pit, so..."

"Don't worry, it's on me," she says. He imagines her wrapped in a towel, fanning herself with a stack of stolen cash. "What do you want?"

"I'd kill for a milkshake."

After vigorously washing her hands and taking the longest shower of her life, Marlow stares out the window of her motel room and wonders what's next. She can't imagine continuing Tony's schemes now that he's out of the picture. She never really liked sticking a gun in people's faces or playing getaway driver.

Speaking of... She hopes Arnie got away. She hopes he's home, or soon will be, and that his family missed him, and that they won't be too pissed, considering the circumstances.

And that makes her think about her mother. The last time they talked, their conversation ended in a screaming match, so going home isn't an option.

She wonders about Dean, about how he just up and quit his job. What would he do now?

There were no easy answers. Not without her tarot cards or at least the day's horoscope.

He's for sure a Virgo, she decides. According to their star signs, it would never work out between them.

Still, she picks up the phone and asks the motel manager to connect her to Dean's room.

There's a bus stop down the road, across the street from an all-night diner called Skippy's or Bippy's or

Slappy's, or some shit. They make plans to meet there before dark.

"Just like old times," he teases.

The diner's actual name is the Dine-In Delight. Dean sits in the back booth, peering over the rim of a cup of coffee.

Marlow slides her tired, aching body across the vinyl seating and paws through the menu. Her stomach growls.

The server, a middle-aged woman sporting a blue beehive and a grim expression, shuffles over. Before she can complain that Dean is missing a shoe, Marlow plucks $100 from her bra and leaves it on the table. The server snatches it up and, in exchange, gives them her finest shit-eating grin.

"What can I get you folks?"

Dean holds up a finger. "Lemme see if I've got this right—two chocolate milkshakes with whipped cream and a cherry on top?"

Marlow nods, impressed but trying to hide it.

The server backs away, but Dean's not finished. He orders two big plates of greasy breakfast food and a side of fries—because why not? Now that he's out of a job, it'll probably be awhile before he eats this well again.

"Thanks for meeting me," she says.

He leans across the table. "Sure. Not like I have any work to catch up on. Not anymore." He frowns, looking down at the scratched tabletop. "Though I might draft something to Burke and Gelman's families when I figure out what to say."

"Your boss has probably covered it up by now."

Dean makes a face that doesn't confirm or deny it. They sit in silence until the waitress returns with their milkshakes. Dean offers Marlow a straw. They clink their glasses. Whipped cream spills down the side. Dean takes a long, hungry sip.

"No wonder you wanted one of these so badly," he says. "Fucking delicious."

"I know, right?"

They sit in ecstasy for a while. Then Marlow sighs, looking out at the bus stop across the street. A few folks are lined up, ready to get wherever the hell they're going to. "So ... I'm gonna go."

He follows her line of sight. "A bus? That doesn't seem like your style. I thought you were all about hot-wiring Mercedes and classic cars."

"I never said I hotwired that Mercedes. Some dude let me take it for a ride and I just never went back."

"How come? Oh, right—your ex hijacked you and it was happily ever after."

"You sound jealous..."

"Maybe I am."

She plays with her straw to avoid his stare. His eyes are bright, sharp, hungry. She cracks a joke to relieve the tension. "Tony wasn't your type anyway."

He smiles. "So where's the bus gonna take you?"

"Somewhere, anywhere. I'll figure it out. I just have to go."

"You're not supposed to leave. Director's orders."

She crosses her arms. "When have I followed any-one's orders? I'm a career criminal with loose morals and maybe twenty grand left in my bra. You can't expect me to stick around."

He can't argue there. "Fair enough."

"But if you've got nothing better to do, maybe you should come. Might be good for you. Loosen you up."

"You don't want to see me loose, sweetheart," he says, grinning.

"I do."

Amused, he rubs his face. He could use a shave and a good night's sleep. But the wheels are turning in his head. He reaches into his jacket and slides his room key across the table.

"I thought you only liked redheads."

"I was wrong."

She traces the key's ridges, almost picks it up. But at the last second, she slides it back over to his side. "We can't do this... Whatever this is."

Face turning pink, he takes his key back and fixes his eyes on the glistening red cherry sinking into the remains of his milkshake. "A one-night stand that didn't pan out."

"A simple hook-up," she adds. "Supposed to be easy breezy."

"Everything got so complicated."

"I don't want complicated. I just want to get laid."

"Same."

Their eyes meet. He's holding her hand, turning it over to reveal her *What the hell?* tattoo. They're both thinking the same thing, but neither dares to say it out loud.

She shrugs, standing up, and throws some cash down to cover the meal. When he follows her out of the booth, she tells him to stay and finish.

He holds out a hand to shake hers. "I still don't know your last name."

"Does it matter?"

"Just curious."

Hand clasped in his, she stands on her tiptoes to

whisper in his ear. His eyebrows rise as her breath caresses his cheek.

"Don't try using your government connections to track me down, okay?" she warns.

"Scout's honor," he promises, pulling her in.

She reaches up to brush her lips against his, just a quick goodbye. But he holds her close until she can feel his heart pounding. Hers is louder, thundering. Blood rushes to her face. She parts her lips, drawing a breath, and just when she decides she's not ready to say goodbye, he lets go.

Her skin is too hot. Her thighs stick together. If she doesn't get away soon, she might do something stupid.

"If this whole taking off on a bus thing doesn't work out, you know where to find me." He nods in the general direction of the motel. "I'll make sure I have those mini vodka bottles you like."

"Thanks," she says, halfway out the door, "but it's probably best if we never see each other again."

He pats his chest. "Never say never—that's my motto."

🔥 🔥 🔥

Only steps away from his motel room, Dean digs around in his pocket for his room key. He's juggling a six-pack and a plastic liquor store bag filled with sample bottles of tequila, vodka, and gin. They clink together.

Sighing, he sets everything down and does a thorough search. Still nothing.

Through the big panel window, he sees the red numbers on the clock radio. It's almost time—Marlow's bus departed ten minutes ago. He knows this because in his pocket (where his key should be) is her folded-up ticket. He picked it off her at the restaurant.

She's not the only one with sticky fingers.

He's getting impatient. He must have lost the key on his way to the liquor store.

Before he heads to the motel office for a replacement, he surveys the area. Marlow should be storming across the parking lot any minute—unless she bought another ticket; he never actually touched her money.

The parking lot is dead quiet. No red boots clicking across the pavement. It was a stupid idea anyway.

A light comes on in his room. He expects Officer Friendly or the judge to make an appearance—one last scare, one final reminder that his nightmare will never end.

But it's neither. Marlow stands in the window, tapping his room key against the glass. *Looking for this?*

He holds up the bag of sample-sized goodies. A gesture of goodwill. An offering.

He waits in the glow of the room's light as she moseys to the door. Maybe she'll let him in or maybe she'll lock him out. Maybe she'll chew him out for his little prank or maybe she'll take him in her arms and—

He grins.

Whatever comes next, whatever tomorrow brings, he's ready—because the future can't be any crazier than the night before.

THE END

THANK YOU

This is the part where the author thanks a huge list of people who helped make the book possible. I would do that here too, but indie authors like myself are a bit like lone wolves with smaller packs, if any.

The people who have lent their support to my little venture, however, have been incredible every step of the way. Most importantly, YOU the reader.

I'm amazed at the ways people find my books. You are the people who matter most to an author, and without your interest in my stories, I'd just be talking to myself. Thank you for your purchases, downloads, requests at your local libraries and bookstores, and so many more places. Thank you for rating and reviewing my books (hopefully this one too), and talking about them on social media. It truly means a lot when you mention my work to your friends and followers. I could write a whole book of THANK YOUs and it would never capture just how much your time and your own words mean to me. Thank you.

And a huge thank you to my husband and son. Your patience and understanding when I slip away on weekend mornings to bang my head against my keyboard and mutter to myself is nothing short of astounding. I hate leaving you both for any reason, even if it's only to sequester myself in a room a few feet away, so thank you for not making the journey too painful. I love you both so much.

– *S.S.*

PLAYLIST

One more thing... I jokingly refer to this book as a "love story." There's not much love lost between Dean and Marlow, but a soundtrack full of romantic '60s music was an amusing funny contrast to their worst night ever, so I kept this playlist of schmaltzy jukebox songs as a little inspiration.

Thought I'd share it if you'd like to listen or follow me on Spotify.

"Rhythm of the Rain," The Cascades
"Son of a Preacher Man," Dusty Springfield
"Another Saturday Night," Sam Cooke

"Just One Look," Doris Troy
"These Boots Are Made For Walkin'," Nancy Sinatra
"Fever," Peggy Lee
"Blame It On The Bossa Nova," Eydie Gormé
"Chains," The Cookies
"What A Man," Linda Lyndell
"(Today I Met) The Boy I'm Going to Marry," Darlene Love
"Town Without Pity," Gene Pitney
"Stay," Maurice Williams & The Zodiacs
"Could This Be Magic," The Dubs
"Nowhere To Run," Martha Reeves & The Vandellas
"Dedicated To The One I Love," The Mamas & The Papas
"Five O'Clock World," The Vogues
"Money (That's What I Want)," Barrett Strong
"Our Day Will Come," Ruby And The Romantics
"Love Me," Elvis Presley
"Lover Please," Clyde McPhatter
"What Becomes Of The Brokenhearted," Jimmy Ruffin
"Cry to Me," Solomon Burke
"You've Really Got A Hold On Me," The Miracles
"Twenty Five Miles," Edwin Starr
"I Will Follow You," Ricky Nelson
"Save the Last Dance for Me," The Drifters
"Will You Love Me Tomorrow," The Shirelles
"Don't Let Me Be Misunderstood," Nina Simone
"You Don't Own Me," Lesley Gore
"Rescue Me," Fontella Bass
"Baby, I'm Yours," Barbara Lewis
"Chapel of Love," The Dixie Cups
"Cupid," Sam Cooke
"Hold Me, Thrill Me, Kiss Me," Mel Carter
"Knock on Wood," Eddie Floyd
"Bring It On Home to Me," Sam Cooke
"Such a Night," Elvis Presley

ABOUT THE AUTHOR

STEPHANIE SPARKS writes stories reminiscent of classic '70s and '80s slasher and monster movies. She loves scream queens, final girls, and the masked maniacs who stalk them. Her books feature action, thrills, dark humor, and sarcasm. She prefers cats to people and when she's not lost in a paperback from hell or listening to 1980s movie soundtracks, she's daydreaming ideas for her next book or writing furiously.

She is a member of the Horror Writers Association and is always working on her next novel.

Visit her online at StephanieSparks.ca where you can learn more about her other books, *Scream Queen, Kill the Babysitter, The Stepchildren,* and *Mandy.*

ALSO AVAILABLE

KILL THE BABYSITTER

Jane's first babysitting gig comes with a lot of rules, and after a hellish night, she breaks an important one: *Don't let the kids play with the Ouija board.* Now the mischievous spirit in the board wants to play a deadly new game: *Kill the Babysitter.* Jane must fight tooth and nail against a murderous horde of possessed children—and if she doesn't team up with her worst enemy, she may not survive the night.

SCREAM, QUEEN

1984... Beautiful, do-good student Becca has been nominated for the coveted role of queen of her town's Harvest Festival. But when she starts looking into its history, she discovers that each of the past queens died under mysterious circumstances — including her mom. There is something insidiously rotten about the festival, and if Becca can't escape her queenly duties, she will have to make the ultimate sacrifice.

THE STEPCHILDREN

Jamie had always suspected something was wrong with her stepfather. Burt wasn't just a man on the hunt for the perfect life — he was a fugitive family annihilator. Years after surviving his attack, Jamie and his other stepchildren come together in group therapy where they learn he has died in prison — or has he? Turns out, even in death, daddy dearest has a few deadly surprises left for his wayward stepchildren.

MANDY

In the dead of night to make a distraught stranger go away, Mandy uses her secret gift to bring a young man back from the dead. Her "gift" becomes a curse when Robbie turns out to be anything but the golden boy she expected. With an insatiable hunger for death and destruction, Robbie will stop at nothing to exploit Mandy's secret for his own gain. But messing with the weird girl will get him more than he bargained for...

See more at StephanieSparks.ca.

MANDY

The last thing Mandy Fisher expected to hear in the dead of night was a fist banging on the door. It woke her like a thunderclap. Unexpected, jarring. She slowly sat up, holding her covers close to her chest. She listened, but couldn't hear beyond the blood rushing to her head, outside of which there was only silence. And the knocking.

When the frantic pounding began again, it wasn't a dream or her imagination playing tricks. She was all alone in her father's house on an acreage that was a two-hour hike to the nearest town. Visitors in the middle of the night were rare, even in her father's line of work.

She laid back down, pulling the blankets over her head. She couldn't fall asleep, nor could she make the knocking stop. It became louder, more urgent, and then a voice cried out.

"Help us!"

Us. Meaning more than one.

Meaning Mandy would be outnumbered.

"Go away," she whispered, breath hot under the covers.

But they wouldn't go away. The back porchlight was on. She had forgotten to turn it off and so it became a beacon for her midnight guests.

The stranger called out again. "I know you're in there!"

She pushed the covers aside, easing off the bed. Her feet touched the cold, hardwood floor. The planks creaked. She bit her lip as if to quiet her movements, as if the panicked stranger down below could sense her exact location.

He knew someone was in the house and he wasn't going to stop banging on the door until either she answered it or he had smashed his way inside.

"Help us, please!"

Mandy grabbed her robe from the hook on the door. She wrapped it around herself, cinching the belt tight. Against her better judgment, she kept the lights off so that under the cover of darkness she could see who was at the door, get a description, and report them if necessary.

Not that she had anything against visitors, but something about strangers in the dark turned her stomach to ice. She never cared much for the company of others — with one exception, but he was long gone.

And he was definitely not coming back.

She tiptoed down the stairs, keeping her back against the wall but also careful not to brush against the family photos trailing downward. Her father and mother on their wedding day in a tiny church. A family photo of the three of them, Mandy just barely able to hold her own head up on her wobbly infant neck. A photo taken before cancer claimed her mother's life. Kindergarten, grade school, junior high pics. Braces clamped on tight and shining in one awkward school photo.

Her graduation photo's frame hung in the exact spot it had been placed years ago; the photo conspicuously absent. Her father hung it in earnest, but after everything that happened that spring, the last thing on his mind would have been to take the frame down.

Mandy gripped the tie around her waist as she approached the front door. She could see through the glass arch out onto the porch, but that light was off and no one was there. She waited for a bloodied hand to slap against the window, like in the movies she was advised to avoid, lest they aggravate her condition.

Mandy rounded the stairs. She passed by the sitting room where her father kept stacks of books and magazines. Then the formal dining room where he handled the bulk of his paperwork. Then the kitchen where he thankfully did not conduct any of his work.

No, that had been Mandy's mistake.

Her crime scene.

At the end of the hallway was a half-lite door, and just before the door, if Mandy turned left, was the entrance to her father's business. It was where the Fisher house became the Fisher & Sons Funeral Home.

There were no sons, however. Just Mandy and her father, and the occasional hired hand when business picked up. Her father thought the "sons" made the name sound homey and personal.

While Mandy was quite satisfied with being an only child, tonight she wished she had some big, strong brothers to protect her because she could see the stranger at the backdoor. His chin dropped onto his chest as he rested his head against the glass. He was young. Maybe Mandy's age. It was hard to tell in the dark, the porchlight casting harsh shadows across his brawny features. His hair fell in a sweaty mess across his cro magnon forehead and heavy brows. A gash above his hairline oozed blood. His nose was busted and bloody. He was a thick boy — a man built for tackling, running, crushing, destroying. If he wanted to, he could make short work of the tired door. But he didn't. Not yet. He was at least that little bit civilized.

All Mandy had to do was stay out of sight. Eventually he would have to go away. She was about to go back to bed. Her slight movement caught his attention. The second he glimpsed her, peeking down the hallway, his eyes widened and he started knocking all over again.

"Oh, shit, hey! You gotta help! My friend— There was an accident. I don't know what to do."

Mandy knew what to do.

Don't let them in.

Go back to bed.

Forget this ever happened.

Her father's words made her pause and reconsider. In the two years she spent in the rest home, he never once brought up the incident that put her there or forced any fatherly wisdom upon her. Not until the hot summer day he arrived to take her home. Then he let it all out.

"Make good choices, Mandy, and be kind to others," he said, wiping the perspiration off his ruddy face. As usual for a workday, he wore a full suit and tie. The heat was cruel to his jolly body, but never affected his friendly disposition. "You're an adult now, so more than ever, you're responsible for what happens to you. It's easy to wall yourself off from others and keep your head down, but you can still do good in this world. You just have to make the right choices."

In the car on that long drive home, Mandy stared out the window and listened to her father's sermon. She didn't know if he meant what he was saying or if he was just trying to fill the silence, but his words stuck with her.

And he was right. All she wanted to do was shut out the world and try to move on with her life. The problem was she worked for her father, and his business was a people-facing, customer service one. It would reflect terribly on the business if she ignored a stranger's pleas for help, only for her father to come home and find him, and then do what she should have done in the first place: Help him.

Make good choices. Be kind to others.

She sighed, dislodging her teeth from her bottom lip. Coming out from the darkness, she went to the door.

The stranger pawed the glass, like a sad, desperate puppy.

"Please."

Mandy turned the lock. The brass slipped between her fingers as the stranger shoved his way in, invading her space. He reeked of blood, sweat, musky cologne, and beer. He loomed over, breathing hard.

Just as quickly, he moved aside and pointed outside to a crumpled mess at the bottom of the steps. A young man's unmoving body.

"You gotta do something."

Want more?

Order your copy today:

Amazon
Barnes & Noble
Blackwell's
Booktopia
Kobo
Waterstones
And more...